HONEY FROM A LION

The Sequel to *South Wind Rising*

Frederick W. Bassett

HONEY FROM A LION
Copyright © 2014 by Frederick W. Bassett
All rights reserved. No part of this book may be reproduced or transmitted in any form or by any means without written permission of the author and publisher.
This is a work of fiction. Any resemblance to actual persons, living or dead, is purely coincidental.

ISBN 13: 9780989403269

Library of Congress Control Number: 2014930178

Cover Art: "The Wading Pool at Carrick's Creek" by Garry Turpin
Cover design by All Things That Matter Press
Published in 2014 by All Things That Matter Press

For Peg, always

Acknowledgments

Special thanks to Bettie Rose Horne, Carole Mauldin, Virginia Pulver, and Denise Waldrep. I am indebted to these wonderful readers for giving me excellent feedback on the first draft of *Honey from a Lion*. The final version of the novel is much improved because of their insights. It is my story, however, so hold me responsible for it, not them. I also thank Deb and Phil Harris at All Things That Matter Press for editing and publishing the first two books of my planned trilogy.

> . . . *he turned aside to see the carcass of the lion: and behold, there was a swarm of bees and honey in the carcass of the lion. And he took thereof in his hands, and went on eating.*
>
> Judges 14:8-9

> *The real voyage of discovery consists not in seeking new landscapes but in having new eyes.*
>
> Marcel Proust

PART I

CHAPTER ONE

Barsh Roberts pulled into the driveway and cut the engine. The house was dark, except for pale light spilling from the den windows. No chance that Hannah was still up. He sat in the car, feeling a tinge of guilt that the day had slipped away and he had not spent any time with his daughter. Poor child, she had no idea what life was about to throw at her.

He dreaded facing Debbie. Try as he would, he had not been able to make her happy. She had endured the first four years of their marriage in Atlanta while he earned a Ph.D. at Emory University, and contrary to his promises, things didn't improve for her after he accepted a professorship at Cooper College. She was always miserable around academics and she hated living in Ashland, a small town in Upstate South Carolina.

Her old boss had offered to make her a partner at Dugan, Johnson and Bennett, Certified Public Accountants, and she couldn't wait to get back to Louisville, her favorite place in the whole world. Although Barsh had given up all hope of revitalizing the marriage, he felt duty-bound to keep the family under one roof for Hannah's sake and offered to resign his position at Cooper and move to Louisville. He could find something there. It didn't have to be a professorship. But Debbie rejected the proposal. She and Hannah would be moving to Louisville without him, although she had not set a definite date.

She didn't want a divorce but insisted on a trial separation for a year, which left him wondering what she really did want. He certainly didn't trust Henry Dugan, a tailored-suits kind of man who seemed to have an eye for Debbie when she worked for him. And she definitely held him in high esteem. It was years before she stopped talking about *Henry* on a regular basis.

Barsh entered the house, expecting to find Debbie watching TV, but finding the den empty, he quietly made his way to Hannah's room. She was sleeping peacefully, the nightlight gently bathing her sweet face. Down the hall, the door to the master bedroom was closed and wouldn't be opened by him. He had moved into the guest bedroom after Debbie insisted on a trial separation.

He thought about going to bed but realized that would be foolish. It would be hours before he settled down enough to sleep. He was reading a brilliantly written book about Baruch Spinoza, which would take his mind away from his troubles if he could get back into the world of this extraordinary philosopher.

He went to the study, his inner sanctuary in this house divided. The walls were lined with floor-to-ceiling bookshelves, except the one with the big window onto the backyard. Beyond the yard, the remnant of a hardwood forest dropped sharply to Coleman's Creek and then rose to the top of a hill. It was those woods that sold him on the house, and they had given him much pleasure over the years.

He kept a record, year by year, of the different species of birds he observed in that little patch of nature. For the seasonal species and those just migrating somewhere else, he noted the day he first observed their arrival. Of the permanent residents, he especially enjoyed a pair of barred owls that hallooed the evenings. His favorite was a red-shouldered hawk that occasionally perched in the tallest oak beyond the creek. One winter day, he watched the magnificent creature swoop down upon a squirrel's nest in the branches of a barren poplar and fly off with the prey clutched in its talons.

Settled at his desk, he noticed that someone had moved *Spinoza*. He picked up the book and smiled at Hannah's bookmark on page five. This was not a book for an eleven-year-old. Still, it pleased him that she was already developing a critical mind. He placed the book aside and reached for his favorite picture of his parents taken by a traveling photographer during the first year of their marriage. His mother, who had kept it on her bedside table, told him the story when he asked about it as a boy. When he asked why he was an only child, she told him about the miscarriages and the stillborn daughter.

How often he had wished his parents could have lived to see Hannah. They would've doted on her, and in time they would have wondered why she was an only child, although they would never have asked. He had wanted more children, but Debbie was terrified by the idea of a second pregnancy.

He returned the photo to its place and counted the years since that eighteen-wheeler crashed into their car, killing them instantly. His mother was only nine years older than he was now, his father fourteen.

They were so happy when he and Debbie finally got married. From their point of view, the marriage was made in Heaven and they would have been severely distraught if they had lived to learn that she had asked for a trial separation. He thought of a passage from the Book of Job on how the dead are utterly cut off from the living: *Their children come to honor, and they do not know it; they are brought low, and it goes unnoticed.*

At least he could take solace in the fact that they would never know his marriage was a failure. No, *failure* wasn't the right word. How could a relationship which produced Hannah be a failure? He wouldn't judge the marriage by what it had become.

He stared out the window into the darkness. For weeks he had searched for a way out of his impending crisis, but the vision he sought wouldn't come. He was a tenured Professor of Religion and Philosophy at Cooper College, but he couldn't see himself teaching there after Debbie moved to Louisville. It was a matter of conscience and honor. How could he teach about spiritual things with his own household torn asunder? He would have to resign, although he had no idea what he would do.

More importantly, he had to find a way to prepare Hannah for the separation. Debbie had given him more time to work on that before they broke the news. She knew, all too well, the trouble she would have if he couldn't ease their precocious child into accepting the separation. The stress, however, was taking its toll on him.

Tomorrow would be another long day with no time to spend with Hannah. In addition to his regular duties on campus, he had to drive to Charlotte to pick up Angela Kundera, who was flying down from Providence, Rhode Island, for a job interview. Her flight was scheduled to land at six o'clock, and he was responsible for taking her to dinner before checking her in the Ashland Hotel.

He felt sure the interview would be a wasted effort. The search committee had lost touch with reality to think that lowly Cooper College could land this woman. Her resume and references clearly placed her in a different league. When he called two weeks ago to invite her down, he fully expected her to decline the invitation, but she seemed to be genuinely enthusiastic about the visit. It made no sense to him. But what puzzled him even more was the fact that Angela Kundera's voice had been buzzing in his head ever since their twenty minute conversation.

There was a stirring down the hall as Hannah's feet were pattering toward him. He turned the swivel chair toward the door.

"Daddy, you're home," she said and ran to his embrace.

"What's wrong, my child?"

"I had a horrible dream. You were lost and I couldn't find you."

"I'm sorry. Nightmares can seem so real. I had lots of them when I was a boy. Some of them kept recurring, but they went away when I got older."

"What kind of nightmares?"

"Things that a boy my age would be afraid of back then."

"Like what?"

"Are you sure you want to hear about my boyhood nightmares?"

"I want to know what they were about."

"Well, snakes for one thing."

"But you're not afraid of snakes. You told me they have their place in the scheme of things."

"Yes, but I was scared of them when I was a boy. One day when Dad was taking me down to the swimming hole in the creek, he almost stepped on a big rattlesnake. You and I would have eased on by and left the snake alone. But Dad killed it because it was poisonous. Then he warned me that I might die if a poisonous snake bit me. Because I was too young to know which were poisonous, he told me to run away as fast as I could when I saw a snake of any kind. So I grew up hating snakes.

"Now I give them their place in the world. We should be open to change. There's always something new coming our way, challenging us to deal successfully with it."

"I know. You've taught me well."

"Now let's get you back in bed. We should both be sleeping the night away."

"Can't I stay up a little longer?"

"Five minutes. You want some milk?"

"No, I want to talk."

"I have an idea. Let's you and me go to Table Rock State Park on Saturday. We'll take a picnic lunch and hike to the top of the mountain."

"Yes, and I'm going to make it all the way to the top without having to stop and rest."

"Okay, but stops are good when you're hiking in the mountains. They give you a chance to listen to the sounds of nature and take a closer look at things along the way."

"Daddy, I hope you don't have to work late tomorrow."

"I hate to tell you, my sweet girl, but tomorrow and Friday are both going to be long busy days for me. I probably won't get home before your bedtime either day. If it would do any good, I'd complain. Speaking of which, I haven't heard you complaining lately about school. Are things going better?"

"Like you say, what good would it do me to complain? My classes are mostly boring. I can't wait to get to college."

"I see you started reading *Spinoza* today. I like old Baruch Spinoza. He was way ahead of his time, which got him into deep, deep trouble. Could you make any sense out of what you read?"

"Not much. You'll have to tell me about him. I can understand you."

"Not tonight. You have to get some zzzz's. We'll talk about Spinoza on the way to Table Rock. Come on, I'll tuck you in."

With Hannah back in bed, he returned to his study, where he sat searching for an underlying anxiety that had caused her to dream that he was lost and she could not find him. He wondered if she had overheard any of the conversations about the separation. He didn't think so, but she did know he had started sleeping alone in the guest bedroom. Maybe that was troubling her. Maybe he should broach the subject with her. No, that didn't seem like a good idea. He would leave it to her to query him. She had never been hesitant to question him about anything.

His first reaction to the impending separation was to draw his daughter closer to him. Now he was having doubt about that strategy. Maybe Housman got it right: *train for ill and not for good*. Should he be pulling back to prepare her for the separation? He didn't think he could do that.

He picked up *Spinoza*, flipped to his marker, and started reading. After a few pages, he gave up and decided to go for a walk. After checking on Hannah, who was fast asleep, he stopped in the driveway to study the heavens, a simple act which often transported him into that infinite realm of awesome wonder. The sky was clear, but he was too earthbound for the flight.

The new moon spoke to him of earthly things. Like its phases, the seasons of his life were changing in an irreversible course. But unlike the moon's recurring phases, he was on a journey that would never repeat itself. The best he could hope for was to live until he was an old man, stilled at last to face the sting of death.

He left the driveway, intent on walking through the whole neighborhood at a fast pace. Most of the houses were dark. He wondered how many of them held secrets the inhabitants were hiding. People were unpredictable. Who could have imagined the problems next door that caused John Young to knock his wife's brains out with a frying pan? Why were men so prone to violence in marital conflicts?

That question got him wondering about one of Robert Frost's narrative poems. What Barsh remembered about "Home Burial" was the husband's callous response to his wife's despair over the death of their child. On some level, the man understood that he had failed his wife, but rather than taking responsibility for contributing to her despair, he threatened to bring her back by force if she left him, which she planned to do.

Barsh knew that he had failed to meet Debbie's deepest needs. Now that she wanted a separation, his only moral recourse was to support her plan to move to Louisville, which he had resolved to do. His primary duty, however, was to Hannah. He had to prepare her for the separation. He could live alone, but he could not live with the consequences of failing his daughter.

CHAPTER TWO

He waited for Angela Kundera at the airport, the room filled with chatter and movement, but he was deep within himself, struggling to regain his stoical equilibrium and rise to the demands of duty for he was, above all, a man of duty. Although he had no idea what the woman looked like, his mind kept fashioning her after someone he had known in graduate school. Whatever she looked like, she was good with words. The cover letter for her resume, although excessively long by conventional standards, pulsed with a vibrant energy which left him wanting even more.

Dr. Kundera was well credentialed and highly qualified for the position, just what the search committee said they were looking for. But what was she looking for? Maybe she'd move to Atlanta, but certainly not Ashland, South Carolina. Perhaps she was simply casting a broad net.

A raspy voice announced that her flight was arriving. Eager to be on their way, people gathered their belongings and started forming a line. Several individuals stood back, waiting for their party to disembark. He joined them, holding a manila folder with his name printed in bold black letters. Now he was wondering if he could spot her first from the impressions which had formed in his mind. Why not give it a try? She'd never know, he thought.

The passengers disembarked: several business men; a few older folks; a handsome couple with two small girls. Then a petite woman with short, frosted hair came bouncing through the door, carrying a briefcase. That's her, he thought. She certainly had high energy. His eyes followed her as she hurried across the way, but she didn't even look at him.

"Dr. Roberts," a woman called as she made her way toward him.

Smartly dressed in a white silky blouse and black slacks, Angela Kundera was tall, willowy, with dark eyes, long black hair, and a pleasant face adorned with dangling silver earrings. She extended her hand with total confidence.

"Welcome, Angela," he said taking her hand as her exotic perfume struck his nostrils.

"Thank you, Dr. Roberts. What a pleasure to meet you at last."

"Please call me Barsh. We're informal at Cooper as you can see by the way I'm dressed."

"Barsh. A family name I presume?"

"Yes, indeed. Needless to say, I know who's being summonsed when I hear it."

"Don't ask me why, but it's a perfect fit for you. I hope you know how excited I am to be here. There's something about Cooper College that intrigues me."

"And we're all pleased that you're interested in Cooper. Do you need a restroom before we get underway?"

"A good idea. I'll be right back."

There's something sweet about this woman, he thought, as he watched her walk away. He had known she was intelligent and sophisticated. But *sweet?* Was that a Southern expression? He couldn't imagine her being flattered by such a tag. He had met too many hard academic women at conferences who would consider it male condescension.

Pacing, he felt strangely energized. He had been so emotionally devitalized by Debbie's decision to leave him that duty alone had kept him going in a perfunctory way. Now he was thinking about the students. The English majors would love Dr. Kundera. He knew it was unlikely that Cooper would be able to bring her on board, but he decided to make every effort to sell her on the college. It just might be his last chance to do something significant for the students.

***

With her suitcase in hand, he led the way to the airport exit, the heels of his boots clanking hard against the floor and Angela gliding along as if she were walking on air. They went side by side through the parking lot in a graceful silence, saving their conversation for the confinement of the car.

He was reconsidering his plan to take her to Jackson's Steak House near Ashland. She might be a vegetarian. Perhaps he should take her to a restaurant in Charlotte that had a more diverse menu.

"Here's the car. Sorry, but this was the closest parking space I could find."

"Not a problem. I enjoyed the walk."

Having deposited her luggage in the trunk, he turned to face her. A breeze lifted her glossy hair across her face. She brushed it aside and looked down at his boots.

"I've been admiring your boots," she said looking him straight in the eye. "What kind are they?"

"Durango harness boots," he said and dropped his eyes for a moment.

"Brown is definitely your color. I mean with your light brown hair."

"I wore boots like these all through high school. I had a pair for school and a pair for riding my horse. I always chose brown to match the saddle leather. These, however, are the first I've had since I left home for college. Bought them the first of the year, and I'm sticking with them for the foreseeable future."

"What about the ponytail and beard?"

"They go back a few years, the summer of 1970 to be precise. I think I was the only man in Ashland that year with a beard and long hair."

"Well, I like them both, especially the way you trim your beard. That's a short ponytail. Do you trim your hair, too?"

"I try to keep it about shoulder length. That suits me better."

"Good choice. And the Durango harness boots go well with your height and broad shoulders. Frankly, I don't know anyone rugged enough to wear them. Take it as a compliment, but I would never have guessed that you chaired the Division of Humanities at Cooper or anywhere for that matter."

"Then I'll accept it as such."

He opened the passenger door and held it for her, a bit apprehensive that she'd think him too patronizing. He was all for women's liberation, but he was never sure about what a new woman expected of him. He had been taught to open doors for women, always, and to shake hands only if the woman offered hers first. Now he didn't know what was expected of him, so he followed his old habits but with some hesitancy, or social stuttering as he called it. Angela gracefully eased into the leather bucket seat and looked up at him with an engaging smile.

Okay, he thought as he walked behind the car. She's certainly pleasant to be with. Then settled in his seat, he keyed the ignition, buckled up, and turned to face her.

"Angela, there's a first-rate steakhouse on our way to Ashland. We can stop there for dinner or we can dine here in Charlotte. Your choice."

"The steakhouse suits me."

"Good. I think you'll like the place."

He left the airport, constantly shifting the gears of the five-speed Audi 5000 as he stopped and started in the traffic.

"I'm looking forward to introducing you to Jackson's Steak House, a rustic place overlooking the Broad River. It's my favorite restaurant around Ashland. Sometimes we leave early and drive along the back roads of the river to Cherokee Falls and then make a loop back through the rolling hills to the restaurant."

"We?"

"My wife and daughter. Hannah is eleven and the light of my life."

"It must be wonderful to have a child."

"It's the greatest joy but also the most horrific responsibility. It's terrifying to think you might fail your own child as a parent."

"That's a somber note."

"Forgive me. I've been rather self-absorbed of late."

"No, it struck home, I'm sorry to say."

He glanced at her. She was staring straight ahead and didn't turn to make eye contact with him. Honoring her silence, he focused on getting to I-85 and out of the Charlotte traffic. Her mental flight was swift.

"You were telling me about the drive to the restaurant. It sounds picturesque."

"It is, but there's something haunting about that drive: the sharp contrast between the natural beauty of the place and the harshness of human life, typified by the crude houses and ramshackle barns scattered along the way."

"Oh my, you have the soul of a poet."

"How I wish that were true, but I'm far too analytical."

"Have you ever written poetry?"

"My freshman year in college. But the Dean, who was an honored poet, gave me such a devastating critique that I never tried it again."

"That was so unfortunate that the Dean cut you down that way. I don't praise poor work, but I always find something positive to say about a student's effort before I start making constructive comments. I believe anyone who has a good eye, feels deeply about things, and loves language, is capable of writing decent poetry. With that bag of tools, which you undoubtedly have, all you need to do is read and write; read and write until you find your own creative voice."

"You make it sound easy."

"No, it is not easy, but it is possible."

"Our English majors will love you, Angela."

"Thanks for the compliment. I trust I will get to meet some of them tomorrow?"

"Definitely. Would you like for me to go over the agenda?"

"Maybe at the restaurant. I've been trying to visualize Cherokee Falls. My parents took me to Niagara Falls when I was nine. They were awesome."

"We're not talking about the same thing here. These falls are quite ordinary. It's just that I love waterfalls. So I like to drive down to see them when we're out that way. We do have splendid waterfalls in our Carolina Mountains, and many are within easy driving distance from Ashland."

"That's a plus for Cooper College. If I get an appointment, I'll be checking them out."

"Well, now that I know you like waterfalls, we could drive to Cherokee Falls before dinner if you'd like. We might even get there in time to watch the sun paint the western sky with its weeping descent into the nether world."

"Ah, a man who can still envision the world mytho-poetically. Yes, I'd love for you to take me there."

"Good," he said and accelerated through a caution light.

She didn't respond further and he found himself uncomfortable with the silence. He could drive for hours without speaking, totally preoccupied with thought. Trying to think of something relevant to say, he acted as if he were concentrating on the heavy traffic.

"This is a fun car," she said breaking the silence. "Watching you shift gears brings back childhood memories of my first efforts behind the steering wheel long before I was old enough for a license."

"Actually, this straight shift is part of my nostalgic jag. When I was in high school, Dad bought a new car and gave me his old Ford pickup. Both were straight shifts. The car had the gearshift on the steering column, but the pickup had a long stick mounted in the floor. I loved that truck. It had a blown muffler and I would leave school every afternoon, double-clutching each gear just for the racket I could make."

"I bet you were a hellion, right?"

"Oh, no, I was quite tame at school, although I did have a different country style. An outdoors boy in those days, I wasn't studious, but the teachers liked me because I respected them and listened to what they had to say.

"Angela, you can relax and rest in silence. Or you can ask me any questions that come to mind. Or you can tell me about yourself. I'll take my cue from you."

"Actually, I'm not tired. What do you mean you had a different country style? Tell me about your youth."

"Okay, but I must warn you that my roots strike deep in an old agrarian culture that will likely bore you to death or else put you on the warpath. First and foremost, I loved hunting, fishing, and camping in the wild. Next, I loved riding my Quarter Horse. That's the difference I was talking about. None of my schoolmates had that combination of interests. There was also four years of varsity football in the mix. And my senior year, I had a Harley-Davidson motorcycle."

"Well, now that you have aroused my interest, please tell me where you grew up."

"Central East Alabama. I was born on a farm, but before I was old enough to know anything about farming, Dad bought a sawmill and got into the lumber business. When I was nine, we moved to town. Then we moved back to the country the summer before I started high school.

"I loved living in the country. None of the roads in our community were paved so they were excellent for horseback riding, which I did frequently late into the night. And I could walk ten minutes, east or west, from our house and be in some forest with my shotgun and hunting dogs."

"Do you still hunt?"

"No, and the hunting days of my youth were not what you're probably thinking. It was not a sport for me but a way to put food on the table. Actually, it was a part of my agrarian heritage. I regret to say that my paternal grandmother's people once owned slaves, and so did my mother's people on both sides. The Robertses were the exception. They were both unionists and abolitionists. No one in my extended family talked about slavery or segregation when I was growing up. Those topics were too controversial for polite conversation.

"I never knew about the slaves until a few years ago, and it really hit me hard. That was one burden I didn't think I'd have to bear as a Southerner. Segregation, yes. I was a part of that system and was far too insensitive to its cruel injustices until I was about seventeen. As an eyewitness to a killing, I was the primary witness for the defense of a black man accused of murdering a white man. Although I testified that he killed the white man in self-defense, the all white jury convicted him of first-degree murder and sentenced him to death."

"That must have been a horrible experience."

"It shook me to the foundation of my being. I probably wouldn't be where I am now if that hadn't happened. Sorry to have digressed, Angela. I was trying to tell you how my hunting days were tied to my agrarian roots before I got sidetracked."

"No apology needed. I'm interested in your story."

"Well, the status of my ancestors had declined over the years from successful farmers, most of whom had owned slaves, to farmers who barely scratched out a living from the land. When my father was growing up on an eighty-acre farm, hunting was an important element in their agrarian life. It was a way of putting food on the table. That's the hunting culture my father introduced me to, and I felt good about being a skillful hunter, who could contribute something to the table.

"I also liked being a part of the wild, that is, what was left of it. I would spend days alone camping in the forest, living off the land. But that was another life."

"You were definitely different."

Focused on telling his story, he had gotten stuck behind an eighteen-wheeler slowly whining up a steep grade of the Interstate, the left-lane traffic flashing by in a steady stream.

"Sorry," he said. "I'm usually a better driver than to get caught this way."

"It happens to me all the time."

"Why don't you tell me about your youth? I'm embarrassed that I've been talking so much about myself."

"I'm intrigued by your background. I've never known anyone like you. Yes, I want to tell you about my youth, but before I get started on that, I'd like to know where you did your graduate work and what your specialty was. You, of course, have read my resume."

"And I reread it this afternoon. You have a most impressive resume. I did my doctoral work at Emory University, and our graduate specialties are only separated by two to three millennia. You focused on Southern literature and I on Biblical literature, which spans almost a thousand years and is written in two totally different languages. As you probably know, Hebrew is Semitic, and Greek is Indo-European. So I've spent a lot of time studying those languages and the culture of the Ancient Near East. I don't get to specialize at Cooper, however. I teach a wide range of courses in religious studies and philosophy. I also teach a few interdisciplinary humanities courses."

"Oh ... I assumed you were a member of the English faculty."

"This search is atypical. The Chair of the English Department is leaving under unpleasant circumstances. There are two contenders who want to become the new chair. Dean Thompson doesn't want to reveal her hand until the end of the semester. So she asked me, as Chair of the Division, to oversee the search, but I won't be voting on the candidates. My job is to keep the committee on task until the position is filled."

"I wasn't questioning your role in the search. I was just surprised. Pleasantly surprised, I should add. Unfortunately, I've never taken any religion courses, but I have recently found myself interested in the subject. Maybe you could tutor me if I get the position."

There was a break in the left-lane traffic and he gunned it past the eighteen-wheeler.

"Yes, of course. Once I find out what your interests are, I'll recommend some great books for you, and we can discuss them."

"I would like that. Barsh, I'm impressed by the breadth of your teaching."

"The critical study of religion is of necessity interdisciplinary. So breadth just comes with the territory. I try to keep up with current scholarship in several related disciplines: anthropology, linguistics, psychology, sociology, and philosophy. Recently, I've been focusing my reading on twentieth-century novels.

"Actually, I've been reading to become a generalist in the humanities. Two years ago, we changed the academic year to include a January Interim. The students spend the whole month studying a single subject designed specifically for the interim. The first year, I taught a course on Perspectives in Black Literature, and this year I taught one on Sexuality in Contemporary Fiction. My approach was to look for ideas, world views, that kind of thing."

"Those are the kind of courses I would enjoy teaching."

"Then Cooper just might be a good place for you. If you're passionate about a special subject, Catherine, that is Dean Thompson, will let you develop that passion into a new course, and only you will get to teach it. Over the years, she has become my closest and dearest friend. The two of us have wide-ranging discussions on a regular basis, and sometimes we're on opposite sides."

"Like what?"

"The Civil War for one thing. Catherine still laments it as The Lost Cause."

"She defends the Confederacy?"

"Yes, but from a philosophical position: the sovereign rights of the states and the rights of the people to assert their independence from old unions and form new ones. She has a point given the philosophical notions found in the Declaration of Independence.

"The difference between us lies in the fact that I can't separate slavery from the political position of the Confederacy and she can. I don't believe the Southern States had a just cause for seceding from the Union. There were significant regional differences, but I do not believe the Southern States would have seceded if it were not for the issue of slavery. Because there is no valid justification for slavery, there was no valid justification for the Confederacy.

"General Grant was only half right in asserting that the Confederate cause was one of the worst for which people ever fought. The South fought, with justification, to defend its homeland from the invading forces of the Union. I only fault the Southern States for seceding without just cause, not for defending their homeland. So I agree with Dean Thompson who calls the conflict the War of Northern Aggression.

"True, South Carolina fired first on Fort Sumter, but they considered it a foreign fort in their homeland. The matter should have been resolved through negotiations, and South Carolina had appointed a commission to do that.

"The Union definitely brought the war to the Confederacy. Therefore, I fault the Union for two things. First, I see no moral justification for the Union to sacrifice hundreds of thousands of its own people to conquer the Confederacy. Second, there was no moral justification for the brutal way the Union ravaged the Confederate States. Although freeing the slaves became a significant byproduct of the war, the primary mission of the Northern armies was to defeat the Confederacy and bring the Southern States back into the Union.

"In spite of all the horrors caused by both sides, I do find two redemptive things about that war: the restoration of the Union and the abolition of slavery. That means the South had to lose, no matter what the cost. And both sides paid a horrific price. It has taken the South a century just to begin to heal from the curses of slavery and the devastation of defeat."

Silence, except for the sounds of the Audi as they sped down the Interstate. What was she thinking? Had he just blown the case for Cooper?

"Angela, I'm sorry I brought up the subject. I'm afraid I've given you the wrong impression of Dean Thompson. She holds the South responsible for its ungodly system of slavery and she is by no means a racist. She led the fight to integrate Cooper."

"Please, I don't have a problem with Dean Thompson. Besides, you just told me she's your dearest and closest friend. You're lucky and I'm envious. I've never had a friendship like that."

"Okay, you're on. Take me into the world of Angela Kundera while I drive us to Jackson's Steak House by way of Cherokee Falls."

"I was born in Peekskill, New York. It's on the Hudson River not far from New York City and I've always lived near the Big Apple."

They were headed south on I-85 with Angela sketching the highlights of her youth, Barsh soaking up every word with pleasure. For the moment, he had forgotten his troubles.

CHAPTER THREE

Barsh kept his eyes on the road as they approached the outskirts of Ashland. He couldn't remember a more enjoyable dinner than he had just experienced with Angela at Jackson's. She had kept him totally engaged with lively discussions of Southern novels.

"I was just thinking about Cherokee Falls," she said. "What a wonderful sunset. Perhaps it was your earlier comment about the sun's weeping descent into the nether world that transformed the moment for me. I definitely felt a strong primal longing. Dinner was delightful and you're an excellent host."

"You're kind to say so, but it's been my pleasure to welcome you to South Carolina. I've reserved a room for you at Ashland Hotel. It's an old establishment, but I thought it would be better for you than one of the motels. Do you need to make any stops before checking in?"

"I don't need anything, but I do like to sense a place at night. Could we possible walk around the campus before you drop me at the hotel?"

"Your wish is my command," he said, surprised that he would be so teasing with a woman he had known for such a short time.

"No sarcasm, please," she said playfully slapping his shoulder. "Wow, you are solid."

"I try to stay in shape."

"I walk a lot to stay fit, but I've never worked out with weights or any of those new exercise machines."

"I walk a lot, too. One of my favorite activities is hiking the trails of our Carolina Mountains. I'm proud to tell you there are a lot of good mountain trails within easy driving distance from Ashland."

"That sounds wonderful. I told you in our phone conversation that I was fascinated by James Dickey's *Deliverance*, especially its setting and the primal yearnings of the protagonist. Do you know the river where they filmed the movie?"

"The Chattooga River. Congress recently named it a Wild and Scenic River, protecting it from damming, logging, and development. There are wonderful trails along the Chattooga, and I've hiked most of them. Rivers and forest used to own my soul, and they still claim a large part of it. I don't think I could live well if I wasn't able to spend time with nature."

"I would dearly love to hike with you along the Chattooga River."

"If you accept the position at Cooper, I promise to take you."

"Accept it? First, I have to get an offer."

"I don't want to jinx you. Let me just say that part is not worrying me."

"Then what part is worrying you?"

"You haven't seen the college. Cooper is as different from Brown as night is from day."

"Good, I'm looking for something very different from Brown."

"Then hope is a wing. You know, that little thing with feathers. Now why would I think of Emily Dickinson? Well, you're both good with words."

"Back to the Chattooga River. Was that a genuine promise?"

"Most definitely, and if you like the Chattooga outing, I'll take you to one of my favorite pieces of wilderness, the Joyce Kilmer Memorial Forest, which far exceeds the aesthetic power of Kilmer's poetry. But that marvelous forest would have been logged years ago if it wasn't for his poem 'Trees' and the devotion of his fans. A timber company was about to cut those giant trees when Kilmer's friends discovered it and stopped them."

"I've never heard of the place."

"It's the last major old growth hardwood forest in the South. Giant yellow poplars that will take your breath away. And huge hemlocks."

"For those two excursions I'll make a special trip back down here even if I don't get the job, unless your promise was contingent on my getting the position."

"Absolutely not. It's based on nothing other than your desire to go there. I'm always looking for friends to join me on my forest treks. Fortunately, Hannah is already taking short hikes with me in the mountains. I hope to get a short window of extended hiking with her before she goes crazy over boys."

"What about your wife?"

"Hiking through the forest is one of the last things in the world Debbie would be interested in doing."

"Well, please count me in. I never dreamed my interest in James Dickey's novel would lead me to this exciting moment. Oh, I just thought of something that should interest you. You were asking me about contemporary poets. Dickey is one of the finest poets writing today. Have you read his poetry?"

"No, only his debut novel."

"In literary circles, he's better known as a poet than novelist. He's served two terms as Consultant in Poetry to the Library of Congress, or

Poet Laureate, as most people say. It may also interest you to know that he grew up in Atlanta with a connection to the mountains of North Georgia. There's an earthy, primal quality to much of his poetry."

"Thanks for sharing that. I'll definitely check out his poetry. Angela, we just turned onto College Drive so I'd better prepare you for your first viewing of Cooper. The campus is a hodgepodge of buildings of various styles. Old Main is older than the college, dating back to the 1830's. It was originally a resort hotel, catering to planters from coastal Carolina who brought their families there to escape the summer heat and mosquitoes of the Lowcountry. But whatever you think of the buildings, the trees are magnificent. Some of them are at least three-hundred years old. There's the Quad, straight ahead."

He turned left and skirted the east side of the campus to park in his usual place beside Kimberly Hall. Someone was practicing on one of the grand pianos.

"Listen to that music," she said. "How wonderful. I like the feel of the place already."

"There are benches on the Quad. Would you like to sit and listen to the music awhile?"

"Yes, that would be lovely."

"This is Kimberly Hall. It has large corner studios for our top music professors and a number of practice rooms for students on first floor. Some faculty offices, including mine, are upstairs."

"Will my office be there if I get the job?"

"Most likely. After I pick you up at the hotel and take you to breakfast, we'll come here to my office. That'll give you some idea about office space at Cooper."

They sat on a wrought iron bench beneath a dogwood tree in front of Kimberly, the night flooding with the music pouring from the open windows. The piece, which he couldn't identify, ended with a flourish and the pianist rose to close the windows of her studio.

"That's Margaret Glenn. Students, faculty, and town folks adore her. Shall I show you more of the campus or have you seen enough for tonight?"

"More, please. I want to get a feel for the whole place."

They strolled around the Quad, which was quiet, Barsh giving a brief history of each building and its current use. The back campus, however, was much alive with stereos blaring, students scurrying from dorm to dorm. He and Angela kept ambling along until they ended up on a bench by the lake.

"Barsh, I didn't fully understand my expectations when I flew out of Providence this afternoon, but I had a strong feeling that something good was in store for me in South Carolina. Please know that feeling is burning brighter than ever."

"That's good to hear. But take your time evaluating everything. Culturally, Ashland is about as far from New York as you can get in the States."

"But aren't you happy here?"

"Only because my interests and goals have changed. When I left Emory, I had big ideas about making a name for myself in the world of Biblical scholarship and teaching in a graduate program at a major university. I got off to a good start by reading a paper at the national meeting of the American Academy of Religion. I felt confident that I had solved a problem that had plagued Biblical scholars for centuries, but even so, I was surprised that my paper was so well received. The next year it was published in an international journal. The solution I charted seems to be winning the day with Biblical scholars everywhere.

"Here's my point. I believe that I had the potential to actualize my earlier goals, but now I have no interest in spending my life studying more and more about less and less, which is what one has to do to become a nationally known Biblical scholar. It's all about specialization.

"I care deeply about the students at Cooper. The most satisfactory aspect of my tenure has been the positive response of the students, most of whom have had little or no introduction to critical thinking. I'm confident that I've made a greater contribution here than I could've at a major university. I'm also confident that you'll be wonderful for our students if you can make the adjustments."

"If it will ease your mind, I'll tell you that I'm looking for a Southern experience with this move."

"Well, there's nothing more Southern than South Carolina."

"I know. Look. The moon is coming up."

They sat watching the crescent moon rising above the distant trees. As it cleared the horizon, a silver wake shimmered across the lake straight into their eyes as if it were bringing some special message just for them.

"I've never seen a more beautiful moonrise," she said. "It's a new moon, too, and I'm taking that as a good omen."

"Then I shall also take it as a good omen," he said thinking how desperately he needed a change of luck. "Angela, I hate to say so but I need to check you in the hotel and get on home."

"Then, reluctantly, I will go."

Silently, they drifted back toward the Quad. One of his religion majors greeted him warmly in passing, her quizzical face announcing surprise at seeing him on campus at night with a strange woman. Back at Kimberly Hall, they met a couple strolling, hand in hand, toward the dorms.

"Ah, to be young and in love," she said. "Do you ever long for your old college days?"

"Heavens, no. I might as well have been a monk. All I did, day and night, was study during the whole school year. Then for two months every summer, I worked hard during the day with a construction company, building houses in the suburbs of Birmingham. After work each day there was more serious reading late into the night. I don't remember having a single date during the whole four years.

"My only break from studying was the month before the fall semester when I toured the country with Uncle Edward, my father's only brother. I was his driver, and we took in most of the United States and parts of Canada during the four summers I lived with him. From Key West to Nova Scotia and San Diego to Vancouver and lots of interesting places in between."

"I'm surprised that you can't recall a single date during your collage years."

"In high school, I had a lot of balls in the air. In college, I was a dull young man. Serious as hell and dull as dirt."

"No, I'm not going to believe that."

"Okay, but it's the truth. For me personally, however, it was a time of tremendous intellectual and spiritual growth. And I should add that the travels with Uncle Edward were very special and rewarding. Unfortunately, I've had only one summer of extended travel since then. The summer before Hannah was born, I toured Europe in a two-seater Fiat convertible all by myself."

"Well, there's nothing dull about you now. And I should add that I'm envious of your travels. Extensive travel is something that I've longed for but haven't yet had a chance to experience."

"Then Cooper could be the place to get you started on that. We have a strong Faculty Development Fund, thanks to the generosity of our alumna and devoted trustee Georgette Wingo, who is Ashland's wealthiest citizen. Each year a number of faculty members enjoy study and travel with grants from this fund. I haven't taken advantage of it, but I'm getting the travel bug again. Just know that you'd be a prime candidate for study-travel grants."

"I'm pleased to hear that."

"Oh, here's something that might interest you. Georgette spent most of her adult life in New York City before returning here to the house she grew up in, and she still maintains her apartment there. Catherine is her closest friend and usually spends time with her at that apartment every summer. Georgette has invited me up several times, but I've yet to accept because of Hannah.

"Here's my point. There aren't many cosmopolitan women in Ashland, and I'm sure Georgette will be eager to establish a friendship with you. She's also a big patron of the arts and will be doubly pleased to learn that you're a poet and novelist. Catherine and I will certainly make the introduction if you're interested."

"As I told you, I'm envious of your special friendship with Catherine so, yes, the possibility of a friendship with Georgette does interest me. I also hope that you and I can become friends. Could we correspond even if I don't get the job?"

"I promise you that I will not be the one to break any correspondence. If you write, I'll answer."

"Then you can be on the lookout for a letter soon."

They left the campus for the hotel. After checking her in, he carried her suitcase to the room and placed it on the luggage rack. When he turned around to leave, there she was, searching his eyes.

"Barsh, this has been an evening of special magic for me, and I hate to see it end."

He wished her a good night, which she returned, and left the room, trembling.

CHAPTER FOUR

Hannah and Debbie were both asleep when he got home. Typically, he would head for the basement about this time for his evening workout. On Sundays, Tuesdays, and Thursdays, his routine lasted about an hour and included heavy weights. The other days, he cut the time to about thirty minutes. There was nothing habitual about this Thursday, however. Even the house seemed oddly strange to him after being with Angela.

He got a beer and went to the study to settle down, but that was impossible. Angela's voice had followed him into his sanctuary. *Barsh, this has been an evening of special magic for me, and I hate to see it end.* What was happening to him?

Always in control of his emotions, he was not in the habit of being carried away with a woman. Why then was he responding so to this woman? She was a candidate for a position in the English Department and would be on a plane, flying north, in less than twenty-four hours. He would probably never see her again.

He took the empty beer bottle to the trashcan in the kitchen and went to the bathroom. On the way back to the study, he thought about April Morehouse, his high school heartthrob, and that thought soon took his mind to Rachel Foster. He had seen neither woman in years and could not remember the last time he had thought about them. Why was he thinking about them now?

Then the connection dawned on him. They were the last two women who had caused him to tremble in their presence before that numinous moment with Angela at the hotel. With crystal clarity, he remembered how strange it was that he had experienced that divine shiver with April and then with Rachel on the same afternoon, almost twenty-seven years ago.

***

It was the last period of the day at Handley High. Barsh walked into study hall in the school library and sat at his usual table with his back to an open window, the expanse of the room before him. April Morehouse, absorbed in a novel, was seated at her place two tables away. Noticing the changing expression on her face, he remembered her amazing confession in English class earlier that year. She had gotten so engrossed in a novel that she fainted at a terrifying moment in the story. What was she reading now? He wondered. If he were a wizard, he would cause everyone in study hall to vanish, except the two of them, while she described for him the setting, characters, and plot of the book she was about to finish.

For two years he had admired her delicate beauty and demure ways. In truth, he loved her ever so dearly in the innermost chamber of his heart, that secret place that only he could enter.

The granddaughter of the late Dr. Albert Norton, she was a member of one of the most distinguished families in town, and he was a fool for loving her. What chance did he, or any country boy, have of winning her love?

At least he hadn't humiliated himself with awkward advances like a couple of classmates. He was always courteous and reserved in her presence. Forwardness had no place in his code of honor.

Love is weird, he thought as he doodled in his notebook. While he yearned for April Morehouse, who had shown no interest in him, a sexy freshman had fluttered her dreamy eyes at him all year. Flattered by her on-going attention that started during football season, he teased her just enough to keep her adoration alive. But April was the only girl he ever envisioned wearing his football sweater. Even a country boy could dream.

He hadn't dated anyone since Amy Burdette betrayed him two summers ago. At first he thought he would never again experience that incredible feeling of being in love, but he had already learned that a romantic heart is as strange as a phoenix. From the ashes of first love, his heart had flickered to life to soar once again on the wings of his fantastic imagination. In reality, he had found a love in April Morehouse, but not a lover.

Study hall was almost over and he had done nothing but muse the period away. Several times he had scanned the room to steal a glance at April, always on the sly. A cool breeze caught the back of his neck and he turned to the window to check the weather. The sky was clear, not a cloud in sight. It would be a good night to ride his Quarter Horse.

April was studying him intently, and she held her gaze for a few moments before dropping her eyes. He had no idea what went on in her head. She was smart. He knew that from her responses in class. But what did she dream about? And why was she studying him? Twice now in one week, he had observed her studying him. Hope was stirring in his heart.

HONEY FROM A LION

It was late spring, 1951, the last week of his sophomore year at Handley High, and he was wishing, for the first time ever, that there were a few more weeks left before summer break. He couldn't recall ever seeing April except at school and school-related activities, and he would not likely see her during the whole summer break. Living five miles out in the country, he rarely came to town during the summer, except for farm supplies. His town friends came to see him often, but he never visited them. There was too much to do in the country, and he enjoyed it all.

April lived on North Main Street in a big house with expansive grounds. Everybody knew it as Dr. Norton's house, although he was long dead. Her mother had grown up in that house and then gone off to the University of Alabama where she met and married John Morehouse, a successful pharmacist. Two years ago they moved into the big house to help care for April's ailing grandmother. Her father opened Morehouse Pharmacy and she joined Barsh's freshman class.

From the first day she appeared in class, he knew she was special. She was slight, almost frail, and her eyes were reticent. Her skin was fair and her long blond hair was striking. To his knowledge, she didn't have a boyfriend. Nor did she seem to have any close girlfriends.

The bell rang ending study hall and the school day. He knew April would go to their homeroom and pack her things. If her mother was not there to pick her up, she would sit on the steps near the sidewalk, waiting for her. He went to his homeroom and looked out the window. Mrs. Morehouse's new Buick was nowhere in sight.

Leaving homeroom, he lingered in the hall, talking with a friend, until April had time to settle on the top step of the stairs. Then he descended the steps with his heart racing and, stopping on the sidewalk, he turned to face her. She seemed unhappy.

"April, your book report last week was very good. I always enjoy your reports."

"Well, thank you."

"I never thought I'd say such a thing, but I'm going to miss that class. Miss Little is the best English teacher I've ever had."

"You just don't know how much I'm going to miss that class. I'm like Miss Little. I'd die if I didn't have good novels to read."

"I wish I had more time to read, but there's just too much to do in this world."

"That was the most fun the other day when you and Miss Little were discussing a story. You think about things that would never cross my

25

mind in a million years. I like that about you. I'll probably have a good cry when school ends Friday."

"I won't cry," he said, "but I'll miss seeing everybody. Anyway, I hope you have a good summer. Do you have any special plans?"

"Summer is always a sad time for me. I'll stay home, except for our vacation at Panama City Beach. What about you? What will your summer be like?"

"Work for the most part. I have a farm to take care of. I'm building up a herd of Black Angus cattle, which means raising corn and hay and taking care of the pastures. I'll also be working at a planer mill during the regular workday Monday through Friday. But I'll find time for fun things, too."

"That's why you're so strong, all that hard work. And all I ever do is sit and read."

"Give me the outdoors, any day, for work or play. The only time I read is late at night or when I'm stuck indoors on a rainy day."

"Oh, that reminds me of something. I just read the most wonderful novel about this girl and her horse. Someone said that you have a horse. Is that true?"

"Yes, that's one of the great things about living in the country. In fact, I'm riding my horse tonight."

"You ride at night?"

"That's about the only time I have to ride, other than Sunday afternoons. It's also a good time, especially on a starlight night with a good moon. But we ride in all kinds of weather, up one dirt road and down another, sometimes until well past midnight."

"Who rides with you?"

"A neighbor. She's just a kid, but she has a special way with horses."

"Do you have a picture of your horse?"

"No, but he's a beautiful animal. I wish you could see him."

"What's his name?"

"Thunder."

"Thunder? Does that mean he's spirited?"

"Very spirited. He loves to run."

"Oh, darn, here's Mother. I'll see you tomorrow. Have a good ride tonight."

"I'm sure I will."

April stood and walked past him, looking up into his gray-green eyes with the sweetest smile. She stopped and turned back, studying his face, as he stood there trembling with excitement.

"I must say that flattop looks good on you. That's the first thing I noticed about you when we moved here. That and your strong arms. And your face is always so tan, even in winter."

"That's because I spend so much time outdoors."

She gave him a big smile, yielded her eyes, and slowly walked away. He would milk that smile for a long time. But what a contrast they posed at that moment. She was the essence of refinement in her pale blue dress, not even reaching his broad shoulders. At almost six feet and still growing, he looked as rugged as the Wild West, dressed in a tan cotton shirt, faded blue jeans, and brown harness boots.

He hurried across the schoolyard to his 1946 Ford pickup. The truck was nothing to brag about, but he was proud to have it. It kept him from having to ride the bus to and from school, and it met his transportation needs for camping, fishing, and hunting.

He felt lucky as he drove out of the parking lot. April Morehouse had actually talked to him with real interest. He wished he had a picture of Thunder to show her, but there was no way to get one developed before school ended Friday. He would have pictures of Thunder before school started again in September.

September ... such a long time to have to wait to see April's sweet face, he thought. Maybe her mother would drive her out to the farm to see Thunder some Sunday afternoon. He had to find a way to invite her without being presumptuous. If she mentioned the horse again, that would be his cue.

He was almost home before he remembered the feed he was supposed to pick up for Joe Foster's cattle. He turned around and headed back to town. At Randolph Farm Supplies, he charged four one-hundred-pound sacks of crushed grain to his neighbor's account and set out to deliver them to the Foster farm, which was on a back road about a mile from where Barsh lived.

Joe Foster had taken over the family farm after his father died and started raising Black Angus cattle to supplement his income as a clerk at Randolph Farm Supplies. Then the Korean War broke out and he was obsessed with the notion of fighting for his country on foreign soil.

His older brother, a decorated World War II hero, had filled him with stories about the glories of war. Now it was Joe's time to fight the communists in Korea so he volunteered for service in the Army. Off he went, leaving behind his wife Rachel, a small son Lewis, and a feeble mother. Before leaving for basic training, he hired Barsh to look after his Black Angus until he returned.

Most days there was nothing for him to do on the Foster farm. He had to bush-hog the pastures whenever they needed it, put out hay for the cattle during the winter months, and see that the bull had extra feed during breeding periods.

Driving up to the Foster farm that afternoon, he was surprised to see Rachel's car. She worked as a teller at First Commercial Bank, and it was too early for her to be home. Was someone sick?

He backed the pickup to the barn to unload the feed, still concerned about Rachel's being home. With ease, he threw a hundred-pound sack of crushed grain on his shoulder and carried it to the feed room. Returning to the truck for another sack, he saw Rachel coming toward him.

"Hey, Barsh. Thanks for bringing the feed."

"Glad to do it. I didn't expect you to be home. Is Lewis sick?"

"No, Mrs. Foster hasn't been feeling well lately so I took her to the doctor this morning and decided to stay home the rest of the day."

"I hope it's nothing serious."

"Her blood pressure is way too high. That's the main thing. She should be all right if she'll take the medicine the doctor prescribed. She can be contrary at times. Barsh, do you know what I'd like to do this afternoon?"

"What's that?"

"Go swimming at the Boy Scout Lake. Joe and I used to swim there a lot. I'm afraid to go by myself. Could you meet me there in about thirty minutes?"

"If that's what you want."

"Oh, thank you, thank you. You don't know how much this means to me. I never get to do anything anymore, except work and look after Lewis and Mrs. Foster. I'll meet you at the lake in thirty minutes."

He drove home, thinking about Rachel all the way. Why hadn't it occurred to him that she was having a hard time while Joe was in Korea? It was a bloody war, and he could be killed any day. Just worrying about that possibility alone would be enough to drive her crazy. Moreover, she was bound to be tired and lonely.

He parked the pickup in the backyard and rushed into the house to get his swimsuit. His dear mother was working in the kitchen.

"I was getting worried about you, Barsh."

"I had to pick up some feed for Joe's cattle. I'm going swimming in the Boy Scout Lake. I haven't been since last summer, and I need a good swim."

"Well, please be careful."

"You know I will."

He found his swimsuit, rolled it in a towel, and left for the lake, which was less than three miles from his house. Driving down the bumpy dirt road, he wished he was on his way to meet April Morehouse somewhere.

He turned off the main road onto the dead-end drive that wound up a steep grade to the lake nestled in a hardwood forest. He parked near the dam and ran up the path to the Boy Scout lodge to change into his swimsuit.

Back at the lake, he dove into the blue water from the dock and swam hard to the upper end and back to the dock, where he stretched out on his towel to await Rachel's arrival. He sat up at the sound of a car. Rachel parked next to his pickup and got out. He assumed that she would be wearing her swimsuit, but she was still dressed as she had been at the barn. This was no place for a woman to change clothes.

"Barsh, come over this way and watch out for me while I change into my swimsuit."

"Okay," he said and started toward her.

"That's good. Stand there and give a yell if you see anyone coming."

She slid into the back seat and closed the door. It was impossible for him to keep his eyes on the road when she began taking off her clothes and draping them over the front seat. God, he could see her breasts as she stretched back against the seat to pull up the swimsuit. Out of the car, she adjusted the swimsuit and then hurried toward him, carrying a big bag.

"Thanks for coming. I want to sunbathe for a while on the dock and then take a swim before I have to go. I don't have a lot of time today."

Rachel settled on her towel and started oiling herself generously. The sight of her spread legs, which were surprisingly athletic, aroused him in spite of his efforts to control himself. She was a married woman. Well oiled, Rachel stretched out on her towel.

"Lie down beside me and talk to me. Is Susan Henry your sweetheart? Tell me the truth. She practically lives with you."

"No, I don't have a sweetheart. Susan is just a friend. We like to ride together. That's all."

"Well, you've certainly changed things around here. Nobody ever rode a horse before you came. You and Thunder were a sight for sore eyes, racing by our place. It wasn't long until Susan got a horse and then John Marshall. You've even got me wanting to join in the fun. You know what I'd like to do?"

"What?"

"To ride double with you some night. Can I?"

"Anytime."

"Oh, thank you. But I don't want Mrs. Foster to know about it. That won't be a problem, though. I can slip off and meet you at the barn after she and Lewis are asleep. We can ride in our pasture, just me and you. No one will ever know about it but us."

"If that's what you want. Just let me know when."

"I will and soon."

Rachel was nine years older than Barsh. He had always admired her and thought Joe Foster was a lucky man to have her as a wife. But he would never again think of her in that same innocent way. He had seen her breasts and trembled in her presence. And now she wanted to ride double with him on Thunder, secretly in their pasture at night.

***

Barsh broke his musing about that school day so long ago and went to the refrigerator to get another beer. Alcohol was not a daily part of his life. He would drink a cocktail at a party or a glass of wine when he ate out at a good restaurant. Occasionally, he would drink a beer at home, careful always not to fall into a rut. Earlier that evening with Angela at Jackson's Steak House, he'd had a whisky sour and then wine with dinner. Now he wanted a second beer. So what? Even an old stoic should break his habits from time to time.

When he returned to his desk with the beer, he was still thinking about Rachel Foster. That day at the lake, he was not absolutely certain what she had in mind for them, but she had given him the most important rule. Whatever the two of them did together, it should remain a secret.

Before two weeks passed, he was entangled in an adulterous relationship with Rachael, which lasted almost a year. It ended abruptly when she received word that Joe would be coming home from Korea without his left arm. The night she told him the news, their relationship immediately reverted back to what it was before, without either of them having to verbalize the new reality.

As acts within themselves, he could accept their sexual liaisons without guilt, but when Joe came home, he could no longer isolate them. Every time he saw Joe, he felt guilty for betraying their friendship. Thus his guilt was chronic because Joe still needed his help with the farm. Sundays were the worst when they attended the same church. Rachel would joyfully sing with the congregation while Joe, by her side, was mute as stone. Barsh knew the source of his silence but could only wonder about Joe's.

Whatever the affair had given Barsh, it cost him double. When school started back that fall, April Morehouse was definitely interested in him. She frequently sought him out and flirted with him, but it was too late. How could he court her in good conscience when he was secretly meeting a married woman for sex? Too artless to untangle himself from Rachel, he never asked April for a single date even though he loved her above ever girl in the world. Before the school year ended, a prominent town boy made a move on her, and she became his girlfriend.

As he sat in the study, wondering what had happened to April, the crescent moon on its westward journey crept into view through the big window and his mind jumped immediately to the scene with Angela Kundera by the campus lake. Had its rising been a good omen as she had suggested? He couldn't see a happy life for himself in the foreseeable future.

There was no doubt in his mind that Debbie was moving to Louisville, never to return. His primary responsibility was to find a way to prepare Hannah for the separation and he didn't have a clue. It was almost midnight and he had to get to sleep. Tomorrow would be another long day for him.

CHAPTER FIVE

Angela was waiting in the lobby of the hotel with her suitcase when he got there. She was dressed in a black skirt and a green silky blouse that rippled over her small breasts with the fluid elegance of a brook. And there was her perfume enticing his nostrils. They exchanged greetings with solicitations of each other's well-being and left the hotel.

He took her to breakfast at Ashland Cafe, a local landmark. Their conversation was light with moments of silent reflection as they studied each other with approving eyes.

Back in the car, he drove toward his campus office.

"Are you ready for today's agenda?" he asked.

"Truthfully, I'm getting anxious now that I know I want this position."

"Just keep a positive focus. You'll impress everyone. I know the students and Dean Thompson well enough to know that they'll love you. Just don't overwhelm the English faculty. Play yourself down a little. They already know you're highly qualified for the position. Your major task is to convince them that you are a team player who's looking for a role to play here at Cooper."

"Thanks for the advice."

"Angela, why did you decide to go to graduate school after working for ten years? If it's none of my business, please say so."

"You know from my resume that I worked in public relations for two different companies after I graduated Columbia with a major in English. That was merely to support myself. My aspiration was to become a famous writer. Most nights and weekends I sat in my room typing away. I wrote poems, short stories, and draft after draft of a novel. I got a few poems and two short stories published in literary journals. After my novel got rejected numerous times, I became despondent about my writing and that made my job unbearable. That's when I started applying to graduate schools. Fortunately, Brown accepted me and gave me a handsome fellowship."

"Did your passion for writing come back?"

"Not really. I started writing short stories again and I finished a second novel, but I'm not pleased with my fiction. Here I am at thirty-eight with nothing much to show for my efforts."

"Isn't that called paying your dues? You exude a real passion for life and I can't see you giving up on your dream at thirty-eight. I predict good things for you and your writing."

"You're right about paying my dues, and I'm still in the red. Strangely enough, though, that dream of becoming a writer is dancing in my head this very moment like never before."

"That's good to hear. Well, here we are back at Cooper."

"You're right, the college does look different in the daylight, but I like it anyway."

He parked and led the way to his office upstairs in Kimberly Hall. As they made their way to the second floor, muted sounds of various musical instruments leaked through the padded walls of several practice rooms. He opened the office door and stooped to retrieve two notes students had slid under it. After flipping the light switch, he stepped back and motioned for Angela to enter.

It was a good-size office and he had made good use of the wall space by building floor-to-ceiling bookshelves on both sides of the room. The other wall space was covered with paintings he'd purchased over the years from starving artists.

"These are handsome shelves."

"Thank you. I built them myself."

He opened the window and stood in front of it, watching her as she moved down the row, calling out a few titles from the sections on anthropology, psychology, sociology, history, and science.

"Please have a seat," he said gesturing toward two comfortable chairs in front of the desk."

"Let me see those photos first," she said easing past him to the file cabinet. "Hannah and Debbie, obviously. Both natural beauties as I imagined."

"They're as fair as the flowers of May, to use Grandmother Roberts' expression."

"And this is you and your horse," she said picking up the photo to examine it closely.

"That's Thunder, my Quarter Horse. I doubt it was true, but the man I bought him from said he was sired by a stallion from the famous King Ranch in Texas."

"You've undergone quite a transformation since those days."

"True, but much of that boy still lives deep within my soul."

"That's a fine testament to you and the boy. I take it you don't have a horse now."

"Debbie wouldn't consider living in the country or I'd have at least one horse, probably more."

They moved toward the chairs, Angela perusing the shelves on the opposite wall where he kept his books on philosophy, theology, Biblical studies, the ancient Near East, and world religions. Then they sat down across from the other.

"You have an exceptional collection of scholarly books. They must have cost you a fortune."

"I don't think you can overindulge yourself with books. I'm rather frugal, expect for books."

"Well, I'm impressed. How I'd love to talk with you about some of these. I noticed you have Herbert Marcuse's *Eros and Civilization*. I checked it out of the library once, but I only read a couple of chapters before giving up the effort."

"Marcuse has a way of wearing you down with his style of writing."

"There was another book that caught my eye, *The Denial of Death*."

"That's Ernest Becker's study of the various ways humans attempt to escape their mortality. Strong meat, as they say."

"Then I'm put it on my reading list. Do the Cooper students know how lucky they are to have you?"

"Most of them seem appreciative. But some have a hard time coping with my courses, although I never tell them what they should believe or not believe. I think it's my duty to point out, without compromise, the things they must wrestle with if they want to live authentic lives. Obviously, this is quite threatening to some of the students who come from very conservative home.

"Most of the ministers around here think I'm the Devil personified. They complain to the president and the trustees about me, but so far Dean Thompson has managed to keep them at bay. Catherine is a remarkable woman. I predict you'll like her, and as I've already told you, I'm certain she'll like you."

"I assume you know I'm a vocal advocate for sexual equality, which a lot of religious leaders oppose even though it's the latter half of the twentieth century. Will those ministers who are after you cause me problems?"

"No, they'll not cause you any problems. And yes, I assumed you were a strong advocate for sexual equality as you should be. I have time to show you Old Main before your appointment with Dean Thompson. Shall we head that way?"

Leaving the office, he stopped in the wide central hall.

"Angela, all the offices have outside window and are similar to mine in size. All the members of the English faculty have offices here. And as I told you last evening, I'm rather certain your office would also be on this floor."

"I'd like that," she said and they left.

They walked leisurely to Old Main passing students who were crisscrossing the Quad on the way to their classes. Everyone they met sized Angela up with approving smiles.

In Old Main he gave her a brief tour of the formal parlors with their portraits of past presidents and other Cooper dignitaries. He showed her the George Washington parlor where the faculty came for coffee, gossip, and light banter every morning.

Then they were off to see Dean Thompson, a Cooper alumna from Charleston who had gone on to earn a Ph.D. in American history at UNC Chapel Hill. A thin woman in her early sixties, she was the epitome of Southern grace, which, in her case, was gilded with a rare intellect, giving her an unassuming power that she wielded wisely. She was the major reason Barsh had stayed at Cooper and probably the only force that had kept him from being fired for his liberal views, given the College's conservative trustees. He introduced the two women and returned to his office.

Later that morning, the Dean stopped by his office on her way back from taking Angela to the library conference room for her meeting with the English faculty. She gave him a glowing report on her impressions of Dr. Kundera and left.

He taught his eleven o'clock class and decided to go home for lunch. Angela was dining with the English faculty in the college cafeteria and he wanted to stay out of their way. After lunch, he read in his office, waiting for her to finish her meeting with the English majors.

A little after two o'clock, three English majors, who were almost beside themselves with excitement, brought her back to his office. He was pleased to see that they were so taken with Dr. Kundera. She embraced each of the girls as they were leaving and told them she hoped to see them in the fall.

"Well, I certainly called that one right," he said and motioned for her to have a seat as he came around the desk to sit beside her. "The students are just as excited about you as I assumed they would be."

"They definitely want me to come, and I do want to be here this fall."

"Then let's talk about housing. Do you plan to rent or buy if you accept the position?"

"I'll have to rent for a while."

"The College owns several rental houses near the campus. They're adequate and the rent is reasonable. My favorite one will be available later this summer. Would you be interested in looking at it?"

"Yes, if you don't think it would jinx my getting an offer."

"I hope you won't think I'm presumptuous, but to expedite matters, I talked with the business manager this morning about this house. If you get the position and want to rent it, he'll send you a lease. I also called Elizabeth Campbell about a possible visit this afternoon. She'd love to show you the house and the rose garden she's created over the years. Elizabeth retired last year and is moving back to West Virginia where she grew up. She said we could drop by anytime this afternoon. No need to call."

"Oh, this is exciting. I've lived in apartments ever since I left home. I'm ready for a house."

"Then let's check this one out."

CHAPTER SIX

The visit with Elizabeth Campbell was pleasant and productive. Angela was pleased with the house and wanted to rent it if she got the job. They thanked Elizabeth, wished her well on her move back to West Virginia, and left.

"Angela, most Cooper faculty members live in developments similar to Fern Meadows where I live. You'll be able to buy in a good neighborhood at any time you choose to do so. The cost of housing and property taxes are quite manageable on Cooper salaries."

"That's good news, but I'll be happy renting the college house for a few years."

"Would you like for me to show you some of the neighborhoods where faculty members live?"

"I'd like to see where you live if you don't mind."

"We'll be there in five minutes. Then I'll show you more of Ashland."

He drove through Fern Meadows, discussing the neighborhood, and stopped in front of his house.

"Barsh, could I use your house to change into slacks for the flight home?"

"Well, of course," he said and pulled into the driveway, pleased to see that their housekeeper's car was missing. On some days Davis didn't come until she picked up Hannah from school.

He carried her suitcase into his bedroom, which he described as the guest bedroom, and went to the study just off the kitchen to wait for her. After a few minutes, the toilet flushed, and he heard her coming down the hall. He rose from his desk and waited for her in the kitchen.

"Oh, thank you," she said smiling. "This is much more comfortable."

"Would you like something to drink before we get on the road?"

"A glass of water would be good."

He poured the water and joined her in the study, where she was browsing his books.

"Thanks," she said taking the water. "I love your study. Do you mind if I sit at your desk a minute?"

"Not at all," he said and sat beside her in Hannah's chair.

"Your parents?" she said holding the framed photo.

"That was taken by a traveling photographer soon after they married. Tragically, Mother and Dad were killed in a traffic accident two weeks after I received my Ph.D. from Emory."

"How sad to lose both parents so suddenly. How did you deal with that?"

"With much grief, although not so much for my own loss as for their loss. They deserved many more good years together. I've never known a couple more devoted to each other than they were. I didn't want to lose them, but I could let them go with eternal gratitude because they had given me the things I needed when I was growing up. I never once doubted that they loved and treasured me. That's a great gift, you know."

"I wish I could say the same about my parents. Not a good scene. It's primarily my fault. I have no patience with them, especially Mother. I should make a greater effort to get along with her, and maybe I will. Who's this?"

"My great-grandfather Paw-Paw Roberts. His grandmother was a full-blooded Creek Indian. He loved the old ways and lived like a frontiersman as far as that was possible. Although we share nothing else in common, I'm sure my love of the wild came from his genes. On his ninety-eighth birthday, he announced to everyone present, and that included me, that he had lived long enough. That night he took to his bed, in good health, and refused all food and drink until he died thirteen days later. Everyone pleaded with him to change his mind, but to no avail."

"What an amazing story."

"They buried him beside a big cedar on a hillside overlooking the home place. He'd built the wooden coffin himself, and as he had stipulated, there was no minister involved in the burial. Following his only surviving son, people would step up to the open grave and tell him what he had meant to them. It was quite moving. Afterwards, I regretted that I didn't say something. I kept thinking I would go back and speak my peace, but I never did."

"That sounds like a good pilgrimage for you."

"You're right. It's on my agenda for the summer."

Silence descended between them as she stared out the study window on a brief flight that left him behind. But soon she was back.

"You've got a bit of the wild here in your backyard."

"That's one of the reasons I bought this place. You can't see it, but there's a creek between us and that wooded ridge over yonder. This is a good place for birding. Are you a birder?"

"No, but I wish I were."

"The college house will be an excellent place for you to begin. You'll need a good pair of field glasses and a field guide."

"What would you recommend?"

"I have extra field glasses I no longer use, and I don't know how many field guides. I'd love to set you up for birding."

"Then I'll take you up on the offer."

"Angela," he said looking at his watch, "I was just thinking about what you said last night about looking for a Southern experience with this move. We've got a good chunk of time before your plane leaves at eight. I can show you more of Ashland or I can take you to Kings Mountain National Military Park on our way back to Charlotte. The Southern patriots won a major battle against the British there. Some historians consider it the turning point in the Revolutionary War. There's a visitors center and a good trail around the battlefield."

"Oh, yes, I'd love to visit the place with you."

"How are those shoes for walking?"

"Quite good, actually. I always wear comfortable shoe, never high heels."

"I certainly approve of that. Here's an idea. When I'm on an outing like this, I pack a canteen of water, some dried fruit and roasted nuts, whatever I have on hand, and take a break somewhere along the trail. What do you think?"

"I love your idea."

"Today, I have dried apricots and roasted almonds. I also have apples and soft drinks if you prefer them."

"Pack the same things for me that you'd take for yourself."

"Okay. I've got a special place in mind for us to take a break: Colonel Patrick Ferguson's grave. I'll pack a beach towel for you to sit on so you won't soil your slacks. These khakis are good for ground sitting. They're also my normal dress as you, no doubt, have concluded."

"I like your informal dress. I assume Colonel Ferguson was killed in the battle. Whose side was he on?"

"The British. He was the commander of their forces in this battle. A citizen of Scotland, Ferguson was an officer in the British army, but the men who fought under his leadership were all South Carolinians who remained loyal to the King. Are you familiar with the Southern strategy the British developed after the war bogged down in the North?"

"No, I'm sorry to say. You're good at summarizing things. Give me a synopsis."

"I'll tell you on the way if that's okay. Let me get my backpack from the pantry and I'll be right back."

She was browsing his books when he returned from the pantry.

"Shall we go?" he asked.

"Ready. This was a treat to see your house. Now I can picture you working at your desk."

"I do spend a lot of time there late at night," he said as they walked to the front door. "Oh, I forgot your suitcase. I'll be right back."

They left for Kings Mountain, Angela telling him how lucky she felt that he was overseeing the search. She had never experienced such genuine hospitality. At her request, he drove her by the rental house again.

"I like this house a lot."

"Then I hope you'll be living in it before fall. The search committee is meeting at one o'clock Monday. It's possible you'll hear from Dean Thompson later that afternoon."

"You said you didn't get a vote, but I hope you'll be pulling for me."

Barsh passed through the last traffic light between them and I-85 and then glanced at Angela who was waiting for his response.

"I certainly will be pulling for you, and I'll be surprised if you don't get an offer."

"Thanks for your confidence. Now tell me about the southern strategy of the British."

"Okay, I'll try to keep it brief. In 1778, the British decided to focus their efforts on conquering the Southern States and they believed they could because there were so many loyalists among them. If the plan worked, they'd then refocus their efforts on capturing the Northern States.

"To execute their plan, the British Navy transported a large force under the command of Sir Henry Clinton to Savannah, Georgia. They soon captured Savannah and then Augusta, the two major population centers in Georgia.

"From those bases, they moved into South Carolina and captured Charleston in May of 1780. George Washington then sent continental forces under the command of General Gates to stop the British advance through South Carolina. Gates and his army, however, were routed by Lord Cornwallis and his British forces at Camden. By the end of that summer, the British had captured all the important forts and outposts in Georgia and South Carolina. The only forces of resistance left in these two states were local militia who waged a kind of guerrilla warfare against the British. Are you still with me?"

"I'm still with you."

"Okay, this is where Colonel Patrick Ferguson comes in."

"And we're eating dried apricots and roasted almonds beside his grave?"

"That we are. Ferguson is buried under a heap of stones, right where he fell."

"Well, this is certainly building up to be an interesting fieldtrip. I hope it's only the first of many more."

"If you join us at Cooper, I'll see that you get a good introduction to this part of the South."

"Then I'll hold you to your word. Can I assume, on the basis of your interest, that your ancestors fought in the Revolutionary War here?"

"At least three of my ancestors fought with the Southern patriots."

"I'm envious of your deep roots in American history. I'm only a third generation immigrant. Oh, well, so much for me. Take me back to your story."

"My story is fast coming to an end, and then I want to hear about your family."

"Would it surprise you to know that you're the first man I've ever met who's expressed an interest in my family?"

"Well, yes, that does surprise me."

"Barsh, you have just confirmed what I had already observed in Southern literature, that Southerners tend to be interested in the families of the people they meet. But do you know what surprises me?"

"You'll have to tell me."

"I'm surprised that I'm eager to tell you about my family."

"Then let me conclude this narrative, and I'll give you the talking stick. Colonel Ferguson's orders were to recruit and arm his own force from the citizens of South Carolina, and being a man of passionate persuasion, he was able to recruit and arm a force of over a thousand loyalists. Their mission was to subdue the backwoods patriots. Those who lived over the Blue Ridge Mountains were especially independent minded, and Ferguson had threatened to march his force over the mountain and burn them out if they did not pledge allegiance to the King.

"As a response to that threat, these Over-Mountain Men, as they were called, marched into South Carolina in October of 1780 to take the battle to Ferguson. Joined by other Patriot forces, they surrounded him on Kings Mountain. Within a few hours, Ferguson was dead and the rest of his men killed or captured."

"Well done," she said. "This is a bonus I never expected on this trip.

My own expert tour guide to a major Revolutionary War site."

"Please, I'm far from an expert on this war, but Cooper does have an expert, Aubrey Morrison, who's a member of the history department. He tells me there were more Revolutionary War battles in South Carolina than any other State."

"Well, your synopsis was most helpful. Now I'm eager to walk the battlefield."

"Okay, Angela, you're on. Tell me about your family."

***

Kings Mountain was always a good outing for Barsh, and he had never enjoyed being there more than with Angela. On the drive to Charlotte, she conversed passionately about the Southern Literary Renaissance. He had never heard of the group of poets and critics from Vanderbilt University known as The Fugitives, to say nothing of their role in the revival of Southern literature. He had read Robert Penn Warren's novel *All the King's Men,* but never knew he was one of the Fugitive Poets and the first Poet Laureate of the United States. Now he was eager to read her favorite Fugitive Poets: Warren, John Crow Ransom, and Allen Tate.

Angela turned to Caroline Gordon, who had been pulled into the literary scene by her marriage to Fugitive Poet, Allen Tate. It turned out to be a turbulent marriage. Nevertheless, Gordon managed to become a successful novelist at a time when American men dominated the literary arts. From her discussion, Barsh could see why Angela would be drawn to Gordon and why she wrote her Ph. D. dissertation on her.

He couldn't believe that Gordon had taught at Emory University during the spring of 1965. He was there, but so deep into his studies of Biblical literature that he knew nothing about her. He felt an affinity with Caroline Gordon just from the way Angela had cast her, and he wished he had met her while they were both at Emory.

Angela had suggested that he might like to start with Gordon's novel *Aleck Maury,* knowing he would appreciate the protagonist's love of nature. But he had set his mind to start with her favorite Gordon novel, *The Women on the Porch.* He didn't need Aleck Maury to show him the value of nature.

Dinner at Emile's Bistro in Charlotte was excellent, and he managed to keep her talking about Southern literature. At one point, she shared with him the major points of a graduate paper she'd written on

Carson McCullers' *The Heart is a Lonely Hunter,* and at his request, she promised to send him a copy.

Back at the airport, he had fallen into one of his pensive moods, which Angela seemed to sense and respect. They sat silently in the waiting room. Time was slipping toward the moment of her departure. The plane was at the boarding gate and she excused herself and went to the restroom. There was the first call for boarding. Then he watched her striding toward him, a broad smile on her face.

"Barsh, I don't know how to thank you for making this such an extraordinary visit in every way."

"It's been my pleasure."

"I'm hoping with all my heart that we'll be colleagues this fall. But whatever happens, I'm claiming you as my friend. Be warned, I can be excessive in my devotion. There's something about you that allows me to be myself without pretense, and at the same time you bring out the best in me. I feel like I'm entering a new stage on life's journey. I'm not saying this well. You do know, don't you?"

Looking into her eyes, he nodded slowly as if he knew what she meant.

An attendant announced that all passengers for the flight should board immediately. Barsh extended his hand and she took it in both of hers. Then she moved against him with a tight embrace. He awkwardly responded with his right hand pulled lightly against her back.

"Goodbye, Angela, and do take good care."

"Goodbye for now, my one-arm hugger. Have a safe drive home and double-clutch the Audi just for me when you leave the parking lot."

She tossed her hair over her shoulder and eased into the short boarding line. At the gate she turned, waved, and disappeared. Now he would wait at the window until her plane was airborne.

CHAPTER SEVEN

As he had promised, Barsh took Hannah to Table Rock State Park that Saturday. They visited the Nature Center, as always, and then headed up Carrick Creek, stopping to admire the wading pool below the first waterfall. Further up the trail, they crossed the creek and turned up the mountain side, stopping occasionally to examine things along the way.

It pleased him that his daughter had taken an interest in shrubs and trees. She knew the distinguishing features of rhododendron and mountain laurel. She could identify several major deciduous trees, and among the evergreens, she could differentiate pines, hemlocks, and cedars.

A little after noon, they stood on the mountain top and looked out on the valley below. Hannah was tired but all smiles. He spotted a moss-covered oak that the wind had toppled and they sat, face to face, straddling its trunk, eating their picnic lunch and discussing environmental issues. Then they descended the trail in high spirits.

"That was fun," she said as they left the parking lot for the drive home. "I want to start hiking different trails with you."

"It was a joy to hike with you today, my sweet girl. I have several different trails in mind for us this summer. I also have plans to hike several trails that are too remote and difficult for you. But they will still be there when you get older, and then we'll hike them together. Okay?"

"That's fine, Daddy."

"Here's the deal. I'll plan the hikes this summer for you and me, and I'll save my long difficult hikes for the fall. How's that?"

"Sounds good. Do you mind if I take a nap?"

"Sleep well and I'll do some thinking."

She reclined her seat and slept most of the way home. He drove the first half of the route worrying about how he might prepare her for the separation. Then he relived the time he spent with Angela Kundera on Thursday and Friday.

***

After dinner that evening, Hannah read him a new poem she had written. He was so moved by her sensibilities that he told her about his first attempt at writing poetry as a college freshman.

"Daddy, could I see those poems?"

"When I showed them to the Academic Dean, who was a respected poet, he gave me such a cold critique that I trashed them. Lately, I've been thinking about giving it another try. Current poetics are more in line with any craft I might be able to develop. But first, I need to start reading more contemporary poetry."

"Then let's do it together," she said.

"Okay, we can make it one of our summer projects. I need to take you to Connemara, Carl Sandburg's last home. It's at Flat Rock, North Carolina, not far from Table Rock. I thought about taking you this afternoon while we were up that way but decided to make that a separate trip. I bought Sandburg's *Collected Poems* on my first visit to Connemara. I'll read you a couple that I think are very strong."

He found the book and read "Fog" and "Chicago". She especially enjoyed "Chicago" and laughed repeatedly as he bellowed out the lines with such bold force: "Stormy, husky, brawling, City of the Big Shoulders . . . Fierce as a dog with tongue lapping for action."

He gave her a brief history of Connemara, which was built before the Civil War as the summer home of a wealthy Charleston family. He talked about Sandburg's habit of writing through the night and about the dairy goats his wife kept.

"It sounds like an interesting place. When can we go?"

"What about next Saturday? We could also do a little hiking at Chimney Rock, which isn't too far from Flat Rock."

"That suites me. Daddy, I'm glad you're going to start writing poetry again."

"I'm definitely giving it another try, but I'm not sure I'll be any good. I have great expectation for you, however. I'm impressed by the poems you're writing."

It was Hannah's bedtime and she turned in without asking for a single extension. Barsh did a light workout in the basement and then sat in the study thinking about Angela Kundera. There was no doubt in his mind that the search committee would recommend her for the English position. But would she accept the offer? Before her visit, he didn't believe she would. Now he was thinking she just might. Otherwise, why would she have acted so enthusiastic about moving to Ashland? Was that just a phony act she had played so well? No, he couldn't believe she was playing him for a fool, although he had to admit he had misjudged people before.

He left the study to check on Hannah who had been lethargic before her bedtime. Standing at the bedroom door, he watched her slumbering breath rise and fall. Then he returned to the study, thinking what a good day the two of them had hiking the mountain to Table Rock. The separation was going to be devastating for both of them.

Debbie turned off the TV and left the den. Listening to her steps as she went to her bedroom, he remembered the early years of their marriage, how awkwardly difficult bedtime had been for him. Would she or would she not? He eventually learned to look for little indicators to tell whether she was in the mood or not. Far be it from him to press a woman for sex. But those days were over for him. After Debbie asked for a separation, he moved into the guest bedroom, and she responded by closing the door to her bedroom when she retired for the evening.

Always conscious about her looks, she had kept a trim figure. She was an attractive woman with beautiful blond hair, but her natural beauty was overshadowed somewhat by her sad countenance. Never had he seen her bubbling over with joy or passion for anything.

A true professional, she dressed the part and played it well Monday through Friday. Saturday was her day. Shopping, relaxing, whatever she wanted to do. Sunday mornings she faithfully attended Sunday school and the worship service at Ashland First Baptist Church.

On a typical evening, one of them prepared dinner on a somewhat rotating basis. After dinner, she usually changed into her pajamas and watched TV, more often than not by herself.

The toilet flushed, and he followed the sound of her steps as she came back down the hall and turned toward the study.

"Can we talk?" she asked.

"Here or the den?"

"The den if you don't mind."

He followed her into the den. She sat in her swivel rocker, and he sat across from her in the big stuffed chair.

"I had another call from Henry Dugan at work yesterday. He's pressing me to let him know when I'm moving to Louisville. He wants me there right away. You can't keep dragging your feet on this. It's time you told Hannah."

"I'm sorry, but I can't do it now. In fact, I'm worried about her."

"What do you mean?"

"Late Wednesday night, she came running down the hall to the study, trembling with fear. She'd had a bad dream in which I was lost. She was searching everywhere but couldn't find me. I talked to her about nightmares, but she was still clingy and didn't want to go back to bed.

We had a good time at Table Rock today, but she still seems anxious."

"Why are you just now telling me about this?

"I don't know. Maybe I was afraid that I was reading too much into the dream because of my own anxiety."

"Barsh, you know that I would already be in Louisville if I weren't concerned about Hannah's wellbeing."

"Yes, and I'm desperately looking for a way to make it easier for her, and hopefully, I'll find one if you'll give me more time."

"I'm trying to be patient. Surely you understand my situation."

"I understand your situation fully, and I hope you understand mine. If you want it done now, you'll have to tell her yourself."

"Okay, I'll give you more time," she said standing to leave. "We both know she'll take it better coming from you, but please find a way soon."

"Believe me, it's my top priority."

CHAPTER EIGHT

The search committee met Monday afternoon at one o'clock. With much praise for Angela, they unanimously recommended her for the English position and quickly dispersed, happy with their choice and delighted that it was the last week of the semester before final exams. Barsh walked across campus to tell Dean Thompson. As he topped the stairs, she was standing beside Sharon's desk, chatting with her receptionist.

"I didn't expect you so soon," Catherine said and ushered him into her office, closing the door behind her. "What's the verdict?"

"They voted unanimously for Dr. Kundera."

"My gracious, when have they ever voted unanimously on anything? Please have a seat and visit with me awhile. I'm delighted with the committee's choice. Dr. Kundera will be such an extraordinary addition to the English Department. Do you think she will accept our offer?"

"She said she would, but it doesn't make sense to me that she would come here. On the drive back to Charlotte, I learned she has an offer from Bennington. She got the offer two days before her visit with us. We can neither match the salary they've offered her nor the prestige of teaching there. Yet, she told me again at the airport that she hopes to be teaching here this fall."

"I didn't know she had an offer from Bennington. Even so, my intuition tells me she'll accept our offer. I think she's looking for something more than salary and academic prestige. As soon as I get the President's approval, I'll call her. He just called me so I know he's in his office. Once again I must thank you for your excellent leadership. You're the best at chairing committees. You always keep them on task until they get the job done."

"Will you call and let me know her response? I'll be in the office until five. Then I'm going home."

"I'll call as soon as I get off the phone with her," she said looking straight into his eyes with a worried face. "Please forgive me, but something seems to be troubling you lately"

"Unfortunately, you're right. I can only tell you that Debbie is exceedingly unhappy."

"I'm so sorry. Is there anything I can do?"

"No, but I appreciate your concern," he said and left for his office.

***

Halfway across the Quad, he remembered Angela's discussion of Caroline Gordon's *The Women on the Porch* and his interest in reading it right away. This would be a good time to see if the library had the novel.

"Ah, Dr. Roberts, I presume," Amanda McGee said. "What brings you our way? Are you looking for me or some rare book?"

"Wouldn't that be one and the same?" he said.

"Well, what did you have for lunch," she said and laughed. "Changing the subject, are we getting that English professor from Brown?"

"We should know soon, possibly today."

"Then she's being offered the position."

"That's a reasonable deduction. Two questions, Amanda. First, do we have Caroline Gordon's novel *The Women on the Porch?*"

"Give me just a minute to check that. Sorry, we don't have anything by her. I can get it through library loan."

"Thanks, but I'll get the bookstore to order it for me."

"Second question?"

"How good is our poetry collection?"

"Poetry?" she said with raised eyebrows.

"Hannah and I have decided to make poetry our summer reading project. I don't think I've told you but she's writing rather insightful poems. And I'm most impressed by her critical reading skills."

"That doesn't surprise me. Judging by the books you've been checking out for her, she's going to be an intellectual. You should bring her with you more often. It's a delight to watch you two. If I knew I could duplicate your achievement, I might change my mind about becoming a mother."

"Maybe Mr. Right will change your mind once you find him. It's not too late, you know."

"I have never been able to envision myself as wife or mother. Now I'm set in my ways. As someone expressed my feeling so well recently: *I'd rather be lonely than bothered.*"

"You don't strike me as the lonely type, Amanda."

"There are days. There are days. But back to your question about our poetry collection. You're in luck. It's quite good, and you can thank the previous librarian for this. They tell me she was a prolific poet who refused to share her work with anyone. For all we know, she may be hailed someday as another Emily Dickinson."

"I'm looking for a couple of anthologies of twentieth century poetry. Hannah will read one and I the other. Then we'll share with each other the poems we like. I'm also interested in James Dickey's poetry. I've heard he's one of the best of our Southern poets. If that's true, I suppose I should know his work."

"Again you're in luck, due to my own acquaintance with Dickey's reputation. You know he teaches at the University of South Carolina, don't you?"

"No, I did not know that."

"Just follow me to the stacks. I wouldn't attempt to judge his poetry, but James Dickey is, without doubt, the most colorful professor at USC. I went to one of his poetry readings while I was a graduate student there, and he clearly had more fun than anyone in the audience."

Barsh checked out a load of poetry books and hurried to his office. He didn't want to miss the Dean's call. After brewing tea, he began reading Dickey's first book of poems. Just after four o'clock, Catherine called to tell him that Dr. Kundera had accepted the position.

"You won't believe how excited she is about our offer. She wants to rent the house that Elizabeth Campbell is vacating. She said you had taken her by to look at it."

"Well, your intuition was correct. There's no doubt that she'll be a tremendous addition to the faculty. I just hope it's the right move for her."

"Time alone will tell, but I'm confident of one thing. You and I will go out of our way to make this a good experience for her. Again, I thank you for your help with the search."

"It was an interesting experience."

CHAPTER NINE

The bell rang and Barsh concluded his last lecture for the semester. The students scrambled for the door, except for Laura Buck who stepped from her front-row seat to his desk.

"Dr. Roberts, I can't tell you how much you've helped me this semester. I have a whole new perspective on my existence. I'm amazed at your ability to analyze things so clearly. You are the best."

"Thank you, Laura. And thanks for your participation. Your comments stimulated several lively discussions."

"There's something I need to talk to you about, but I have a class next period. Will you be in your office this afternoon?"

"I'll sign you up for one o'clock if that's okay."

"Oh, thank you. Could you give me at least thirty minutes?"

"Not a problem."

He gathered his lecture notes and went straight to his office where he brewed tea and ate a sandwich. As he stewed over his situation, he thought it might be a good thing for him to take a trip somewhere by himself. But where would he go? The phone rang.

"Barsh, I just got a lovely letter from Angela Kundera. Have you heard from her?"

"Not yet, but I haven't checked the mail today. She did promise to write me."

"Then I'm sure you have one waiting for you. Do you have plans for Saturday morning? I'd love to have you over for breakfast. It's been too long since your last visit. You don't know how much our breakfast discussions mean to me."

"I'm sorry, Catherine. It has been too long, but I've promised to take Hannah to Connemara and then Chimney Rock. She says she's ready to hike the lower trail to Hickory Nut Falls. Can you join us?"

"I wish I could, but Georgette and I are going to Spartanburg for lunch. Do you have any big plans for the summer?"

"I'm thinking about taking a trip somewhere. I need to get away by myself for a while. But don't give up on me. We'll find time for another breakfast discussion soon."

"Yes, we'll make it happen. Have a great day with Hannah tomorrow. Bye."

He drank the last of the tea and left for the campus post office, wondering if he had a letter from Angela. She had promised to write him soon. But *soon* doesn't mean this week, he reasoned, trying to brace himself against disappointment. But *soon* did mean this week. His mail included a large manila envelope from Angela, and he walked with a lighter step as he made his way back to the office.

Settled at his desk, he shuffled though the mail. Mostly junk. Ah, something from an old classmate. It was an invitation to the twenty-fifth anniversary of Handley High's class of '53, which was taking place in two weeks. There was a handwritten note apologizing for the late invitation. They had just tracked down his address. How fortuitous, he thought as he began to think about his classmates. Yes, he would definitely be there.

He looked at his watch and decided to save Angela's fat manila envelope until after his meeting with Laura Buck. What did she need to talk to him about? She had dropped by a few times during the semester to talk about the course, always lavishing him with praise. She admired his intellect, his compassion, and wanted to tell him so. She felt lucky that she had chosen Cooper College to earn her baccalaureate, otherwise she would have missed the best courses she had ever taken.

Other than what he could see, which was an attractive woman probably in her early-thirties, all he knew about her was that she was a registered nurse from Spartanburg who had decided to earn a bachelor's degree. It would open more professional doors for her.

"Hi, Dr. Roberts," she said standing in the doorway.

"Come in, Laura," he said and rose to greet her.

She closed the door and quickly extended her hand.

He gestured for her to take a chair and then sat facing her.

"I don't know where to start."

"Start anywhere. You'll find your way as you go."

"I told you I'm a nurse, but I don't think I told you I'm married to a doctor. Mark is a highly respected surgeon and has a good practice. The problem is he has lost interest in me. He works hard and then he drinks with his buddies. I assume he has a woman, or more likely several women. The point is he does nothing with me, and I can't take it anymore. He says a divorce would mess up his finances so I need help. Should I pursue a divorce, anyway?"

"I'm not a marriage counselor, Laura. You need to find a good marriage counselor. I think that's the first step."

"You're a professor of religion, and I want your opinion. Do I have moral grounds for seeking a divorce?"

HONEY FROM A LION

"You'll have to make that call. It would be presumptuous for me to advise you one way or the other. You have to decide what your duties are to yourself and to your husband. Have you told him the current situation is unacceptable?"

"Yes, but he doesn't take me seriously."

"I suggest that you demand a serious discussion with him about the issues. Then you can hold him responsible for his reaction and take it from there."

"So as a professor of religion, you don't condemn divorce outright. I was reared a Catholic."

"Definitely not. People often make grave mistakes in choosing a mate. People also change, sometimes for better and sometimes for worse. Relationships can become poisonous, destructive, unbearable, unredeemable. Divorce is clearly the best answer in those cases.

"My advice is to find a marriage counselor who can help you sort things out, preferably with your husband. Fix the marriage if you can. If you can't, get out."

"Do you know how much I admire you? You are so intelligent without a hint of arrogance. That's what makes you so endearing. You would not believe how arrogant Mark is. He has contempt for almost everyone he meets."

"I'm sorry to hear that."

"I was so disappointed to learn you're not teaching summer school. Do you plan to travel?"

"I'm still working on summer plans."

Laura fished a pen from her pocketbook and wrote her name and phone number on a piece of paper.

"Please call me the next time you're in Spartanburg. I'd love to take you to lunch. We'll dine high or low. Your preference, my pleasure."

"That would be nice. But I seldom get to Spartanburg."

"I don't blame you. Anyway, I can't thank you enough for your understanding. See you in class next week for the final exam. Hope it's not too hard."

"You're a good student and should have no difficulty with the exam. Please know that I wish you the best with your marital problems."

He stood and opened the door for her, and she reluctantly left. Alone, he opened his mail from Angela. There was a long letter and the paper on Carson McCullers that she had promised him.

He started with the letter and savored it from the opening *My Dear Friend* to the final *Affectionately yours, Angela*. She had written the letter late Monday evening and promised to write him often. As she had forewarned him, she was excessive with her devotion.

Praise was nothing new to him. Students often flattered him and, occasionally, flirted with him, but it never went to his head. He had never taken advantage of any student advances. Angela, however, was a new experience. Her words were like manna from heaven for a pilgrim lost in the desert. He read again from the letter: *Barsh, you didn't hear the typewriter stop its clacking, but it did while I, alone in this apartment, lifted my glass of wine to you in deepest affection.*

He didn't have any wine, but he'd get some on the way home. "Angela, my friend," he said without breath, "when all the house goes quiet tonight, I'll lift my glass to you." He locked her letter in the file cabinet and put her paper on Carson McCullers in his briefcase. He would read it after Hannah's bedtime.

***

With a bottle of expensive wine in hand, he left the store for home, haranguing with himself all the way. What was wrong with him? He had never bought expensive wine before. He had better get Angela Kundera out of his head.

He remembered the invitation to his class reunion. Twenty-five years ago, he had marched through those final exercises at Handley High without a backward glance and then pursued a spiritual and intellectual life that none of his classmates could have predicted in a thousand years.

In spite of his position at lowly Cooper, his teaching had remained lively and engaging until Debbie asked for a trial separation. Racists, hedonists, and fundamentalists always enrolled in his classes in sufficient numbers to challenge his sensibilities and give him a sense of purpose. And there had always been students who eagerly opened their minds to his discussions of the critical issues of existence, giving him a sense of achievement. But that was the past.

He knew he couldn't teach at Cooper after Debbie left him. But what would he do? For months he had searched in vain for an answer.

He needed a diversion, and the notice of his class reunion could not have come at a better time. With mounting anticipation, he began to look forward to the reunion. How good it would be to see his old classmates again and to discover what had happened to them.

CHAPTER TEN

Barsh counted down the days, eagerly awaiting his high school reunion. He really needed to see his old classmates. Then the day dawned, and he set out alone for the small Alabama town that he had forsaken after his parents moved to Georgia during his freshman year of college. Memories of his youth kept streaming into his consciousness. His experiences growing up were rich and diverse, sad and joyful, and he reminisced about them mile after droning mile.

As he approached his hometown in early afternoon, he thought about checking into a motel to rest awhile before visiting some of his old haunts. Instead, he decided to drive straight to the cemetery of the country church where his parents were buried. The closer he got to the community where he had spent the best years of his youth, the more emotional he became.

Foster's Store had been torn down, leaving no visible sign that it had ever existed. But he could see Mrs. Foster sitting on a high stool behind the counter, vivaciously conversing with all who entered. On the other side of the road, Mitchum's Store was still standing, although it was closed. There was no evidence of the gristmill that had stood next door.

The old church his ancestors had helped build out of heart pine had been demolished and replaced by a larger brick one across the road. He sat in the Audi in the church parking lot, gripping the steering wheel as he tried to calm his emotions. Then he walked to the cemetery.

Standing beside his parent's graves, he was overwhelmed with grief. The tears were flowing, and then he began to sob. Never in his life could he remember actually weeping, to say nothing of sobbing. He remembered a silent tear trickling down his face the day his parents were buried, but nothing more. It was time he had a good cry.

Back in the car, he realized the weeping was as much about the breakup of his family as the loss of his parents. The grief he felt for them was the catalyst for the flood.

From the churchyard, he drove by their old farm, wanting to stop and talk to the current owners but not quite willing to do so. The new owners had done a good job keeping the place up. The pastures were well maintained and filled with Hereford cattle. How he would love to see Thunder, his Quarter Horse, racing across that pasture once again, he thought.

Down the road and around the bend he was pleased to see that the Henry place had been turned into a horse farm. The old cotton fields and corn fields were now well-fenced pastures and the horses grazing the bright green grass were first rate saddle horses. The old wooden house with its tin roof was gone, replaced by a stately brick one. God, he would love to see Susan Henry, his little riding pal from the past. Perhaps the horses were a good sign that she was still connected to the place. He stopped but found no one at home.

Disappointed, he headed for the back road where Rachel and Joe Foster lived. He had no intention of stopping, but he needed to drive by the place. It would be good if Joe happened to be bush-hogging the pasture, driving the tractor without the one arm he lost in Korea. Even a distant sighting of his former neighbor would mean a lot to him.

The house had a new coat of white paint. Joe's Black Angus cattle were grazing across the way in the back pasture near the forest. There was a cow trail through those woods that led to a creek where the cattle went for water. Farther up the creek, ancient storm waters had washed out a good swimming hole below a waterfall. The very thought of that place took him back to one of the most astounding nights of his youth.

***

He had camped and fished for two nights on the Tallapoosa River with Rayford McKay to celebrate the end of their sophomore year at Handley High. They broke camp early Sunday morning so that Barsh could honor his mother's notions about Sunday. She didn't approve of fishing or hunting on the Lord's Day, but thankfully she did not object to horseback riding on Sunday afternoons.

As usual, he and Susan Henry rode their horses for miles along three different crisscrossing dirt roads that Sunday afternoon. Coming back by Corn House Creek, they left the road and rode up the creek to a logging trail, which they followed back to the county road. As they passed the Foster farm, he saw the bull mount one of the cows and made a mental note of what he needed to do before the day ended. He had agreed to look after Joe Foster's cattle while he was fighting the communists in Korea, and that included giving Raymond a good measure of grain and hay on those day when he was servicing the cows.

After super, Barsh drove his old Ford pickup to the Foster's barn to fulfill his duty. As he was filling the grain bucket, Rachel walked into the feed room.

"Hey," she said, "thanks for staying on top of things. I'm sure Raymond is ready for that grain. He's had a busy day with the cows."

"Just following Joe's instructions."

Barsh was shocked that Rachel would call attention to what the bull had been doing. He thought all women played blind to the bull's business. At least he had never heard a woman comment about it even when it was going on before their eyes.

"I'll be right back," he said and took the grain to the bull's feed trough.

Rachel was sitting on a sack of grain with her skirt hiked up above her knees when he returned.

"Have you given him any hay?" she said.

"That's next."

He climbed the ladder to the loft and forked the hay down the chute. Back at the ladder, he stopped at the sight of Rachel below him. She was stretched out on her back on the sacks of grain with her legs pulled up to her butt, exposed. He was frozen in his tracks until she sat up, modestly composed again, and then he descended the ladder as if he had not seen the show.

"I saw you and Susan riding by on your horses this afternoon. Did y'all have fun?"

"We always have fun when we ride."

"You remember promising me that we could ride double, don't you?"

"All you need to do is tell me when."

"What about tonight?"

"Uh … okay."

"Can you meet me here around ten? Lewis and Mrs. Foster should both be sound asleep by then."

"Sure, if that's what you want."

"Please wait for me if I'm late. Sometimes Mrs. Foster has a hard time getting to sleep."

"I'll wait until you get here."

"You are so dear."

True to his word, he waited in the shadow of the barn for Rachel. The lights were out in Mrs. Foster's bedroom. Soon the lights in the living room went out. The whole house was dark. The night, however, was well lit by the moon, which was just a day or two past its majestic fullness.

Rachel, carrying a blanket, slipped out the back door and glided across the yard in the silvery light.

"Barsh," she whispered as she approached the barn.

"I'm here," he said and stepped out of the shadows, leading Thunder by the reins.

"I brought a blanket. I'll ride on it behind you."

"Don't you want the saddle?"

"No, I want to hold on to you."

"You still want us to ride in the pasture?"

"It's safer for me. A neighbor might pass us on the road. I don't want any gossip. Let's ride up the creek to the waterfall."

They crossed the pasture and entered the woods, Thunder following the cow trail to the creek. Barsh turned him up the creek and let him find his way through the woods. Rachel snuggled against his back to shield herself from tree branches.

"I hear the falls," she said holding him tighter.

He wondered if she could hear his heart beating. It had been two years since a woman had pulled herself against him.

"Here we are," he said reining Thunder to a stop at the edge of a small pasture between the woods and the creek.

"Gracious," she said. "Look how bright the moon's wake is on the creek. Let's sit on the bank and talk."

"Okay," he said and dismounted first so he could help her down.

"I'll spread the blanket while you take care of the horse," she said.

"Good boy," he whispered as he tied the reins to a sapling and then joined Rachel beside the creek, where they sat cross-legged on the blanket facing each other.

"Have you ever seen a more brilliant sky?" she said. "All those distant stars make me feel so small and worthless. What does my life matter in the scheme of all this vastness?"

"You're a wonderful person, Rachel. Everyone respects and admires you."

"A few people seem to like me, but I need more than that. I'm sure you have no idea how lonely I get in that old house at night."

"I know you must miss Joe."

"You're right. But this will surely shock you. I don't allow myself to think about Joe anymore. It's as if there was nothing connecting us, not even our letters. When I answer his, I seem to be writing what's expected of me, not what I feel. At first, I could hardly stand it when I knew he was on the frontline in Korea. Nothing I did seemed important. My world seemed like one big waiting room. At work, at church, at home ... I seemed to be waiting for word that Joe had been killed. I thought I was going crazy at one point. Now all I feel is emptiness."

Barsh was shocked as she had warned him he would be. He didn't know what to say. Everything that came to mind seemed useless. But her silence was more than he could bear.

"I'm sorry. I didn't know. You're living in hell."

"I knew you'd understand," she said and stretched out on her back. "A woman I work with at the bank is always trying to get me to go out with her. There's a place on the Wadley Highway where she goes to dance and meet men on Saturday night. I can't do that, but I'm dying for your companionship. Do you know how good it feels just being here with you tonight? I need you to be close to me."

"Okay," he said searching her face in the moonlight.

She beckoned him with her arms and he filled them. Body to body and soul to soul, they rocked gently in tight embrace.

"Do me," she said, and he did her with all his passion as the moon slipped slowly into the western sky.

Never again did she have to ask him to *do* her. He could not count the times he had waited for her in the feed room of that barn. They soon had a pallet in the hayloft. Sometimes they didn't make it to the loft but used the sacks of crushed grain as a love bed. The secret rendezvous ended the day Rachel got word that Joe would be coming home without his left arm.

Barsh thought she would avoid him once Joe was home, but she didn't. At church, she joked with him, teased him, inquired about his activities as if they had never been one flesh.

***

Those bitter-sweet memories followed Barsh all the way back to town. He still didn't know how to deal with what had happened. He could not repudiate what he had done, but he couldn't think about Joe Foster without feeling the throbbing pain of guilt for betraying his neighbor.

He checked into a motel on the edge of town, rested a few minutes, and then drove to his old neighborhood. The Burdette house on the corner of Barkley Street and Britton Road looked basically unchanged. It had been almost thirty years since he last saw his first love, Amy Burdette. In all those years, he always got the feeling that she hadn't had a good life whenever he thought about her.

Britton Road, which was unpaved when he lived there, had been paved. He stopped in front of their house, and it seemed strange that he had ever lived there.

He drove slowly down the road. New houses had been built on every big lot that had once served as a pasture for someone's milk cows. There was no sign of the Wades' junkyard or their big house. It had been demolished, and four new houses had been built on their property. He wondered if any of the Wades lived in the new houses.

When he topped the hill and headed for the end of the road, he was surprised to see that Britton's Dairy Farm had vanished. The tenant house and the big barn were gone. Trees and bushes had taken root in the pastures. Memory after memory continued to emerge in his mind after he left his old neighborhood.

Back in the motel, he showered and dressed for the class reunion. He looked forward to seeing his classmates, especially April Morehouse and Rayford Mckay. He kept trying to imagine how they had changed and what they had done with their lives.

They were both there with their spouses. April had married the banker's son she had dated since their junior year. Rayford, who had also married his high school sweetheart, was now the town mayor. They seemed glad to see him, but the brief conversations with them were most unsatisfactory.

The class president presided over a vacuous program, which included a brief report on the latest class superlatives: the most kids, the most divorces, and so forth. Barsh was recognized for having earned the most academic degrees, four, an achievement no one who had known him in high school could have imagined.

The reunion was over in less than two hours. Then everyone faded into the night, leaving him so empty he felt betrayed.

CHAPTER ELEVEN

Leaving town Sunday morning, he stopped for gas at Brown's Texaco. There, challenging his eyes, stood Wesley Workman, jesting loudly with a tall black man. The voice was unmistakable.

The year Barsh turned fifteen he had formed an unlikely friendship with Wesley, who at seventeen was a skilled garage mechanic and an accomplished womanizer. He used to fill the nights with explicit narrations of his sexual exploits as they sat around a campfire in an old-growth forest. There were other memories, darker ones that Barsh had tried to forget. Now they flooded his consciousness.

It was their common interest in camping that had brought them together. But that was another life. A quarter of a century had coursed its way through the marrow of his bones since those days.

Wesley, dressed in khaki work clothes, was gaunt beyond his years but still handsome in a rakish way. The black man, probably on his way to church, was wearing a gray striped suit with an orange tie and a tan hat. Wesley reeled on his heels, laughing, and then headed toward a battered pulpwood truck.

"Wesley," Barsh called with deeper emotion than he could have imagined before seeing him.

"Yeah," he said trying to figure out who had called him.

"I'm Barsh Roberts."

"God a' mighty, you're the last person in the world I expected to see today."

Barsh extended his hand, and Wesley took it tentatively. Eye to eye, they stared in unblinking disbelief at such a chance meeting.

"By God, you are a professor, beard and all. Rayford told me you was, but I couldn't picture it. Hell, you liked trees better than people back in our old campin' days. I could never figure it out. What you doin' back in this hellhole?"

"Our class reunion last night. First time I'd been back for one. I couldn't wait to see everyone, but it wasn't much of anything. I was terribly disappointed."

"What did you expect from this god-forsaken place?"

The sun, climbing higher in the sky, shimmered on Wesley's truck.

"How long you been hauling pulpwood? The last time I heard, you were still working at your daddy's garage."

"I walked out of that goddamn garage for the last time ... God, it's been twenty years," he said and eased into a guttural laugh. "You know how Daddy was always ridin' my ass. I could out mechanic him, but I could never please him. So it was bound to happen."

Wesley searched his eyes with unyielding intensity. Barsh wondered what he was looking for. Forgiveness? It was finally there. He had a better understanding of that old saying, *the flesh is weak*. But neither man would ever give breath to the betrayal that shattered their friendship.

"How's Jenny, Wesley? Rayford told me you married her. I knew her brother well. He used to hunt with me."

"Oh, she's fine. And a good woman, too. She puts up with me, and I sure as hell ain't changed. Well, I guess I've changed some. I drink a lot now, and I don't take on as many women as I used to. Most of the time I'm too drunk to give a damn. What about you? Did you ever get married?"

"I married a girl from Kentucky, Debbie Whalen."

"I bet you ain't been campin' since you got married, have you?"

"Actually, we did camp once in a state park in Georgia, but Debbie's not much for camping."

"For God's sake, Barsh, who ever heard of takin' your wife campin'? The whole idea is to get away from home for a spell."

"I thought it was to get back close to nature."

"Well, I guess you did. Sorry, but I've got to go. I'm closin' a deal on some timber, and I'm already late. Where you headed? Home?"

"As soon as I gas up."

"And just where would that be?"

"Ashland, South Carolina."

"Well, you take care of yourself."

"And you, too. It's good to see you, Wesley."

"Yeah, it's good to see you. I've thought about you a million times."

There was a tinge of regret in Wesley's eyes. Then he cocked his head, grinning in his special way, and climbed into the truck. The loud muffler roared in Barsh's head until it merged with the memory of Wesley's throaty Harley-Davidson. For a moment, he's fourteen, seated behind him on that black motorcycle. They're flying down the Lafayette Highway, flat-out on the straights and backfiring into the curves.

With a full tank of gas, he set out for home, carrying with him images of Wesley, who was on a fast track to the grave and proud that he could get there on his own. But where was Barsh headed?

For the past twenty-five years, his life had been dominated by rigorous study, critical thought, and passionate teaching. But that was the past. The good life he had worked so hard to build for himself in academia seemed doomed.

The brief encounter with Wesley had awakened old memories of how as a boy he had found strength and grace in the wild, living off the land by his own hunting and fishing skills. At forty-three, he had forgotten how it felt to kill a rabbit and roast it over an open fire, to live wild and unfettered in the forest for days at a time.

Perhaps he should try to capture, once more, that primal essence of life. The idea appealed to him, and he set his mind to camp, alone, for two weeks in some remote forest. Purged by the solitude of the wilderness, he just might find a new direction for his life.

Then a radical thought began to take hold of him. It was an idea that had first popped into his head, years ago, after reading *A Modern Utopia* by H. G. Wells. The samurai, who served the new world order that Wells envisioned, were expected to spend time alone in the wilderness each year to renew and purify their spirit. Reflecting on that notion, Barsh had wondered if he, with preparation, could live alone in the wild through the seasons of one year, stripped of every human tool and product that he couldn't make with his own hands from the raw materials of the earth. At the time, it was only a whimsical thought.

Speeding north on I-85, he turned that whimsical thought into the vision he'd been searching for ever since Debbie had asked for a year-long trial separation. He could see himself living alone in the wild for one year, armed only with Stone Age tools and products he had fashioned himself.

That would be a worthy challenge for any man in the postmodern world. Strip yourself of five-thousand years of material culture and live in the forest by your own strength and wits. Do or die. The vision filled him with an irrepressible resolve as he drove toward his fractured home.

***

Alone in the study that Sunday evening, he thought again about a year-long sojourn in the wild. If he took a Sabbatical, which he was due, he could postpone the decision about resigning from Cooper when Debbie moved out. Who knew what a year would bring? Things might not work out the way Debbie had envisioned them and she'd be ready to bring Hannah home. At whatever price, he wanted Hannah to grow up under the same roof with him. Even if that didn't happen, he'd have a year to find a way forward. But how would Hannah respond to such a plan?

She knew how he loved the wild and would likely support the plan as an appropriate response to Debbie's decision to move to Louisville on a trial separation. But how could he get her to accept Debbie's plan? As he thought about that challenge, a devious notion seized him. If he told Hannah that one of his dreams was to spend a year in the wild, living like his distant Creek ancestors, she'd almost certainly encourage him to go for it. Debbie could then recast the move to Louisville as a reaction to his plan for a wilderness sojourn.

In an odd way, he had stumbled onto a scheme that would probably work with Hannah. But could he pull such a devious scheme on his daughter? Yes, he could swallow the deceit in order to shield her from the truth for at least a year, possibly forever. But would Debbie go for such a scheme?

It would have definite advantages for her. She'd get her trial separation in Louisville without having to take the blame for it, justifying the move in order to be closer to her parents while he was off in the wild, doing his thing.

There was one negative consequence for Debbie, however. She'd have to give him time to learn the traditional earth skills of Native Americans in order to make his own bow and arrows, pottery, baskets, and deerskin clothes and bedding. He was confident he could achieve that objective by the end of the fall semester. But would she make such a concession? It was the first of June, and she was already jumping to go.

He checked on Hannah, and she was sound asleep. It was time to lay out the plan for Debbie, who was watching a movie. She gave him a quizzical glance as he entered the den and sat in his chair.

"How's the movie?" he asked at the first commercial break.

"It's okay. Are you watching the rest of it with me?"

"No, I have something to discuss with you after the movie."

"Then let's discuss it now," she said and turned off the TV.

"I think I have a way out for us with Hannah, but it's a complicated plan."

She listened carefully as he explained and surprisingly, she accepted it and went straight to bed. He returned to the study, overwhelmed by the challenging task before him.

The absolute critical task for him was to be able to make flint arrowheads. Without them, he'd not be able to kill deer. And without deer, there would be no deerskins for the clothing and bedding he would need to survive the winter months. He would have to find someone to teach him this ancient earth skill.

He had fond memories of talking to elderly members of the Eastern Band of the Cherokees in North Carolina. They were always eager to tell him about the traditions of their people. Perhaps they still knew how to make flint arrowheads. He'd drive to their Reservation in the morning and ask the curator of the museum if he knew anyone who made flint arrowheads.

He got a beer and returned to the study, still focused on the things he had to do. It was obvious that he needed his own place in the country. First and foremost, he needed a place that had a deep forest where he could secretly hunt and kill the deer he'd need to make his buckskin clothes and bedding. He couldn't wait until hunting season opened. He also needed a place with outbuilding where he could develop the requisite earth skills.

It was time to buy a farm and he'd pay cash for it, using proceeds from the trust he had established for Hannah with the insurance money he received when the driver for Markland Trucking was judged liable for the death of his parents. The trust had almost doubled in value and he could use the earnings as he chose. He knew just the realtor to help him find a suitable property and made a mental note to call him in the morning before he left for Cherokee, North Carolina.

Hannah would likely want to go with him and that would work out well. He'd let her think his new quest was just a hobby until it was well underway. Then he'd take her to Alabama and there, beside Paw-Paw Roberts' grave, would work his big scheme on her, closing the deal by telling her that time was running out for his dream. He would soon be too old for such an undertaking. It was now or never for him.

CHAPTER TWELVE

Barsh and Hannah were on the road to Cherokee before nine o'clock Monday. Beyond Asheville he decided it was time to tell her about his goal of learning the old earth skills of Native Americans.

"Hannah, I've been thinking about Paw-Paw Roberts a lot lately. I told you how he decided on his ninety-eighth birthday that he'd lived long enough and refused to eat or drink until he died. I don't think I told you about his burial, however."

"No, you never told me that."

"He had already chosen his grave site on a forested hillside overlooking the old home place. Four men carried him there in a wooden coffin he had built himself a month before he died.

"He didn't want a religions service with a preacher speaking over him. When they lowered him into the good earth, his only surviving son stepped up to the open grave and talked to his father as if he could hear him. Then other people did the same. I wanted to say something, but no one my age spoke so I held my tongue. After all these years, I'm going to visit his grave later this summer and tell him the things I wanted to say that day. Would you like to go with me?"

"Yes, I want to go."

"That's what I was hoping you'd say. There are a lot of things in Alabama I want to show you."

"Do you know what I'm really looking forward to seeing?"

"I don't have a clue, my dear."

"The Tallapoosa River. You always describe it as the river of your youth. It's like a mythical place to me."

"Then, I'll definitely show you the Tallapoosa."

"When can we go?"

"I don't have a date. But you and I will be in Alabama sometime before school starts this fall. You know how proud I am of the Creek blood that flows in my body even if it is only a few drops. In honor of that heritage, I've decided to learn the old earth skills they lived by."

"Well, I think you should."

"Paw-Paw Roberts made his own hunting clothes out of deerskins just like his Creek grandmother taught him. I'd like to be able to do that. I intend to ask the curator of the museum if the Cherokee still make them. Maybe they could teach me."

"Good idea, Daddy."

"When I was a boy playing Indians, I made my own bow and arrows. I don't know where I got the idea, but I cut the arrowheads from a piece of heavy tin. Fashioned them just like an Indian arrowhead and filed them sharp as a razor. Now I want to learn how to make the real thing. But finding someone who knows the art of flint-knapping will probably be a big challenge."

"Knowing you, I'll bet you will find someone."

"That's my intention. The Cherokee still weave their traditional baskets to sell as crafts, and the Catawba are still making pottery according to their tradition. I'll have no trouble learning those skills."

"You're really serious about this, aren't you?"

"I'm devoting most of my energy this summer to this and our poetry project."

***

The curator of the museum told Barsh and Hannah about Moon Man who lived at Big Cove, the most traditional section of the Qualla Boundary Band of the Eastern Cherokee. His first language was still Cherokee and he was the only person the curator knew who made buckskin clothes. He didn't know anyone who made flint arrowheads.

After several wrong turns, they found Moon Man's place. Barsh explained his mission and the old man welcomed them. Yes, he knew the art of brain tanning, which was traditionally woman's work. He had never married, so his mother continued to make his buckskin clothes until she got too old. Then she taught him.

With pride, he then showed them his buckskin clothes and made a point of the fact that he only wore them when he was deer hunting. He knew nothing, however, about making flint arrowheads. He had always hunted with a rifle just like his father before him.

"My Paw-Paw Roberts followed the same practice of hunting in buckskin clothes," Barsh said. "His full-blooded Creek grandmother taught him how to make them."

"Bad blood between Cherokee and Creek after white man get between them."

"I know the story well."

"Andrew Jackson no good President. Trail of Blood for Cherokee. But my people stay here in these mountains. No go to Oklahoma. Where Paw-Paw Roberts live?"

"At the foot of Talladega Mountain in Alabama. My biggest regret is that I didn't get him to teach me how to tan deerskins."

"I teach you."

"Mr. Moon Man, can I ask you a question?" Hannah said.

"What, child?"

"How did you get your name?"

"When young man, I study moon every night. Need answers. One night, moon study me. Tell Uncle. He call me Moon Man."

"That's a good name for you," Barsh said. "Have you ever visited the Cherokee in Oklahoma?

"No leave these mountains."

"If you'd like to go to Oklahoma, I'll take you out there. It won't cost you a dime."

"No like Oklahoma. I teach you brain tanning. No cost you dime."

"I'll be honored beyond words."

"Come back with deerskin. Bring brain."

They left Moon Man's place and visited Oconaluftee Village, a reconstructed Cherokee village from the eighteenth century. It was Hannah's first visit and she thoroughly enjoyed it. He promised to bring her back later in the summer for the outdoor drama, "Unto These Hills."

Leaving Cherokee, Barsh felt lucky to have found Moon Man. Now he had to find someone who could teach him how to make flint arrowheads. Tomorrow, he'd call the Department of Anthropology at the University of South Carolina. Maybe they could put him on to someone.

***

Before the week ended, Barsh had learned that Don Crabtree, an archeologist from Idaho, had almost singlehandedly revived the art of flint-knapping. In the 1930's he was giving demonstrations at the University of California at Berkley. Since then, the number of flint-knappers had significantly increased across the country. They were typically white men doing it as a hobby.

The Chairman of the Department of Archaeology at the University of Georgia had directed him to a Park Ranger at the Ocmulgee National Park near Macon. Barsh spent the next week there, visiting the huge Indian mounds and taking flint-knapping lessons. Before he left, he was making crude arrow points.

On his return from Georgia that Saturday, he was pleased to learn that his realtor had found the perfect farm for his needs. He spent most of

Sunday checking the place out.

Located eleven miles from Ashland, the farm was just short of a hundred and sixty acres, a county highway having claimed a portion of the northeast forty. Most of the farm was still forested and its backwoodsy location was just what Barsh wanted. The south side of the farm fronted the Pacolet River, and on the west side, his forest joined an even deeper forest.

Overjoyed with the find, he signed a contract on Monday to purchase the property at an early closing date. Then he drove to the college to pick up his mail. There was another large manila envelope from Angela. With the mail in hand, he headed for his office.

Kimberly Hall was deserted and he was pleased to have the place to himself. Settled at his desk, he opened the envelope, thinking Angela had probably sent him another critical essay. There was a long letter and two chapters of a new novel she had started. He read the letter first. Stunned, he reread the good news section of the letter:

I have good news. I've started another novel, and I'm writing with more joy than I've ever known. I used to write, desperately longing to be that new voice literary critics were waiting to discover and herald to the world. But that never happened, and I grew more despondent about my fiction with each rejection letter I received.

The enclosed chapters are for you, my dear friend. They are somewhat autobiographical as you will no doubt recognize. I've gone back to my youth, searching for a protagonist, and I found her there, awkward and vulnerable. That's something I had avoided in all my previous fiction. My protagonists were always so smart, so sophisticated. They just popped on the scene that way. They had no history, no roots, no family.

You helped me find my true voice. The way you claim your own roots. You are so comfortable with your journey. That was so liberating to me. Remember the drive from the Charlotte airport to Jackson's Steak House by way of Cherokee Falls? I told you about the trauma of my thirteenth summer. That was the first time I had ever talked about that summer to anyone. You made it so easy for me.

I would love to read the enclosed chapters to you, face to face, but I can't wait for the day I can look you in the eye again. I need to share them now.

Barsh, you are my muse. And what a wonderful muse you are.

Never in a thousand years would he have ever imagined the day when a writer would claim him as her muse. He had sparked fire in a few women during the course of his life. Sometimes it was the other way around and he was the one feeling the heat. But after his adulterous entanglement with Rachel Foster, he had kept a strong hand on the rudder of his passion. Now Angela Kundera was claiming him as her muse and he was deeply moved.

He didn't presume to know the ramifications of her affection for him. Perhaps her feelings were purely platonic. He certainly felt spiritually and intellectually connected to her. He also ached for sensual intimacy with her. But duty would block him from drinking from that well, even if she were willing. There was no place in his life for romance in the foreseeable future.

Whatever Angela's true feelings for him might be, she was probably running away from some major disappointment as much as she was reaching out for his friendship. Still, he could feel the undertow of troubled waters. Hannah was his North Star. Whatever the challenges, he must not fail his daughter.

Maybe he should write Angela about his plan for a sabbatical. She might change her mind about the move if she knew, and that might be best for both of them. The Dean would let her out of the contract. Was there a way to tell her without sounding like a presumptuous fool? If there was, he couldn't think of it.

Setting the letter aside, he focused his attention on the two chapters of the new novel and relished each sentence to the very last word. God, she could write. What was she doing that minute? How he would like to pick up the phone and talk to her about the novel. But he couldn't do that. He would have to respond by letter, which he did with great care and caution.

He couldn't remember ever being so conflicted about another person. He loved her, but knew he had no business loving her. It was difficult for him to steer a steady course of collegial friendship in his letters to her, but that was always his objective. He locked Angela's letter and the two chapter of the novel in the file cabinet and left for home by way of the post office to mail his letter to her.

Davis was watching TV in the den when he got home. He told her that she could leave whenever she wished, that he would take care of Hannah the rest of the day. She was happy to leave early to do some shopping. He found Hannah reading at the desk in her room.

"What's up, my sweet girl?"

"Just reading poetry."

"That's good. We'll have another session of sharing poems tonight."

"Did you buy the farm?"

"I have a contract to buy it. We're closing the deal as soon as they can do a title search and a new deed to the property. I'm paying cash from the earnings of the trust fund, which will speed up the process considerably."

"When can you take me out there?"

"As soon as we close the deal. I can't tell you how excited I am about owning this property. I hope you'll like it."

"You know I will."

"It will be an excellent place for me to develop my earth skills. Meantime, I plan to work on flint-knapping in the basement. All I need is a tarpaulin to catch the flakes. You want to go with me to the hardware store me to get one?"

"Yeah, let's go. I want to see how you do flint-knapping."

CHAPTER THIRTEEN

Barsh left the lawyer's office with the deed to the property that Jeremiah Keeble first settled in 1792. The deal was done and he was headed for the farm that now belonged to him and his heirs. He had bought the place as it was which included all the household furnishings, the farm tools, and an old Ferguson tractor with a bush-hog mower.

The drive was pleasant and he was eager to hike again to the Pacolet River. As he passed Horton's Store, he took note of the fact that it would be a good landmark if he needed to give anyone directions. The farm was almost a mile past the store.

He turned off the county highway and stopped to unlock the gate, which had been installed by the previous owner to open up more land for his cattle to range. But Barsh was delighted to have the gate for the privacy it would afford him as he pursued his earth skills. He then drove up the lane that curved through the woods to the cleared land and then the old farmhouse which was totally hidden from traffic on the highway. He couldn't have dreamed up a better place for his current needs.

He parked at the edge of the yard and walked around surveying the place. The old fields, which were originally cleared for corn and cotton, were now green pastures. He had been told it was not uncommon to see deer in the pastures early in the morning before they disappeared into the adjacent forest to bed down for the day. The forest stretched all the way to the Pacolet River and up the river past his land. He didn't know how extensive the forest was beyond his property, but he intended to explore it Sunday afternoon. He had access to a large forest and should have no trouble killing the deer he needed for buckskin clothing and bedding.

He retrieved his hiking boots and backpack from the trunk of the car and sat on an old bench beneath a massive white oak to change shoes. A mockingbird, perched nearby on a fencepost, broke the silence with a spirited melody. He paused a minute after lacing his boots, letting his spirit rise with the mockingbird's fine notes, and then made a quick tour through the old farmhouse before heading south across the pasture for the forest and the river.

The mixed hardwood forest had seen the ax and saw from time to time, but it had never been clear cut. He noticed a stump here and there and he passed a few stump holes so old the wood had rotted away. There was little underbrush, which made for good walking, and he hiked with purpose at a good pace.

Well into the forest, he stopped to take in the beauty of the rolling woodland. The only sound he heard was the distant cawing of a crow. As he set off again for the river, he caught sight of a Cooper's hawk darting through the canopy of the trees, hard on the tail of a small brown bird, probably a sparrow. He didn't see how the chase ended, which suited him just fine because he couldn't take sides. The fate of the wild was the fate of the wild.

At length, he stood on the north bank of the Pacolet where its headlong rush from the mountains of North Carolina had slowed to a languid pace.

He hiked up the riverbank until he came to a bluff with a big granite ledge that caught his interest. Descending the bank onto a sandbar, he took note of the tracks of raccoon, fox, and deer. He couldn't resist the urge to skip a small flat rock across the river's surface, which he did twice before walking up the sandbar to the granite ledge.

He climbed onto the ledge and sat thinking how lucky he had been to find this particular property. A lone turkey vulture circled gracefully overhead. He lay back on the warm granite and watched the vulture until it drifted out of sight.

What a contrast between the vulture's placid search for carrion and the fierce thrashing of the Cooper's hawk after a song bird on the wing. The vulture and the hawk, scavenger and hunter, each filling its niche in the biosphere.

He recalled the position of anthropologists who claim that scavenging for carrion had been a critical step forward in early man's adaptation of hunting. How ironic that the ancestors of the deadliest hunters on earth had once scavenged for carrion. Like most civilized people, Barsh had moved beyond hunting. He was always mindful, however, that slaughterhouse workers did the dirty work of killing and processing the meat he had consumed since his youth.

Could he turn his own cultural clock back and stoically wash the blood of a kill from his hands without guilt or sentimentality? He would have to make that adjustment if he followed his plan to live in the wild for a year.

Then his mind turned back to the idea of scavenging. It was common to see vultures eating roadkill, including deer. Occasionally, he would see a dead deer on the side of the highway before vultures got to it. Perhaps he could work out an agreement with the highway department to remove such roadkills for their hides. If so, it would limit the number of deer he would have to kill for his buckskin clothes and bedding. But he would have to kill as least one deer with bow and arrow made by his own hands to prove his capability.

The parts of his plan were coming together much faster than he had imagined. It was time to talk to Dean Thompson about a sabbatical.

***

Late that afternoon, Barsh climbed the stairs to Dean Thompson's office. Her secretary was nowhere in sight and for a moment, he watched Catherine reading some papers. He tapped on the side of the open door.

"Oh, Barsh, come in," she said and rose to greet him. "I haven't seen you in … what? Three weeks? Have you been out of town?"

She gestured for him to sit in his usual place and then sat beside him.

"I've been busy with a new project."

"Please bring me up to date."

The Dean's secretary was back talking to someone at her desk. He paused and looked at the open door before answering.

"Catherine, could I stop by your house for coffee in the morning? I've got a lot to share with you, including my new project."

"Oh, yes, but I'm fixing breakfast just like it was one of our regular Saturday morning discussions. Is eight too late for you?"

"That's good," he said and stood to leave.

"I'll walk out with you. I need some fresh air."

He knew he had set off an alarm and would have to clue her in before he left campus. They walked in silence onto the Quad.

"Okay, my friend, give it to me straight. What's going on?"

"It hurts me to tell you, but Debbie is leaving me. She doesn't want a divorce, at least not now. She's asking for a trial separation for a year."

"I don't know what to say. I knew Debbie was unhappy, but I assumed it was with life in general. I can't believe she wants a separation. I thought you held her together. I mean with all her depression."

"No, no. In spite of her bouts of depression, she's a determined woman with her own goals and needs. Her old boss in Louisville has offered to make her a partner in his accounting firm. She was his assistant when I first met her. She tells me the only time she's ever been happy was when she lived in Louisville. So I can't blame her for going. She hasn't been happy here with me, and she deserves a shot at happiness."

"I am so sorry, Barsh. How is Hannah taking this?"

"We haven't told her yet. Debbie will be taking her to Louisville, and that's going to be a real problem for Hannah. You know how close we are. But I have a plan I think will make the separation easier for her."

"Well, that's a small relief. What's the plan?"

"It's quite complicated. I'll explain everything in the morning. I can tell you that I'd like to take a sabbatical after the fall semester. I've talked Debbie into waiting until then to move."

"You know I'll support your plan for a sabbatical."

"Thanks, Catherine. What would I do without you in my corner?"

Dean Thompson proceeded to the library and he left for home, eager to tell Hannah that he had closed the deal on the farm.

CHAPTER FOURTEEN

During breakfast with Dean Thompson that Saturday, Barsh filled her in on everything and she promised her full support for his sabbatical plan. They left the breakfast table and sat in the den, conversing about an article Catherine was writing about Varina Anne "Winnie" Davis, the youngest child of Jefferson Davis, President of the Confederacy.

Winnie was a mere baby when Richmond fell and the Civil War ended. At twelve she was sent to school in Europe for five years and then lived with her parents at their plantation near Biloxi, Mississippi. For a time she made public appearances with her father at Confederate veterans' conventions, but her mind was grasping for bigger things in the North, including romance. After her father's death, she moved to New York City where she was befriended by Kate and Joseph Pulitzer. She wrote as a correspondent for Pulitzer's newspaper and completed four novels before dying at a young age.

Barsh had assumed incorrectly that she was a typical Southern bell because she was hailed as the Daughter of the Confederacy. Now he found himself eager to learn more about her and her novels. He commended Catherine for her research on Winnie Davis, thanked her for support, and left for home.

Hannah, who was waiting for him in the den, jumped from her chair at the crack of the door and hurried to greet him.

"Daddy, can we go to the farm now?"

"As soon as we load up. Did you pack us a lunch?"

"Lunch is all prepared."

"Good girl. Do you have books and a blanket?"

"I have everything I need. I am your daughter, right?"

"Just checking. You can read in the hayloft while I work at flint-knapping in the feed room. I'm taking the *Complete Poems of Robert Frost*. We'll take turns reading to each other over lunch and then we'll hike to the Pacolet River this afternoon."

"Sounds like a fun day to me," Hannah said as Debbie entered the den.

"I don't suppose you've changed your mind about going to the farm with us," he said.

"No, I'm going shopping in Spartanburg. When will you two be home?"

"Probably around five. You want to eat out?"

"Maybe, I know I don't want to cook."

"I'll cook something if you don't want to eat out."

"We'll see how I feel. Hope you two have a good day."

"And the same to you."

He drove away from the house, eager to show Hannah the farm, but he was still thinking about Debbie.

"Maybe we can get your mother to the farm Sunday afternoon, just to show her the place."

"I wouldn't count on it. You know how Mama feels about farms."

"Do you know your mother's favorite place in the whole world?"

"I have no idea."

"Louisville, Kentucky."

"Louisville?"

"That's where she lived after finishing college. She worked at Dugan, Johnson and Bennett, the foremost accounting firm in the whole city. She was Henry Dugan's assistant and loved it. Then we got married and moved to Atlanta so I could enroll in the graduate school at Emory University. She was the primary bread winner in those days, although I did have a stipend as a Teaching Assistant. It was a great time for me but a bad time for her. She missed Louisville and hated living in Atlanta.

"After I finished my Ph.D. program, I applied to every college and university that advertised an opening in religious studies. The only offer I got was from Cooper College and I grabbed it, thankful to have a teaching position anywhere. And guess what miraculous wonder happened right here in old Ashland? You, Hannah Marie Roberts, made your grand entrance into the world."

"You can be so dramatic, Daddy."

"Ah, but it was a dramatic time for me. I was as proud as any father who ever lived, and I still am."

Hannah quietly observed the country scenery. He glanced at her every few minutes and gave her a big smile if she returned his glance. They were fast approaching the farm.

"Do you know what I'm thinking?"

"What?" she said smiling.

"Just how much you remind me of my mother. Did I ever tell you that you have her dark features. Your hair, eyes, and complexion are so like hers."

"No, you never told me, but I noticed it on my own, studying your photographs of her. I used to wonder why I looked so different from you and Mama. Then it hit me one day as I was studying a photograph of your mother."

"Well, I should have told you myself long ago. Of course, it would not have mattered to me who you favored. Here's an awesome truth you should never forget. You are uniquely you. There's never been another you and there never will be."

"Do I have your mother's personality?"

"No, your grandmother Roberts was not a critical thinker like you. She was all about love and compassion."

"Are you saying it's wrong for a girl to be a critical thinker?"

"Heavens, no. I love you just the way you are."

"That's what I thought."

"There's nothing in the world more important to me than your wellbeing and happiness. Look to your right. Our farm begins there with that barbed-wire fence."

A minute later, he turned onto the dirt lane and stopped to unlock the gate.

"This is the entrance to the old Keeble farm, which is now the Roberts farm. I just had a good idea. After I pull through the gate and stop to relock it, I'd like for you to drive to the house. This private lane will be a good place for me to teach you how to drive."

"Great, I'm ready."

After several demonstrations of clutching, accelerating, and braking, he turned the car over to Hannah, who drove up the lane all the way to the house in first gear.

"You did just fine, my sweet girl. Next, I'll teach you how to shift from first to the second gear. This will be your job from now on. I'll unlock the gate, you'll drive through and wait for me to lock it again, and then you'll drive us to the house."

"Job accepted. Driving is fun."

He gave her a tour of the old farmhouse and led her to the screened-in porch that faced the west pasture and the forest beyond it.

"Let's try out this double swing," he said. "You have no idea how excited I am to own this place. I plan to redo the kitchen and bathroom. Of course, I'll buy new mattresses for the beds, and I'll buy a few pieces of furniture to go with this old stuff. Which bedroom do you want?"

"I like the one with the blue walls."

"Then that'll be yours. Okay, I'm ready to show you the barn."

"And I'm going to read in the hayloft just like you used to do when you were a boy."

Hannah got her book and blanket, he got his flint-knapping materials, and they headed for the barn.

"There's nothing like a barn for a country man," he said. "This one has never been painted, and I have no plans to paint it. Look at those old boards that are weathered gray. I like them this way. I do plan to replace the rusty tin roof and I'm doing the same for the house. Let me show you the feed room. It's perfect for my flint-knapping. By the way, the hayloft is also a good place to daydream about the things you want to come your way in life.

"Hannah, I was just about to ask you to tell me about your daydreams, and then I realized that I never shared my boyhood dreams with anyone. I held them close to my heart. I guess that's the way it should be."

"Daydreams are private."

"But anxieties and troubles are different. You should be able to talk openly about these with Debbie and me, right?"

"Don't worry, Daddy. I know I can talk to you about anything."

"That's the way I want it to be between us."

He opened the padlock to the feed room and waited for Hannah to enter.

"Look at this old table. It's made out of solid oak. Weighs a ton. No telling how old it is. I found it in the tool shed. It makes a great worktable. I plan to work on my projects Monday through Friday this summer, but I don't expect you to come with me. You just tell me anytime you want to join me. Otherwise, you can stay home with Davis. She's agreed to change her schedule for the summer so I can get an early start. She'll come every morning before Debbie leaves for work and stay until five. I'll be home by then if Debbie has to work late. Oh, guess what I'm buying next week?"

"Some cows?"

"Good guess, but, no, I'm buying a new Ford pickup. A man with a farm needs a truck."

It turned out to be a good day at the farm. Hannah was relaxed and pleased to see him pursuing his new quest with such determination, and she enjoyed the hike to the Pacolet River.

CHAPTER FIFTEEN

Week after week as the summer slipped away, Barsh worked hard at the farm, preparing for his wilderness sojourn, and his determined efforts had paid off. With growing proficiency at flint-knapping, he had fashioned a good collection of stone tools and arrowheads. He had made two bows and a quiver of arrows. With the aid of the road commissioner, he had scavenged six deer from road kill and brain-tanned the hides the way Moon Man had taught him. He had formed a friendship with a Catawba Indian near Rock Hill, who taught him how to make clay pots using their traditional method. Using his own ingenuity, he had built fish traps out of split bamboo, modeled after wire fish traps his father once used, and tested them in the Pacolet River.

By the second Sunday in August, he was ready to kill his first deer with his handmade bow. This was something he had to do in order to authenticate his sabbatical plan. If he could kill one deer, he could kill more. Thus he could accept the fact that he had made all the buckskin clothes and bedding to date from road kill.

As a mental preparation for the deer hunt, he had reread parts of Leslie Silko's novel *Ceremony*, looking for the chapter where Tayo, the mixed blood Laguna Pueblo protagonist, performed a ceremony over the deer he had just killed. Barsh had been deeply moved by that scene when he first read the book and now he wanted to emulate the ceremony whenever he killed a deer.

He spent the first part of that Sunday evening with Hannah. She read him her latest poem, which was about their first hike to the Pacolet River and the joy of being close to nature with her father. Then they read to each other several poems they had selected from the anthologies they were reading.

Just before her bedtime, he told her his plan for killing a deer. He would leave the house as soon as she was asleep and spend the night at the farm. Two hours before dawn, he would hike to a good stand in the forest and wait for a deer to come by on its way to bed down for the day. He'd follow that pattern daily until he made a kill

Fortunately, he killed his first deer the second morning, stoically pulling the bowstring and releasing the arrow. Standing over the dead buck, he followed his own version of Tayo's ceremony before skinning it with a flint knife.

Later that afternoon, he drove home from the farm with a lot on his mind. The first workday for the new academic year at Cooper had been scheduled for Thursday week, and he had not taken Hannah to Alabama to sell her on his sabbatical plan. He wanted to be in Ashland when Angela moved down and was waiting to hear from her about the moving date. As soon as he could clear that, he'd know when he could take Hannah to Alabama.

He parked the Ford pickup, as usual, on the side of their driveway. Debbie's space in the two-car garage was empty. She was late. Davis exited the den with Hannah following her.

"How was your day, Dr. Roberts?"

"I had a good day. How was yours?"

"Every day with Hannah is a good one. She's getting smarter by the hour. What do you think she's gonna be when she grows up?"

"That's a good question. Maybe we should ask her."

"I just did but she doesn't know."

"I always tell her that she'll find her way and it'll be a good one."

"Well, I better get going. See y'all tomorrow."

"Daddy, Angela Kundera called. She wants you to call her."

"When did she call?"

"About an hour ago. I answered the phone, and she knew my name."

"That shouldn't surprise you. You know it's hard for me to talk to anyone five minutes without telling them about you. I guess she told you she's our new English professor."

"Yes, and she said she was looking forward to meeting me."

"Did you get her number?"

"It's on your desk."

Hannah followed him to the study and sat watching him as he dialed.

"Hello," she said after the second ring.

"Hi, Angela. Hannah said you called."

"Sorry to call you at home, but I couldn't get you at Cooper. I'm leaving for Ashland this Thursday. The movers will be here at seven that morning and I'll get on the road as soon as they finish loading my things. I should be there sometime Friday afternoon."

"We're all set for you here. I checked with the business office last week and the house is ready. It even has a fresh coat of paint."

"I'm so excited about having my own house. No more apartments. And I'll have a rose garden, too."

"What can I do to help with the move? Have you contacted Ashland Public Works to have the water and electricity turned on?"

"I thought I'd have to wait and do that in person."

"Let me do it for you. Then you'll have water and electricity when you get here. If they want a deposit, you can pay me back."

"Oh, thank you. You are such a thoughtful man. One more thing. Would you pick up the house keys from the business office, just in case they close before I get there Friday? The movers said they'd be there by nine Saturday morning. They have a side delivery in western Pennsylvania."

"Consider it done. I'll also pick up your office key."

"You are the best. I can't wait to see you."

"I'll be working at the office Friday afternoon."

"Good, I'll come straight to your office."

"Did you get my directions?"

"Got them. Tell Hannah I said hello. I was delighted to talk with her. Bye for now."

"Bye. And do be careful driving down."

He hung up the phone and turned to face his daughter.

"Dr. Kundera said to tell you hello. Guess what? Not only is she an authority on Southern literature, she's a poet and fiction writer."

"Then maybe she'll help you become a poet."

"I don't know about that. It'll be a long time before I'm ready to have my efforts critiqued by someone with her credentials. Hannah, summer break is almost over, and you and I have yet to make our pilgrimage to the sacred soil of Alabama. Let's head that way early Sunday morning."

"I'll be ready. How long can we stay?"

"I have meetings at the college that Thursday so we'll have to drive home Wednesday. But we'll have two full days and three nights. There are a lot of places I want to take you and I just added another one to the list this morning."

"What's that?"

"Cheaha Mountain, the highest point in Alabama. I used to camp in those forests. I wonder what's keeping Debbie. I guess I should start dinner."

"I'll help you."

They worked as a team preparing dinner, but all the while, he kept thinking about Angela Kundera.

PART II

CHAPTER SIXTEEN

Barsh stood at his office window in Kimberly Hall looking down on the parking lot, which was empty except for his Ford pickup. The shadow of a huge red oak was taking a lazy afternoon stretch across the asphalt pavement. He remembered how Angela had embraced the stately tree before she left campus back in the spring. Now she was on her way back to join the Cooper faculty. He tried to envision her driving south and realized he didn't know what kind of car she owned. The phone rang. It was Catherine.

"Barsh, I need a break."

"Can you come over? I'd join you there, but I'm waiting for Angela. I thought she'd be here before now. I'm getting a little worried."

"I'm on my way."

At the sound of her shoes tapping on the hardwood floor, he rose to greet her at the office door.

"Well, it looks like we've got the place all to ourselves. Aren't we lucky?"

"Margaret Glenn was the last to leave, maybe thirty minutes ago. I trust all is well with you."

"Things are hectic as usual for this time of the year, but I can't complain."

They sat opposite each other in the two comfortable chairs, their eyes trying to read the other's face. She looked at the open book on his desk.

"Am I to assume that you and Hannah are still working on your poetry project?"

"Yes, and I'm amazed at her aesthetic and critical abilities. I find it hard to believe she won't be twelve until November."

"She is amazing, and you deserve most of the credit for her development. You're such an extraordinary father."

"I don't know about that. Sometimes I think I've done it all wrong. Maybe the inaccessible father is the best model for the child."

"No! I know about the distant father. Barsh, I feel so for you and Hannah."

"I'm taking her to Alabama this Sunday for a few days. I intend to share my sabbatical plan with her while we're there, and I'm growing more anxious by the day."

"You know I'll be thinking about you."

"Thanks for caring. If she does support the plan, I think she and I'll both be better prepared to face whatever lies ahead of us. For Hannah's sake, I hope Debbie will get Louisville out of her system and be ready to come home by the time I return from the wild. But even if she doesn't, Hannah will be a year older and better prepared for a permanent separation or divorce. She could even be into boys by then and happy to be in Louisville. At what age does that happen?"

"I think I was fifteen. But you know there was only one boy for me. I loved John from the day we met. It was all I could do just to breathe when word came that he had been killed in Germany. He was twenty-one and I was eighteen."

"You've been so heroic, Catherine. Yet I wish you had found someone to share your life with. There's a man somewhere who's missed out on a good wife."

"I've never told anyone this before, but I was actually open for the right man after I turned thirty. Maybe my expectations were unrealistic. Anyway, I never met anyone who came close to winning my heart. Changing the subject, does Angela know about your sabbatical?"

"I thought about telling her as soon as I decided to take one, but that seemed presumptuous. Now I plan to let her get acclimated to Cooper before I tell her. You haven't told anyone, have you?"

"The President. But only that you wanted to take a sabbatical starting in January and that I approved your plans. Without any questions, he signed off on it."

"Let's keep it to ourselves for a while. I'll tell Angela before I go public. I owe her that much."

"I think you're taking the right course. I brought up the subject because I knew it was likely troubling you."

"One of the things Angela is looking for in this move is, to use her words, *a Southern experience.*"

"And she's counting on you to be her guide."

"That's what she says."

"She can experience a lot of the South under your guidance between now and January. Maybe I can take up some of the slack while you're gone. There's nothing more Southern than Charleston and I'd love to be her guide for that part of the South. My ancestors were there in 1693. It would also be a good thing for me if Angela and I could become friends. You do know that I'm going to miss you, don't you?"

"I'm confident you two will become friends. Angela knows about our special friendship. In fact, she said she was envious. I get the feeling she's leaving a bad situation."

"That wouldn't surprise me. Based on her correspondence with me, she certainly seems anxious to get on down here. Just don't let her root me out of your life."

"That'll be the day. Your place in my life is as fixed as Robert E. Lee's is in your pantheon."

"Then I have nothing to worry about. Well, I have to get back to the office and finish my work for today. Don't forget to tell Angela I'm bringing ham biscuits for breakfast in the morning, and please call me sometime tonight to let me know what time to be there. You're bringing a card table and three folding chairs, right?"

"Yes, and let me bring the coffee. I have a big thermos."

"Sounds good. See you then."

He walked with her to the stairs, thankful that he had such a dear friend. Back at the desk, he picked up the anthology and began reading the editor's selection of poems by Richard Eberhart. He didn't remember Eberhart from his year-long sophomore lit class at Samford until he got to "The Groundhog."

The sentiment of that poem had followed him across the years. He even remembered the opening lines: *In June, amid the golden fields, I saw a groundhog lying dead.* He also remembered the lines about the angry stick because he had poked a dead dog with a stick when he was a boy: *Half with loathing, half with a strange love, I poked him with an angry stick.* He read the poem with renewed appreciation for Richard Eberhart and, locking his name in his memory, he added "The Groundhog" to the poems he intended on reading to Hannah that evening.

A car whined into the parking lot and stopped near his truck. He closed the book. The car door slammed.

"Hello, Ford truck," Angela said.

There was no doubt about the voice. He hurried to the window to wave a welcome, but she was on her way to the front of Kimberly Hall, that silky black hair dancing with her long strides. He took a deep breath and walked to the office door. Up the stairs, she bounded and broke into a broad smile when she saw him.

"Welcome to Cooper, Angela," he said as he walked toward her with an extended hand.

"I'm so happy to be here," she said taking his hand in both of hers and looking deep into his eyes. "I'm sorry I kept you waiting all afternoon. I pushed the Volvo as hard as I dared."

"I didn't mind the wait at all. I've been reading. But I was getting a little worried, afraid you might have had car trouble. It's a male thing, I guess, worrying about women on the road. Anyway, it's something I can't seem to slough off in spite of the women's movement."

"How dear of you. By the way, I like your truck."

"Thank you. Would you like tea?"

"Yes, please, I'll be right back. The bathroom's downstairs, right?"

He nodded ever so slightly and watched her walk away. He had already filled the kettle with water and broken out his new tea set for the occasion. Soon he heard her coming back. She had refreshed her lipstick and added a touch of her exotic perfume.

"What can I say? I've never been so excited about a move. I can hardly believe I'm here."

"The news of your coming has created unusual excitement. Three members of the English faculty called today to ask if you had arrived. Do you take sugar?"

"No, thanks."

They sat facing each other, sipping green tea and drinking deep drafts of joy with their eyes.

"Dean Thompson and I plan to help you and the movers unload your things tomorrow if that's okay with you."

"Wow, what Southern hospitality. I'd love to have your help."

"I always offer to help new members of the Humanities Division when they move here, and Catherine usually joins me."

"Ah, for a moment I thought I was getting special attention," she said with arched eyebrows.

"We have to appear evenhanded with the faculty, but we'll both find ways to let you know how pleased we are to have you here. Truthfully, I never thought you would accept the position. But here you are."

"If you only knew. I've never felt so good about myself. I'm trusting my intuition like never before. This move seems so right for me."

"Then I trust it is the right move for you. Before I forget, I need to ask you about breakfast. Catherine wants to fix ham biscuits. Is that okay?"

"How could I refuse such an offer?"

"As you requested, I picked up the keys from the business office this morning. Then I checked out the house. The water and electricity have been turned on. While I was there, I set up a card table and some folding chairs in the kitchen just in case you agreed to Catherine's offer of ham biscuits. Earlier this afternoon, I left a bottle of Chardonnay, a basket of fruit, and one of Willard's famous roast beef sandwiches in the refrigerator. I hope the sandwich is still edible. Oh, and I left two small gifts for you on the card table."

"Barsh, you're going to make me cry. But rest assured I'll find a way to pay you back."

"Your office is across the hall. Well, actually it's not a typical hall but a huge room as you can see. Your office is number 203."

"Thanks. Let's check it out."

He handed her the key and followed her across the hall. She unlocked the door and gestured for him to enter.

"After you," he said.

"I like this location," she said sitting behind the desk. I can see your office door across the way. I'll be able to keep track of the goings and comings in number 212."

He unconsciously looked at his watch and then regretted it.

"I know you must be eager to get home, but I have a special request. Could you join me for a glass of the Chardonnay you left in the refrigerator? I want to welcome you as the first guest in my new home."

"Well … yes. Do you remember the way or do you want to follow me?"

"I'll follow you, and thanks for everything."

***

Out of habit from attending parties at the house, he parked in the backyard near the porch steps. Angela stopped beside his truck and jumped out.

"Yes," she shouted lifting her arms to the sky. "Barsh, you have no idea how excited I am to have this house and I love being able to park here next to the backdoor. Please call on me at the backdoor."

"Very well," he said and followed her through the screened-in porch into the kitchen.

"Oh, you remembered the field glasses and the field guide to birds. How dear of you. Thank you … thank you. I do want to become a birder. Welcome to my home. Now join me as I check it out again."

They walked through the house, which had been cleaned thoroughly, and ended up back in the kitchen.

"Okay, time to toast our friendship."

She opened the refrigerator, took the wine, and picked up the corkscrew he had left on the card table. Should he offer to open the wine? Normally he would, but she seemed intent on doing it herself.

"I'd be glad to open that for you," he said becoming uncomfortable with his first decision.

"Well, thank you, I'm not used to having a gentleman around."

He opened the wine and she poured a glass.

"How interesting," she said. "We have to drink from the same glass. You are my guest so you must drink first, which means you get to make the first toast."

"To friendship as true as the North Star," he said and drank and handed her the glass.

She drank to his toast and lifted the glass.

"To friendship as true as the sun and the moon," she said and they both drank again. "Now we must break bread together before you go. We'll eat the sandwich and some fruit."

She got them from the refrigerator, and they sat at the card table.

"We'll just pass the sandwich back and forth," she said and passed it to him. "The first bite belongs to you."

They ate the sandwich and drank the wine, passing them back and forth. The conversation was light and lively.

"I've said it before. You are such a thoughtful man. But here's a confession. I now know why one side of me trusted you implicitly from the day I met you even though the other side kept calling me a fool."

"Caution is usually a good policy in my estimation. I will never deliberately betray our friendship, but I have unintentionally failed more than my share of good people."

"I'll take my chance. I'm here, happy and expectant."

"Angela, I don't know how to say this without sounding like a presumptuous fool, but I need to tell you that true friendship is all I can offer you."

"Then we're on the same page. I made a vow last winter that I'd never again get romantically involved with a married man. Three years ago, I began an affair with a member of the English Faculty at Brown. He was married, with children, and told me that he and his wife were estranged and soon to be divorced. I was still a Ph.D. candidate at the time, and like a fool I believed him."

"Please forgive me. I feel totally ridiculous."

"All is well. I appreciate your honesty."

"You do know that I treasure your friendship, right?" he said.

"There's not a doubt in my mind."

Silently, they studied each other, weighing the gravity of the moment. Then he broke eye contact and looked at his watch.

"Yes, I know you have to go. I trust I haven't delayed you too long."

"No, but I must go," he said and stood to leave. "Oh, I almost forgot to ask you. What time do you want Catherine and me to come in the morning?"

"The movers said they would be here around nine. What about eight?"

"That's good. Where are you staying tonight?"

"The Ashland Hotel."

"Sleep well. I know you must be exhausted from the long drive. See you tomorrow."

"Yes, tomorrow."

She followed him to the back steps and waved as he drove away.

CHAPTER SEVENTEEN

The moving truck pulled away from the house, headed north, and Barsh joined Angela and Catherine in the kitchen.

"Let's sit at the table and relax," Angela said. "I can't believe how well this went. Having both of you really made a difference and I can't thank you enough. I've never been welcomed anywhere so warmly."

"Barsh and I like to help when new faculty move in. He's good with the heavy stuff and I'm fine with the light boxes."

"Well, you both are dear to take your Saturday to help me. What a relief to have all my things in this house. I'm actually looking forward to getting everything in order, but now it's time for me to do a little something for you two. Please be my guest for dinner somewhere this evening."

"Well, yes, thank you," Catherine said and turned to Barsh.

"I wish I could join you, but I have a family commitment. Angela, let me take some of your office things to the college in my truck. Those boxes of books marked *office* are too heavy for you to carry from the parking lot to the second floor and I have time to do it this afternoon."

"Aren't you too tired?"

"No, but if you are, I can help you when Hannah and I get back from Alabama. We're leaving early in the morning and plan to be back Wednesday afternoon."

"Well, let's get it done today. How could I refuse such a generous offer?"

"I'll see you two later," Catherine said. "Angela, what time shall we go to dinner?"

"Is seven okay?"

"That's fine, and I'll come by for you."

"Thank you, Catherine."

He followed the Dean to the car and opened the door for her.

"I do hope you and Hannah have a successful trip to Alabama. I'll be anxious to hear all about it."

"I'll give you a report Thursday before I leave campus."

Angela waved from the porch as Catherine drove away and then ushered him back into the kitchen.

"Would you like a glass of wine?"

"I'd like coffee if you don't mind. I see you have the makings."

"That does sound good. Have a seat at the table while I make a pot."

There was a grace about her that was pleasing to watch. With the coffee dripping, she got the fruit from the refrigerator, sat down across from him, took a cluster of grapes, and passed the basket to him.

"Thanks for taking care of lunch," she said. "Willard's barbecue sandwiches were just the thing. Did you see how the movers gobbled them down?"

"Just remember, Willard's is the place to go if you want takeout sandwiches."

"I'll remember. Now tell me about the Alabama trip. Is this your pilgrimage to Paw-Paw Roberts' grave?"

"That and more. I want to show Hannah where I grew up. We visit Debbie's parents in Kentucky several times every year, but Hannah has never been to Alabama. She's heard my old stories about growing up there so often she can tell them as well as I. Earlier this summer I promised to take her before school started back. Then I got involved in other projects and the summer slipped away. This is my last chance to keep that promise."

"A man who keeps promises. I like that. I look forward to meeting Hannah. I could tell she's special just in the few minutes I talked with her on the phone Tuesday. The coffee's ready. Let's sit in the living room."

She poured the coffee and they moved to the living room.

"Your furniture seems tailor-made for this room."

"I must say I'm pleased with the way the room is shaping up. I can already envision how it will look when I get the paintings hung and all the accents in place."

He chose an easy chair beside the fireplace. She sat on the end of the sofa next to him.

"I love this log-burning fireplace. I've never had one before. I can't wait to start a fire this fall."

"As the proud owner of a farm with woodland, I've already cut more firewood than I'll burn this winter. I have split oak and round hickory logs that are just the right size to sizzle the evening away. I'll bring you some of both."

"How generous of you. Your joy over buying the farm jumped from the pages of your letters."

"I was there almost every day this summer working on several projects that I'm excited about."

"Like what?"

"For one thing, I'm making pottery according to the traditional method of the Catawba Indians. A small group of them live near Rock Hill, which is not far from here, and one of their potters has been helping me."

"How did you get interested in making traditional pottery?"

"It's a long story. Have you read any of William Gilmore Simms' novels?"

"No, but I know he was an important Charleston writer and a prolific one as I recall. Early nineteenth century?"

"That's right. Simms, like Cooper, understood the epic dimensions of the doomed Native American culture. His novel, *The Yemassee*, has been compared by some to Cooper's *The Last of the Mohicans*. I think both are important books, but I'm not qualified to compare them on their literary merits.

"Anyway, I once read Simms' description of the Catawba Indian on their annual journey to Charleston, laden with pottery to trade for European goods. When I recently learned that they were trying to establish a reservation near Rock Hill, I paid them a visit to see if I could help. During my conversation with their leaders, I made reference to Simm's account of the Catawba trading their pottery in Charleston, and they told me they still made traditional pottery. I became friends with one of their potters and learned enough to try my hand at it"

"You know the farm is on my list, don't you?"

"I'll take you as soon as the weather cools down a bit and we'll hike to the Pacolet River."

"Speaking of my list, do you have any idea when you might be able to take me to the Joyce Kilmer Memorial Forest? I've moved that outing to the top of my list."

"I can take you in a week or so, but I'd rather wait until the trees have lost their leaves. I want you to be able to see the bare structure of those giant yellow poplars. How their massive limbs spread out in all directions in the top of those trees like giant sculptures."

"Then I'll wait for that day."

"Believe me, it'll be worth the wait. Meantime, there are other places I can take you to experience our Carolina Mountains. Oh, I know the perfect place to begin that journey. Do you like surprises?"

"Good surprises are wonderful."

"Then you'll like this one. Unless something comes up, I can take you on a fieldtrip to the Carolina Mountains a week from this Sunday. That's the day before the students arrive. If you need more time to settle in, we can go later."

"Please, I'll be ready. Could I prepare a picnic lunch?"

"That would be good. Without giving the detail away, I can tell you we'll share your picnic lunch high on a mountain top in North Carolina."

"Sounds divine," she said.

"Would you also consider bringing cassettes of your favorite music? We'll have a lot a driving time on the way there and back."

"I'd love to do that."

"Now let me take all of the boxes marked *office* to 203. The movers and I stacked them on the back porch."

In about an hour, he had moved all those boxes to her campus office. Back in the kitchen, he needed to touch her before leaving. Not a handshake. Not a hug.

"Give me five for the road," he said with a smile and she did. "Call Catherine if you need help with anything. If she can't help you, she'll know who can. I'll see you Thursday morning at the faculty meeting."

"A million thanks, Barsh. Be safe and have a good time with Hannah in Alabama."

She followed him to the truck and waved as he drove away.

CHAPTER EIGHTEEN

Their bags were stashed in the Audi and they were all set to leave for Alabama. Debbie followed them to the car and hugged Hannah long and hard.

"Bye, my dear girl. Hope you two have a great trip."

"We will, Mama."

"Barsh, please be careful."

"Don't worry. We'll be just fine."

He backed out of the driveway and looked back at Debbie who was drooping with anxiety. She was counting on him to sell the sabbatical plan to Hannah. He, however, was beginning to have doubts about the plan. Hannah was unusually subdued as they left the neighborhood. He turned to smile at her, but she was looking straight ahead, holding a book in her hand.

"I hope that's an interesting book. We've got a long drive ahead of us."

"I want to talk."

"You name the subject and we'll have at it."

"You and Mama."

"What about Debbie and me?"

"Why did you stop sleeping with her? It's been worrying me for months, and you said we should talk about anything that was bothering me."

"Yes, we definitely need to talk. I assume you know that means Debbie and I no longer have an intimate marriage."

"That's what worries me."

"Okay, I'll give you my perspective on what has happened. You can ask your mother what she thinks happened if you wish."

"Your account is all I need."

"As you well know, Debbie and I have very different worldviews and hold very different beliefs about a lot of things. For example, she doesn't believe in evolution because it contradicts the Biblical account of the origin of all living things. For me, evolution is totally evident from a modern scientific point of view.

"This kind of difference has always been there, but rather than converging over time, the gulf between us has grown wider. She's remained conservative and traditional and I've become much more liberal. At first I tried to share my intellectual and spiritual journey with her, but it was too threatening for her to embrace.

"I'm not sure what happened between us in the bedroom, but I think she found it more and more difficult to be intimate with me as the gulf between our worldviews continued to grow. I do know that our bedroom kept getting colder and colder until there was no lovemaking. Things between us came to a head last spring and I decided that having my own bed would be less complicated for both of us.

"If anyone is to blame, I guess it's me. I'm the one who's changed, although I don't think it does any good to assign blame. I certainly don't blame her for being who she is. She's a good woman, just traditional in many ways.

"The cold truth is that she and I are no longer lovers in the romantic sense of the word, but I love and honor her as your mother and always will. I also respect her needs as she does mine, which means we often go our separate ways.

"The summer before you were born, I wanted the two of us to take an extended tour of Europe, but she had no interest in traveling in Europe. She insisted, however, that I go by myself, and I did. I spent two extraordinary months traveling over Europe all by myself.

"She never complains when you and I do things that she doesn't enjoy. And she never complains when I leave for some hiking trip or any other trip I choose to take."

"Okay, I understand."

"I trust you know that we both love you unconditionally and always will no matter what our relationship may be."

"I know that. I think I'll read. Do you mind?"

"You read and I'll drive. And between us, we'll rack up the miles. Look out Alabama. Here we come, ready or not."

***

The drive from Ashland to Atlanta had gone well. Barsh did a lot of thinking while Hannah read. In Atlanta, he made a detour to show her Emory University.

Back on course, they stopped for lunch at Sprayberry's Barbecue in Newnan, Georgia. His mind flooded with memories of Wesley Workman and the trips they had made on his Harley-Davidson. Once they had roared in and out of Atlanta on that black motorcycle just for the hell of it and then stopped at Sprayberry's on the way home. He could see Wesley flirting with the sassy waitress and recalled that he was quite the womanizer.

Those memories got Barsh thinking about Amy Burdette, his first heartthrob and victim of Wesley's seductive powers. She had such potential as a young girl, but she was pregnant at fourteen. What had happened to her? he wondered. He hadn't seen her since her family moved away that fall.

After he and Hannah left the restaurant, he decided to tell her about his first experience of love. Perhaps it would be helpful to her when she started down love's treacherous pathway, he thought, since he hadn't been very lucky with it.

"Hannah, you know that we moved from the country to town when I was nine. Did I ever tell you about Amy Burdette who lived next door?"

"I don't think so."

"Amy was a tomboy, almost a year younger than I. She'd come to our house practically every day. We played in the house, under the house, and in the yard. Later, we played in and around a tepee that I'd built in the meadow below our house. Adjacent to our backyard, there was a small grove of mixed trees, mostly hardwood, where we developed our climbing skills. We especially enjoyed climbing this big magnolia tree. Its foliage spread out from the ground up and was so dense that no one could see us when we were hanging out there.

"For five years she was my best friend and could've been a boy for all I cared. About the time she turned fourteen, her parents stopped her from coming over to play with me, but I didn't care. I had started rambling beyond our neighborhood to places that were unsafe for her to go. We continued to walk to school and back each day, however.

"Then this astonishing thing happened after school one afternoon. Standing on the sidewalk in front of her house, I looked into her eyes and fell in love with her. Soon I was crazy in love with her. She was the girl I wanted to marry when we grew up and she seemed to be just as committed to me. But things don't always turn out the way you expect them to.

"Before summer ended, she was infatuated with Wesley Workman, one of my camping buddies, who had made a move on her. He had a reputation for using girls for his own pleasure and in keeping with that reputation, he seduced Amy. She then dumped me without the courtesy of telling me. She just started avoiding me completely. My heart was shattered. Her life, however, was turned upside down when Wesley got her pregnant. The family moved away that fall and I never saw her again.

I heard her parents put her in a home for unwed mothers in another town."

"A home for unwed mothers?"

"This was a way of protecting girls in her predicament and their families. When the baby was born, it would be put up for adoption and the girl would return home to grow up."

"What a sad story, Daddy."

"A sad story, indeed, and a painful experience for me. In spite of my broken heart, I've always wished her the best, and I hope she has had a good life."

"Wouldn't you like to find out what happened to her?"

"Truthfully, I'm afraid to. I fear things didn't turn out well for her. Promise me that you'll never let anyone abuse or mistreat you because you're in love with them."

"How could I? I'm your daughter."

"And that makes me one proud father."

They both fell silent, Hannah writing on one of her pads and Barsh pushing the Audi down the winding highway.

***

Mid-afternoon, Barsh and Hannah checked into a motel on the edge of town. After a short rest, they left for a brief tour of the place. He pointed out the stores that he had frequented, noting how shabby the places looked now, especially the once glorious Martin Theatre where he had spent many happy Saturday mornings as a boy. From Main Street, he drove by the schools he had attended and then headed for his old neighborhood. In spite of his effort to point out all the changes that had occurred, he knew there was no way his daughter could envision the place as it was to him when he lived there.

"Well, that was my old neighborhood," he said as they left.

"I'm sorry, Daddy, but it seems strange to me that you once lived here."

"That's understandable. It even seems strange to me now. If you don't mind, I'd like to visit Edna Peters, the widow of Coon Peters, who taught me how to live off the land."

"I remember your stories about him. He gave you his 12 gauge pump shotgun."

"I never saw him again after my parents moved to Georgia, but I wrote to him occasionally until he died. For all I know, Mrs. Peters is dead. I haven't heard from her in years. Anyway, I need to drive out there. We'll be back in less than an hour. Then we'll find a place to eat and call it a day. I've got a busy schedule for us tomorrow."

His mind filled with memories associated with Coon Peters as he drove to the farm. Surprisingly, the old house hadn't changed much. There was a late model Chevy sedan parked in the yard. Hannah followed him onto the front porch. The wooden door was open, but the screen door was latched with an old fashion hook. He knocked and a woman cautiously approached the door.

"Good afternoon. I'm Barsh Roberts, an old friend of Mrs. Peters."

"Gracious goodness, Barsh, I never dreamed I'd get to meet you. I'm Suzy, the youngest daughter, and I've heard all about you. Y'all come on in."

"Pleased to meet you, Suzy. This is my daughter Hannah."

"I'm so glad y'all came for a visit. But I hate to tell you that Mama died eighteen years ago from breast cancer."

"I'm sorry to hear the sad news. She never answered my last letter and I was afraid something had happened."

"I was home when that letter came. Mama was too near dead to answer it. Do you still live in Louisville?"

"No, we live in Ashland, South Carolina."

"I guess you know Daddy thought you was the best boy in Alabama back then. He wanted a boy like you but all he got was girls."

"The year I turned fifteen, I stumbled upon your father sitting by a fire at his old camp on the west bank of Wehadkee Creek. That was pure luck for me. He taught me how to roast fish and squirrel over an open fire. I wasn't sure he could make it home on his own so I went with him. He had a hard time, even with me carrying all his gear. He told me that working in the cotton mill had ruined his lungs.

"That was my second time to camp in that old growth forest and his last. After that, I'd stop by to see him on my way to and from Camp Wehadkee, as I called it. He was just the friend I needed back then. Do you know he gave me his old pump shotgun when I was fifteen?

"Mama told me he wanted you to have it because he didn't have a son to pass it down to. Daddy kept all your letters and so did Mama. I've read them all at least a dozen times."

"Suzy, we've got to go, but it sure is good to meet you. I'm back in Alabama to show Hannah where I grew up, and I needed to come by and check on your mother."

"Oh, I wish y'all could spend the night with me."

"Thanks but we have a lot to do in a short time."

They exchanged goodbyes, and he and Hannah were on their way to find a good place to eat.

"Well, my sweet girl, I trust you can appreciate how much that visit meant to me. Now I can close that chapter of my life."

CHAPTER NINTEEN

After breakfast Monday morning, Barsh drove through town and headed north on the old U.S. 431 and then turned west on the Wadley Highway. As a high school boy, he had taken that route countless times in his old Ford pickup, eager to get back to their farm. It was a beautiful day and he was full of stories.

"Hannah, we're coming up on High Pine Creek. Look to your right as we cross the bridge and you'll see its rippling currents. I've fished and hunted along this creek from its headwaters to its mouth at the Tallapoosa River. About two miles up the creek from here, there's a cave in the side of a bluff called Coot's Cave. My elders used to tell me about Coot Pitman who lived in that cave when they were young. He would tramp the roads, near and far, and people called him a boogeyman. Parents would tell their children you better look out or old Coot Pitman will get you."

"I thought I'd heard all of your stories."

"Oh, no, I have a good stock and I'm not near the bottom of the barrel."

He left the state highway, turning right onto a county highway.

"Okay, we're ascending the hills to the sacred soil of Broughton. Before we leave the community, we'll visit the cemetery where Mother and Dad are buried. First, I want to drive by the farm where I spent the happiest days of my youth. Then we'll stop at the Henry place to see if anyone is home. You know the stories about my little pal Susan Henry and our horseback riding days."

"Do you think she still lives there?"

"I don't know but I hope to find out today."

"Have you seen her since you moved away?"

"Not a single time."

Oh, the memories of this community, he thought, as he turned right at King Marshall's Store onto another county highway. He was almost there.

"Look to your left, Hannah."

"Is that where you lived?"

"That's it. Not much to brag about, but I wouldn't have traded it for a royal palace when I was a young man. I'm pleased that the current owners are keeping the place up. They're raising Hereford cattle. That fence running away from the road up ahead is the property line between this farm and the Henry farm. Susan's grandparents owned the place and she and her mother lived with them. Her mother was never married, but I called her Mrs. Henry."

Barsh turned into the driveway, pleased to see a new Buick parked in front of the garage. A strange feeling came over him as he headed for the door with Hannah following hard on his heels. He took a deep breath and rang the doorbell. Mrs. Henry opened the door and stared intently at him.

"I'm Barsh, Mrs. Henry."

"Lord o' mercy," she said and rushed to embrace him, "I couldn't believe my eyes. And who's this pretty girl?"

"My daughter Hannah."

"She's sure got your mother's features," she said reaching for a hug. "Hannah, you are a beautiful child. Barsh, you don't know how happy I am to see y'all. Come on in."

She led the way to the spacious den. There, above a well-crafted stone fireplace, was a large oil portrait of Susan. Wearing tall boots and a fancy riding outfit, she was sitting astride a magnificent black stallion. Following Mrs. Henry's directions, he sat in a big stuffed chair and Hannah sat beside her on the couch.

"Barsh, I ain't married no rich fool if that's what you're thinking. Papa left the place to me, and I sold it to Susan after she married Terry Halford, a doctor up in Nashville. They live on a big horse farm. She built this house for me and turned Papa's old fields into pastures for some of her broodmares."

"Well, I'm pleased to hear she's doing well. I know you must be proud of her."

"Oh, she's done good for herself. If you met her for the first time now, you'd think she was born a princess. Look at that painting of her dressed out in them fancy pants and boots. Does that look like the Susan you knew?"

"Her outfit is definitely an upgrade and so is the horse. But there's a good resemblance to the girl who once rode a horse named Dan up and down the dusty roads of our days. Susan was beautiful then and she's beautiful now."

"She owes her love of horses to you. When y'all moved out here and you got Thunder, nothing was ever the same with Susan. She was driving us all crazy until I bought her that horse. Then she didn't care about nobody or nothing but you and y'all's horses.

"When you went off to college, all she talked about was going to college herself and becoming a horse doctor. Nobody ever believed she could do it, but she did. Susan was a spunky girl. You got to give her that. Oh, my Lord, she about went crazy when your parents moved and she lost you. It was her love of horses and her dream of being a horse doctor that pulled her through."

"Susan was a natural with horses," he said. "Sometimes she would curry Thunder while waiting for me to finish some chore, and he loved it with her taking her gentle time and talking to him like he could understand everything she said."

"Daddy, how old was Susan then?"

"I believe she was about your age when we moved here. She was fifteen or sixteen the last time I saw her."

"Hannah, I'll tell you something else. Susan would have followed Barsh to hell if he'd a-wanted to go there."

"Don't believe that. True, Susan was my little riding pal, and I was determined to look out for her. I always believed she would do well in life, and I'm delighted to learn she's excelled."

A hush settle over them. Barsh studied Susan's portrait and suddenly he had a longing to see her.

"Barsh, tell me about yourself. Do you still hunt and fish? Lord, I missed all the fish and game you used to bring us. You were so good to share with us."

"I gave up hunting and fishing when I went off to college. I don't camp anymore either, but I still love the wild. I do a lot of hiking in the Carolina Mountains."

"What about a horse? I can't imagine you without a horse."

"Thunder was my one and only horse. I married a girl from Kentucky. She was born on a big tobacco farm, but she hated living in the country. So horses and country living were out of the question for us."

"That's a pure shame."

"Daddy, you could have a horse now that you bought the farm."

"You bought a farm?"

"It's just a place for me to get away. We don't live there."

"Hannah's right, Barsh. You, of all people, should have a horse. And Hannah should have one, too. She can be your little riding buddy now. Susan would love to fix you both up with a horse. You must go see her. It would do her a world of good."

"Yeah, Daddy, let's visit Susan. I think you should buy us each a horse from Susan. You can teach me how to ride."

"Well, maybe we could visit Susan and check out her horses."

"I can't wait to tell her y'all are coming to see her."

"Hold off on that until I call her."

"Then promise me you'll call her."

"Okay, I'll call her."

"That will tickle her to death. She has won about every prize there is when it comes to riding Tennessee Walkers. Let me show you some pictures of her riding."

Mrs. Henry retrieved a thick album and he and Hannah sat beside her on the couch as she narrated the photos. He was most impressed.

"I'm giving you this picture. It's just like the painting up there."

"Thank you very much. I'll treasure this photo."

"Barsh, can y'all spend the night with me?"

"Thanks for the invitation, but we have to go. There are lots of places I want to take Hannah and we don't have much time. But I have to ask you about some people first."

All the people he asked about were dead, except Joe and Rachel Foster.

"Please tell Susan that I love her portrait, that she is as beautiful as she was the last time I saw her. Tell her I'm proud of all her accomplishments."

"Oh, I'll tell her, for sure. Now let me give you Susan's phone number."

They exchanged phone numbers and said their goodbyes, promising to stay in touch by phone. Hannah was beaming with joy as he drove away. He showed her where all the people who had meant a lot to him lived, and then they stopped at the cemetery to visit the graves of his parents. He didn't break down this time, but talked about his mother and father until Hannah started crying.

"What's wrong, my dear," he said and took her in his arms.

"I don't know, Daddy."

He felt sure she was crying because of his and Debbie's estrangement, but he decided not to go there.

"Hannah, my dear, it's time for me to show you the Tallapoosa River. We'll cross the river in about fifteen minutes just before we get to a little town called Wadley. I've camped at a dozen or more places upriver and downriver from that bridge. We're going to a place called Horseshoe Bend, which is downriver. In 1814 General Andrew Jackson defeated the Creek Indians at this site and ended their last war against the whites who were settling on their traditional land. It's now a National Military Park, but when I camped there, it was just a wild place on the river where I like to fish and camp.

"When we leave Horseshoe Bend, I'll take you to Lake Martin, which was created by a hydro-electric dam further down the river. My father used to take me fishing there with his friends before I was old enough to drive myself. We'd leave after Dad got off work on Friday and come back Sunday morning. I was the only boy among those men and it was quite an experience for me. I'll take you to our favorite place to camp and fish.

"From Lake Martin, we'll head back this way with Cheaha Mountain as our destination. Hopefully, we'll have time to do some hiking on one of the trails there. We'll dine at Mountaintop Restaurant, which has a spectacular view, and then spend the night at the lodge there."

"Daddy, I'm glad to see where you grew up. But you know what?" she said and paused.

"What?"

"I don't know how to say it. How did you get to where you are from here?"

"That's a good question. We'll talk about it tomorrow when we visit Paw-Paw Robert's grave. Okay?"

"That's fine with me."

It was a good day for both of them. Hannah seemed to enjoy it all, including Cheaha Mountain, their final destination for the day. He went to sleep that night, dreading his task for the next morning.

CHAPTER TWENTY

After two wrong turns that forced Barsh to stop and ask for directions, he spotted Paw-Paw Roberts' old home place and turned up the lane that led to the house. There was neither car nor truck in sight. He stopped at the edge of the yard, his heart sinking with fear that no one was home. A bluetick coonhound announced their arrival and scrambled from beneath the house. Hannah, who was silently taking it all in, seemed anxious.

"Don't worry, my sweet girl. If anyone's home, they'll soon come to the door."

The house looked just as he remembered it, an unpainted wooden structure with a tin roof. The two huge water oaks shading the front yard were anchored by massive roots, humped up as they stretched out from the trunk of each tree. He remembered sitting on one of those roots as a small boy and talking with a blond-headed girl in a faded blue dress.

He looked across the way for the little shed built over a spring where Paw-Paw used to keep milk in the summer. Not a vestige of the structure remained. He couldn't recall the name of the girl who showed him the spring, but he could see her squatting on the opposite side of the little pool of cool water bubbling up from the earth.

A stooped woman with gray hair opened the front door and stepped onto the porch.

"This is the place, but I don't know that woman. You stay in the car and I'll talk to her."

"Aren't you afraid of that dog?"

"No, it's a good natured hound, just letting the home folks know they have company."

Barsh walked toward the house, talking calmly to the barking dog as he offered it the palm of his hand. The woman, who had moved from the door to the porch steps, shouted for Jaw Bone to hush up and get back under the house. Instead, the dog accepted Barsh's friendly overture and followed him to the steps.

"Good morning, I'm Barsh Roberts. My great-grandfather Roberts used to live here"

"Lord o' Mercy, Barsh, I'd a never recognized you, but I remember you when you was just a boy. Never knowed of another boy named Barsh. You're Bill Roberts' boy, ain't you?"

"Yes, ma'am."

"You don't likely remember me, but we're kinfolks, probably first cousins five or six times removed. If my mother-in-law was yet alive she could count it up sure and square."

"No, I don't remember you. Who are you?"

"Arrie Roberts. Call me Cousin Arrie. I was a Hammell before I married Johnson Roberts. We bought this place from the heirs after Paw-Paw died. My husband up and died on me two years ago. Dropped dead without a warning, but I ain't complaining. Mama lost Daddy when she was just forty-seven. Besides, I got a son who keeps a regular check on me. Those are his white-face cows grazing down yonder by the creek. Who's that in the car out there?"

"My daughter, Hannah."

"Well, you get that girl and y'all come on in this house and talk to me."

Barsh hurried to the car for Hannah, thankful that relatives still owned the property.

"We struck gold," he said bending toward the open window. "She's a distant cousin who remembers me. Let's visit with her awhile and then we'll be on our way to Paw-Paw's grave."

He opened the door and she followed him to the porch.

"Hannah, this is our Cousin Arrie."

"My Lord, you're the prettiest girl I ever laid my eyes on. Y'all come on in."

She led them through the house to the back porch which had been screened in since Barsh was last there. They sat patiently answering the questions she threw at them, her hungry eyes shifting back and forth between Hannah and him.

"Cousin Arrie, I'd like to visit Paw-Paw's grave if that's all right."

"Lord, yes, and I'd go with you if I was able."

"Paw-Paw always told me to be proud of the Creek blood flowing through my body. And I am. That's why I brought Hannah with me today. I wanted her to see where he lived and died and was buried."

"Do you remember the way?"

"I think we walked straight up from here to a place just before the mountain got steep. I remember standing beside a big cedar, looking out across the valley."

"That's right. You won't have no trouble finding the grave. Look for that cedar. It's the only one up there. All the rest have been cut and sold.

HONEY FROM A LION

***

They sat beside the grave, satisfied with the carefully chosen words each had poured from their hearts. Barsh searched for a good segue to the task before him.

"Did I ever tell you about the time I camped in a cave for a week one winter?"

"No, sir."

"This is how that came about. The summer before my senior year at Handley High, I discovered a cave in a high bluff about three miles up the Tallapoosa River from where I was camping. Sitting in the mouth of that cave, I wondered if Indians had ever camped there. Then I thought about possible camp fires and found signs of smoke on the roof of the cave so I named it Soot Cave.

"On my way back to camp, I saw deer tracks. From that moment, I started making plans to camp at Soot Cave that winter and try to kill a deer, something I'd never done. When I was growing up, deer were rare in our part of Alabama. They'd been practically wiped out from over hunting. Fortunately, they're now plentiful because of restocking programs and strict hunting regulations. Out of curiosity, I called the game warden earlier this summer."

"What happened that winter? Did you kill a deer?"

"The day after Christmas I left for that cave prepared to camp until New Year's Eve. Each morning I'd get up before dawn and hike to a different stand where I'd wait half the morning hoping a deer would come by on its way to bed down somewhere for the day. They forage at night. Midmorning, I'd leave the stand and hunt until I killed some small game to roast for supper. Then I'd eat the leftovers for breakfast. Two meals a day, an early supper and breakfast before dawn. I did that all week and never saw a deer."

"Didn't you get discouraged and want to go home?"

"Not at all. That camping trip remains one of my cherished experiences. Every evening I'd sit in the mouth of the cave and watch the sun set in the distant horizon across the river. I did a lot of thinking about a lot of things. I was confused and bewildered about what I wanted to do with my life.

"While working with a logging crew the summer before, I witnessed senseless racism that caused a black man to kill a white man with an ax in self defense. Then the black man was unjustly convicted of murder and executed by the State of Alabama. The racial bigotry and legal injustice that I experienced firsthand had shattered my trust in our social system. I started thinking seriously about going to Alaska and living in the wild. In the end, I realized I couldn't do that to Mother and Dad. They wouldn't know what was happening to me, and I wouldn't know what was happening to them.

"Dad and I had worked out a plan for me to go to Auburn University and major in civil engineering, but that no longer appealed to me. So I limped along my senior year uncertain about my future."

He was studying Hannah, who seemed shaken by his narration. She was so young, so innocent, so vulnerable. At that moment, he knew his sabbatical scheme was dead. There was no way he could abandon his daughter to Debbie's care for a year.

Debbie could take their daughter to Louisville but not under false pretense. He would tell Hannah the truth and he would remain an integral part of her life. They would visit back and forth as often as possible and they would stay in touch by phone and correspondence.

"Well, my sweet girl, I guess you know I'm glad I decided not to go to Alaska. Otherwise, I'd not be the father of the best daughter I could ever imagine."

"What happened to cause you to want to be a professor?"

"The summer after I graduated high school I had a profound religious experience. It left me with a clear sense of calling. I came to realize that my mission in life was to be a voice for justice and righteousness and a servant to a broken humanity. That fall I enrolled at Samford University to major in religion and soon learned that I could best carry out my mission by becoming a college professor of religious studies. You know the story from there."

"I like your story, Daddy. Everything makes sense to me now."

"I'm glad you think so. It's meant a lot to me to be able to show you where I grew up."

"Yeah, it's meant a lot to me, too. Now I can fit everything together."

"Okay, it's time for us to take leave of this place. We're spending the night in Birmingham with Uncle Edward, who influenced me as a young man second only to Mother and Dad. He gave me my first field guide to birds when I was twelve. He was so pleased when I called and told him we were coming.

"We'll get there in time for me to show you Samford University and the colossal statue of Vulcan standing on a tall pedestal on Red Mountain, looking down on Birmingham. They used to say this was the largest cast iron stature in the world. You and I'll climb the stair to the top of the pedestal and cast our eyes down on the city. We'll take Uncle Edward out to a nice restaurant somewhere. He's a great story teller so we'll get to hear some of his tales before bedtime. Then we'll head home tomorrow."

CHAPTER TWENTY-ONE

Back home in Ashland by mid-afternoon on Wednesday, Barsh left Hannah with Davis and drove straight to Debbie's office to give her a report on the trip, knowing how anxious she'd be to talk to him. She was counting on his selling Hannah on the sabbatical plan.

Debbie was with a client so he waited in the reception area. He always felt strangely out of place in her domain and never stopped by except to take something to her or to pick up something. His presence had aroused the curiosity of the receptionist who, unruffled by his terse responses, pressed on with her effort to uncover his reason for being there.

She had once questioned him about his views on the Bible, just to make sure the community gossip about his liberal assessment was on the mark. He'd learned to respond to her kind by turning the questions back on them. As he expected, she gave a dogmatic response about the inerrancy of the Bible, which she insisted must be interpreted literally. He responded by asking if she were open to any other views on the subject. "None whatsoever," she said. To which he responded, "Then it would be foolish for me to attempt to explain something that you've already rejected outright with no openness to changing your mind regardless of the evidence." And after that response, she clammed up.

Now she was after something other than his views on religious dogma. The way she kept nosing around led him to suspect that she knew about Debbie's plan to leave him and move to Louisville. She screened Debbie's phone calls, and he wouldn't put it past her to have listened in on Henry Dugan's calls.

The door to Debbie's office opened and she exited with Georgette Wingo, one of Ashland's wealthiest citizens, who was also a trustee and generous benefactor of Cooper College. He rose to greet them.

"How good to see you, Barsh. I can't tell you how distraught I am that you've given up teaching our Sunday school class. It's fallen apart in two weeks as we all knew it would once you resigned. But I'll never be able to repay you for all you've taught me. I had given up on the church before Ellen Moore talked you into starting a class for some of us disgruntled women."

"It was my pleasure to be a part of that class for the past nine years."

"Well, you've helped us all. Can you join me for lunch one day next week? I want to invite Catherine, too."

"Any day except Friday."

"Then I'll call Catherine and let her pick a time."

Georgette turned to thank Debbie for her help and left. Barsh followed his wife into her office.

"Thank God, you're back," she whispered and closed the door. "Did you tell Hannah?"

"No."

"Why? I was counting on that."

"I realized that I couldn't leave our daughter for a whole year. She needs me to stay involved in her life. That was a bad plan, and I'm ashamed I ever thought about such a deceptive scheme."

"Then how are we going to deal with this?"

"We have to come clean with Hannah. I think she'll soon be able to handle the separation. During our trip, she asked me why I started sleeping in the guest bedroom. I blamed it on our philosophical differences. I told her that I was the one who had changed over the years and that we now found it difficult to be intimate with each other."

"And how did she respond?"

"She seemed to take it in stride. I assured her that whatever happened to our relationship, we both loved her unconditionally. Don't worry. I'll tell her about the separation in a way that supports you. Let's give her time to process the things I told her about us, and then I'll tell her about the separation. My only request is that you allow me to stay involved in her life."

"Of course, I want you to stay involved in her life. You can visit her at any time and she can stay with you during holidays and summers. I promise you full cooperation on this."

"That's what I needed to hear," he said relieved that Hannah would spend holidays and summers with him. She clearly said *summers,* which confirmed his suspicion that she would not be coming back.

"Okay, I'm feeling better about this approach." she said. "It's a much better plan."

"One more thing." He said. "I'm taking a break from church."

"You just gave up your Sunday school class, and now you're quitting church?"

"I'm not quitting church, just taking a break. I feel hypocritical sitting together in the sanctuary as if nothing was wrong. So I'm planning a lot of Sunday hiking trips to the mountains during the coming months."

"Then I'll leave that between you and God."

***

After dinner, he worked on a presentation he was giving at the faculty meeting the next day. His heart wasn't in it, but he couldn't let that drag him down. Angela Kundera would be there, and he wanted his presentation to be fresh and sharp.

Hannah was in her room working on a new poem she had started that afternoon. Just before her bedtime, she came into the study with the poem. They chatted, and then she read him the poem which addressed the Tallapoosa River, praising it for all the joy and pleasure it had given her father.

"What a beautiful poem, my sweet girl. Do you know what literary critics call this kind of poem?"

"What do you mean?"

"A poem that addresses an inanimate thing like the Tallapoosa River or a person who is absent is called an apostrophe."

"You just gave me an idea. I'm going to write an apostrophe addressed to your horse Thunder about the sorrow you experienced when you had to sell him."

"I hope my sad stories don't turn out to be a burden for you."

"Don't you remember telling me that sad stories have their place in children's literature?"

"Then it must be true," he said with a smile. "Do you know what I kept thinking about on the drive home from Alabama?"

"What?"

"Camping at Soot Cave during Christmas break. This time I want to test my survival skills for two weeks, using only the things I've made with my own hands."

"You mean your bow and arrows and stuff?"

"That's right."

"Knowing you, I bet you can do it."

"You wouldn't object if I were not with you Christmas?"

"Not as long as you are doing something that's important to you."

"Well, I shall make my plans. Thanks for understanding how important this is to me."

***

The house was quiet when Barsh came up the stairs from the

basement after a hard workout. He went to the study to cool down. Working the body to near exhaustion had a way of calming his mind and it was easy to do that when he worked with heavy weights.

He sat at the desk, feeling a bit optimistic about easing Hannah into accepting the separation. Now he had to come up with a new plan for his sabbatical. The obvious thing would be post-doctoral studies at some university.

He had once dreamed of studying the Hebrew scriptures of the Bible with Gerhard von Rad at the University of Heidelberg during his first sabbatical. Barsh's own scholarship had been influenced by von Rad's approach to the Old Testament known as *tradition history*, and the idea of living in Germany for a year had been very appealing at the time. That dream had vanished, however.

His interests now were much broader. In addition to his diverse courses in religion and philosophy, he had introduced several interdisciplinary courses into the humanities curriculum. The question for him was a simple one. What studies would help him expand his expertise in the humanities? The answer was obvious. Contemporary literature. Yes, that's what he would like to study. He would run the idea by Dean Thompson tomorrow to see if she would support such a plan. Feeling better about his situation, he left the study to shower and go to bed.

CHAPTER TWENTY-TWO

Angela stood in his office door, looking a bit wilted from the long, tedious meetings that teachers, especially new faculty members, have to endure in preparation for the new academic year.

"Come in," he said rising to welcome her.

"Could we have tea?"

"You're just in time. The water is hot."

He fixed green tea and they sat facing each other in front of the desk.

"It's been a long day," she said, "but the meetings were helpful. I should get the Cooper system down quickly. I got my course schedule for the semester and I'm pleased with it."

"That's good news. I can tell you, without doubt, the students are going to respond enthusiastically to you and your courses."

"Thanks for your confidence."

"How are you adjusting to your new house?"

"I couldn't be happier. It's such a joy to have a house and yard of my own."

The phone rang and he took the call. It was Dean Thompson.

"That was Catherine. She wants me to stop by her office before I leave campus. She's eager to hear about Hannah's response to our Alabama trip."

"I'd like to hear about that, too."

"She enjoyed the trip immensely. It was a great experience for both of us. Surprisingly, she came home wanting a horse, although she has never even been around a horse."

"Are you buying her one?"

"That's the plan. She's always been fascinated by the stories about my horseback-riding days in Alabama with my little pal Susan Henry. We stopped at the Henry place, which joined our farm, and had a good visit with her mother. I was pleased to learn that Susan is a successful veterinarian. She's married to a doctor and they lives on a horse farm near Nashville where she raises Tennessee Walkers. She has won all the big riding competitions in her field."

"I assume Tennessee Walkers are a breed of horse."

"They're known for their high-stepping gait. I wanted one as a boy, but they were beyond my means."

He retrieved from his desk the photograph of Susan astride her black stallion and showed it to Angela.

"And this woman was once your little riding pal?"

"For almost five years. Before I went off to college, we rode at least once every week."

"I know nothing about horses, have never even touched one, but as a young girl I wanted one more than I can tell you. I guess I was in love with the *idea* of having a horse."

"Maybe that's the case with Hannah. We'll see. She was impressed by all the photos we saw of Susan and her horses. When Mrs. Henry suggested that Susan would love to fix us up with a horse, Hannah was ready to go. I promised I'd call Susan about a possible visit. The idea of owning a couple of Tennessee Walkers is appealing to me now that I own a farm with good pastures."

"Are you looking forward to seeing Susan?"

"Truthfully, I have mixed feeling about it. I haven't seen her since spring of my freshman year at Samford. That was the year my parents sold the farm and moved to Georgia. I got two letters from her before the semester ended. The first one just told me how much she missed me, and I responded to it. The last one was a heart-wrenching love letter. I didn't love her, but I couldn't bring myself to tell her. It hurts me still when I think about the fact that I didn't answer that letter."

"When are you going to visit her?"

"I don't have an invitation and may not get one. I'm working up the courage to call her. Anyway, I wouldn't blame her if she never wanted to see me again."

"Oh, I think she'll want to see you, but I understand your concern. Changing the subject, is our trip to the mountains still on for Sunday?"

"It's on my calendar."

"Great. I've already picked out the music and I've decided what we're having for our picnic lunch. Can you give me a clue about where in the mountains we're going?"

"The top of Mount Mitchell, the highest place in the United States east of the Mississippi River."

"Wow. That's amazing. Will there be a lot of hiking?"

"Just the last few steps. There's a good road up the mountain and also a visitor's center. I'm adding two other attractions that are in the area if you're interested."

"Great. I'll let you surprise me with those."

"I hope the outing will live up to your expectation."

"Have no doubt. I've been beside myself with excitement ever since you left my house Saturday."

"Sorry to rush off, Angela, but I have to give Catherine a report and then head home."

"Off with you, then. I'll clean the tea set."

"Thanks, but I'll swing by and clean up after I see Catherine."

***

Barsh gave Dean Thompson a report on the Alabama trip, including the fact that he had scuttled the plan for a year-long sojourn in the wild and replaced it with plans for a two-week sojourn during the Christmas Holidays, something he felt like he owed himself. It was now or never.

"Catherine, I'm now thinking about studying contemporary literature during my sabbatical. Preferably at a university within a six or seven hour drive of Louisville. I have this strong premonition that Debbie will not move back once she gets to Louisville. If she doesn't come back by the end of the sabbatical, I'll probably have to resign from Cooper unless you could get me an appointment as Professor of Humanities."

"I never dreamed Cooper might lose you. If you'll accept my advice, I urge you to commit to the idea of studying contemporary literature somewhere. Meantime, I'll begin shaking heaven and earth to find a way to get you reappointed as Professor of Humanities. Truthfully, that's what you are now."

"Catherine, I trust you know that I would hate to leave Cooper, but I don't want to put a heavy burden on you either."

"Working to keep you here will not be a burden."

"Okay, I'm committed to studying contemporary literature somewhere, and we'll see what happens."

"One way or another, I'm going to get you an appointment as Cooper's first Professor of Humanities. You'll still be able to teach philosophy and your favorite religion courses, but we'll bring in a Professor of Religion to teach most of those courses. That'll take a lot of pressure off both of us. Now back to Hannah, do you have any new ideas about how to prepare her for the separation?"

"We had good adult conversations that focused on marital issues during our Alabama trip and I'm beginning to think she may adjust better than I first imagined. I now plan to tell her the whole truth. Debbie is on board with the new strategy. Most importantly, she wants me to remain an integral part of Hannah's life. I can see her anytime and she can spend holidays and summers with me. Whenever I break the news about the separation and move, I'll emphasize the fact that I'll stay involved in her life."

"I do believe Hannah will adjust just fine once she knows you'll still be an integral part of her life."

"I'm a bit optimistic for the first time. Be assured that I'll keep you informed."

"Oh, I'm counting on that."

The gravity of the situation weighed upon them both as he stood to leave. Forcing a smile, he kissed her on the forehead and left. He took the Kimberly stairs two at a time and hurried to his office. Angela had cleaned the tea set. He got his briefcase, locked the office, and stopped at her door.

"Thanks for cleaning up."

"Thanks for the tea."

"See you tomorrow."

"Yes, tomorrow. And then we're going to Mount Mitchell on Sunday. I'm so excited about this outing."

"It's a special place," he said and left for home.

CHAPTER TWENTY-THREE

He drove into Angela's backyard early Sunday morning and parked beside her car. As he opened the Audi's door she came bounding down the porch steps with a picnic basket. She was wearing a silky purple blouse with short sleeves, black slacks, and sandals. Her hair was in a ponytail, flying high as a Tennessee Walker's. They exchanged smiles and greetings, and he took the basket.

"I'll be right back," she said.

He put the picnic basket in the trunk, and she was back with a big cloth bag on her shoulder.

"Okay, I'm ready," she said. "I can't wait to have lunch with you on top of Mount Mitchell."

"There's an interesting story about the man for whom the mountain is named. He's actually buried there on the mountain. I'll tell you what happened when we visit his grave."

"I love it when you share the local lore with me. It makes me feel connected."

He opened the door for her and admired the graceful way she eased into the seat. She looked up at him with a winsome smile before he closed the door. Buckled up, he shifted to reverse and was surprised to find her hand on top of his.

"Can I shift the gears with you?" she asked in response to his quizzical look.

"Well . . . yes. Would you like to drive?"

"No, I just want to shift gears with you."

"All you have to do is tell me whenever you'd like to drive."

"I definitely want to try this straight shift but not today."

They drove through Ashland, shifting gears together, and were soon in the country cruising at a decent speed as they wound their way over the rolling hills. They were relaxed, playful, chatty, and mindful of the scenery. Even the moments of silence were sweet.

"Would you like to know the other two places I want to take you?"

"Please, I'm all ears."

"First, there's Linville Caverns inside Humpback Mountain. It's on our way to the Blue Ridge Parkway. We'll stop for a short guided tour if you're interested."

"Sounds like a wonderful experience to me."

"So you're not afraid of caves?"

"The New York subway is as close as I've been to experiencing a cave. As long as I can hang on to you, I'll be just fine."

"It's not far from the caverns to Linville. We'll stop for coffee and a bagel or something and then drive north on the Blue Ridge Parkway for a quick visit to Grandfather Mountain. The last time I took Hannah people were hang gliding from the mountain top. It's quite an experience to watch them launch and glide into the valley below."

"Oh, yes. I'm with you all the way."

"At the top of the mountain there's a swinging bridge that we'll cross and walk to an overlook. Hopefully, we'll get to watch some hang gliding from there."

"I can't wait."

"Leaving Grandfather Mountain, we'll drive south on the Parkway to the exit for Mount Mitchell, which is a part of the Black Mountains of North Carolina. They form a relatively short range of about fifteen miles, but six of the ten highest peaks in the Eastern United States are found there, including the highest."

"Truthfully, I don't know when I've been so excited."

"A day in the mountains is always good medicine for me."

A lone vulture, drifting in from the west, caught his eye, and he leaned forward for a better view through the top of the windshield. Turkey vulture, he thought and righted himself. Angela was looking at him with a quizzical look.

"That's an old habit I've carried with me from boyhood. Whenever I see a vulture, I keep eyeing it until I can identify it as a turkey vulture or a black vulture, our two Carolina species. I know that sounds pointless and probably silly to you."

"I can't deny it's a rather strange habit. Yet somehow it doesn't surprise me that you'd do that. I must confess I have such negative feelings for vultures that I turn away as soon as I see them scavenging road kill."

"The connotations of *vulture* have all turned negative, but I've grown to admire the feathered ones. I think of them as the Jains of the bird kingdom because they never strike a blow at a living thing."

"Jains?"

"Those totally passive people of India who have such reverence for every form of life, plant and animal, that they'll only eat food that was prepared for someone else. The leftovers, if you will. The analogy isn't perfect. It's just that I've learned to give the vultures their place in the scheme of things."

"I can see that you would. I'll try to be more understanding and less repulsed by them. You have a way of changing my perspective on things if you haven't noticed."

"I'd hate to corrupt a good Yankee."

"Like I said before, I'll take my chance with you. Are you ready for some music?"

"Sure. What did you bring?"

"Several things, but I'd like to start with a James Taylor song, "Carolina in My Mind."

"I like the title but I'm not familiar with it."

"I'm a big James Taylor fan. I remembered this song on the way home from the job interview and played it when I got back to the apartment. If you want to know the truth, I played it throughout the summer, singing along *in my mind I'm going to Carolina.*"

"Then play it for me," he said.

"What do you think?" she asked.

"I like the song, and I like James Taylor's voice. But most of all, I'm glad you had Carolina in your mind. Your friendship is good for me."

"If you only knew. Do you like Bob Dylan?"

"Truthfully, I don't know him that well, either."

"He's one of my long-time favorites. Did you know he took his professional name from the Welsh poet, Dylan Thomas?"

"No, and I wouldn't have recognized that name before this summer. The anthology I'm reading has three poems by him."

"What do you think of them?"

"There's something quite moving about them. I felt the emotion as I read them, and yet I was often confused by his strange usage of words. I knew he was using language figuratively, but even so, some of the words made no syntactical sense to me. I couldn't make a figurative connection to anything concrete, just an emotional feeling."

"You're right on target about their emotional impact. His poems evoke a certain mood that you can't miss. That and the music of the lyrics are what I admire most about his work. Critics talk about *sound and sense.* Both have their place, although not equally so in most poems. Dylan Thomas usually gives a bigger nod to sound or music than sense. You don't have to make sense out of every expression to get the essence of his poems."

"Well, that's helpful. I thought I was supposed to make sense out of every word. I'll read his poems again tonight and listen for the music and feel the emotions."

"Now for a little Bob Dylan. This cassette has some of his early recordings."

"I'm ready," he said shifting down a gear for the gravity of the rising highway.

Angela inserted the cassette, and they settled back to let Bob Dylan take over. Barsh listened attentively. He thought the instrumentation was good, but he had a hard time understanding some of the lyrics because of the way he mumbled the words. Angela paused the cassette.

"The next song, *I Want You,* is my favorite. Do you know it?"

"I don't think so."

He had a difficult time catching the lyrics, and those he did understand seemed to have no logical relationship with the refrain, *I want you.* She paused the cassette when the song ended.

"You look puzzled."

"I couldn't make out a lot of the lyrics."

"Some of his words are difficult to catch and some of the lyrics are somewhat disjointed, even corny. But I know them all by heart. You have to understand my state of mind when I first heard this song. I was too tall, too awkward, and my boyfriend had just dumped me for another girl. I desperately needed someone to tell me he wanted me. In my imaginary world, I could make believe that Bob Dylan was singing this song to me. Then I fell for Joe Snyder, who already had a girlfriend, but I could fantasize myself to the heights of delirium by believing he was the one singing *I want you.*"

"I can relate to that. A new girl joined our freshman class in high school and captured my heart immediately. I had just been dumped by my first love who shunned me at every turn until the family moved away that fall. I think the shunning hurt worse than the rejection. Anyway, I fell for the new girl, knowing I didn't have a chance to win her. I was a country boy, and she belonged to the town elite. Still, I loved her for four years without ever asking her for a date."

"Why didn't you ask her for a date if you loved her so? What did you have to lose?"

"My pride, I guess, at least at first. By our junior year, she was interested in me, but by then I had gotten entangled in an adulterous relationship with an older woman. It started innocently enough. Her husband was in Korea, and she was lonely. She was nine years older than me. It was all about companionship at first and then sex. I was never a matter of romantic love for either of us.

"Although I wanted to respond to the overtures of the girl I loved so dearly, there was no way I could as long as I was involved with the married woman. I wanted out of that relationship so I could follow my heart, but because I had willingly entered it, I felt honor bound not to be the one to end it. She was always telling me how desperately she needed me. The woman broke it off immediately when she got word her husband was coming home from the war, but it was too late for me. One of the prominent town boys had won the girl's affection by then. Believe me, I know the depths of unrequited love."

"Well, I never dreamed that Bob Dylan's music would lead us to this moment. If it's okay with you, I'd like to save the rest of the music until later."

"That's fine with me. Angela, you're the first person I've ever told that story, and now I'm regretting it."

"You don't think I'm untrustworthy, do you?"

"No, I consider you very trustworthy. It just seems wrong to talk about something I did with a woman, even if I didn't identify her. Wesley Workman, an old camping friend from my youth, used to spill his guts in graphic detail about the women he'd had. He wanted just one thing from a woman and didn't care what the ramifications might be. More innocent and naive than you can imagine, I was both intrigued and repulsed by his erotic rants. I actually knew some of the girls he talked about. I vowed that I would never spill my guts that way."

"What you told me was quite different from what your friend was doing. You weren't bragging about your sexual exploits. You were explaining a dilemma."

"That's true. Thanks for your understanding."

"I have the highest respect for you and I trust you implicitly. I surprise myself at the things I want to share with you."

"You'll never guess what my monkey mind just latched onto."

"Then tell me."

"Remember our conversation about Caroline Gordon on the way back to Charlotte for your flight home last spring. I didn't know about the woman, but I felt a deep connection with her as you told me about her and how her novels became the subject of your dissertation. That Monday I checked the Cooper library for her books. Finding none, I order four, including *The Women on the Porch*, which I had moved to the top of my reading list because it was your favorite.

"As I read the novel, I felt the same close affinity with the protagonist Catherine Chapman that I had when you were telling me about Caroline

Gordon. You did tell me this novel was somewhat autobiographical, right?"

"Would you like to read my dissertation? It'll give you a better idea of the autobiographical dimensions of *The Women on the Porch*."

"Yeah, I was going to ask if I could."

"I'll bring it to you tomorrow. I'm intrigued that you felt such a strong connection with Chapman so let's take a look at her. After she discovered her husband's infidelity, she fled New York for Swan Quarters, her ancestral home in Tennessee, which was also the home of the women on the porch. I loved Gordon's symbolism of the porch as the portal to the land of the death. It was obvious that the women living at Swan Quarters were idling their lives in relative disjunction from the world as they waited for death."

"I liked the way she did that, too. But I knew Catherine had too much fire in her bones to choose that porch for her final destination. I didn't know, however, if she would leave Swan Quarters for the neighbor, Tom, who wanted her, or for her husband, who came seeking reconciliation."

"Well stated. Which man did you think Catherine would choose? And did she make the right choice in your opinion?"

"I felt like she would go back to her husband, which she did, although I couldn't see that choice working for her in the long run."

"That's interesting because Caroline Gordon made the same choice. She actually divorced Allen Tate, remarried him, and then divorced him for good because of his repeated infidelity."

"Did Gordon ever find her true love?"

"I think Tate was her true love, meaning she truly loved him, but unfortunately for her, he wasn't a true lover. To my knowledge she has never found a true lover."

"That's sad."

"Very sad. But Gordon ends *The Women on the Porch* with the reconciliation of Catherine and Jim so we don't know how she envisioned the ultimate end for them. But you couldn't envision a happy ever after for them. Why?"

"Jim seemed to be remorseful and to regret having lost Catherine, but I didn't see any transformation of his character that would keep him faithful to her."

"Well, that was certainly the case with Gordon's own husband. Do you think Catherine should have chosen Tom, her new lover?"

"I couldn't see that working, either. They matched up well in the department of lovemaking and they both shared a love for the land and horses. But Tom was not an intellectual, and I think Catherine needed an intellectual man who was also a true lover. She seemed a bit daunted at times by her husband and his intellectual friend, but I saw her as a woman with a questing mind. I understand why she'd give Jim another chance. But truthfully, I didn't see a man in the story who was both capable of and willing to meet her needs. So in my opinion, life didn't give her the choice she needed. Unfortunately, I've know a lot of people with Catherine Chapman's dilemma."

"I'll have to agree with your analysis. You're a wise man, Barsh."

"That is highly debatable."

"Not in my mind. I've spent my adult life choosing men that weren't good for me or choosing to live by myself. You just helped me see that the man I needed to choose was never available for me."

They fell silent as the Audi hummed over the rolling hills. He knew that he hadn't been lucky in love, and now Angela had confessed that she had struck out in love. He looked at her and she turned to meet his eyes. Her face lit up with a smile.

"Look, Angela, you can see the Blue Ridge Mountains. Let's enjoy the scenery?"

"Yes, let's enjoy the scenery."

CHAPTER TWENTY-FOUR

He parked near the Visitor's Center on Mount Mitchell. Angela, animated by the drive to the top of the mountain, scrambled out and shouted, "Hello, Mount Mitchell."

"I need a pit stop," he said.

"The same here. See you in a minute."

At the urinal in the Welcome Center, Bob Dylan's *I want you* kept spinning around in his head. Yes, he wanted her. How could he deny it? Control yourself, he murmured in his head and left the restroom.

Angela walked toward him, looking happy, her lipstick and perfume refreshed. She raised her hand for a high five, which he rejoined.

"Let's take the trail to the observation tower. We'll enjoy the view and pay our respect to Elisha Mitchell, who's buried nearby. Then we'll pick out a good place to eat lunch and come back for the things. There are picnic tables here, but I'd rather sit on a blanket somewhere off the trail. Does that suit you?"

"Oh, yes, lunch on a blanket any day."

A few other visitors were going and coming as they made their way up the trail. The view from the tower was spectacular: the Blue Ridge Mountains to the east and range after range of mountains to the west.

"I'm filled with the beauty of this place," she said.

"Being here, even alone, is good for the soul, but far better with a friend."

"Definitely better with a friend. This was an excellent choice for our first outing to the Carolina Mountains. Flying home after the interview, I was so afraid I'd never get to experience these mountains with you. But here we are on Mount Mitchell," she said with a shiver and rubbed her arms with her hands.

"You're chilled, Angela. I have a jacket in the car."

"I'll take the jacket when we go back for the picnic basket. I want to hear about Elisha Mitchell."

"You need a jacket. I'll tell you on the way."

They exited the observation tower and headed for the car.

"Elisha Mitchell was a multi-talented intellectual who taught science at the University of North Carolina at Chapel Hill in the first half of the nineteenth century. One of his many accomplishments was the measurement of the height of this place. Afterwards, he declared this mountaintop to be the highest point east of the Mississippi River. Prior to his measurement of this peak, Mount Washington in New Hampshire held that honor.

"Soon after Mitchell established this place to be the tallest, Thomas Clingman claimed that he had discovered an even higher peak in the Great Smoky Mountains, which is now known as Clingmans Dome. His claim, which had disturbed Mitchell, was later proved to be incorrect.

"To double check his work, Mitchell set out alone for the top of this mountain to re-measure it. Back then there was no road so he hiked in, never to be seen alive again. His son organized a search party of mountain men to look for his father. One of them was an old bear hunter named Big Tom Wilson. He tracked Mitchell from this spot to a forty-foot waterfall, and there was his body floating in the pool below. Some think he was trying to hike down from the mountain at night or in a thunder storm when he fell from the cliff. They buried Mitchell first in Asheville, and later they reburied him here."

"Barsh, I'm so impressed by your knowledge of local history."

"Most people are bored by such stories, but they always interest me. I'm grateful for people who record them. I got my account from Wilma Dykeman's *The French Broad,* which is part of the *Rivers of America Series*. Dykeman covers the whole French Broad Basin which includes the eastern side of Mount Mitchell, which drains into the Swannanoa River, which merges with the French Broad at Asheville. From there the French Broad wanders west to Knoxville where it joins forces with the Holston to form the Tennessee River. That's a lot of river-talk just to say we're on the western side of the Continental Divide."

"You're the first man I've know who truly loves rivers, and I honor you for that."

"Well, it's good to be honored for something. One final note on Dykeman. She was a prolific writer, mostly nonfiction, but she has three novels. I've read her first novel *The Tall Woman* and am quite fond of it."

"I'm not familiar with any of her work. What's the novel about?"

"It's set in the French Broad Basin just after the Civil War. The protagonist is a mountain woman, strong of body, mind, and heart. Someone I could have loved if I had lived in her time. I like the fact that the characters are multidimensional people, not Appalachian stereotypes. That's one of the things I don't like about Dickey's *Deliverance*. Of course, I know he had to create some villains to achieve his objective. So why not drag in a few Appalachian degenerates?"

"You're right. It was a cheap shot at the local people, but like I told you, I was fascinated by the setting and the primal yearnings of the protagonist."

"Here, let me get the jacket for you," he said and unlocked the trunk of the car. "I forgot to tell you that the temperature is much cooler up here."

"Thanks," she said as he held the jacket for her. "This is much better."

"I saw the perfect place for us to eat lunch."

***

Finished with the picnic, they sat cross-legged on the blanket, buoyed by the presence of the other and the beauty of the mountains.

"This is a day to die for," she said. "Halcyon is the only word that does it justice."

"As always, the mountains have renewed my spirit, but you've added good music, delicious food, and interesting conversation. I join you in declaring this day halcyon. And now I think I'll try a little ground therapy."

He stretched out on his back as she sat studying him.

"You look so peaceful lying there."

"In spite of the chilled air, the sun feels warm on my face, and grounding one's self like this is great therapy for the soul. You should try it."

She lay down on her back so near him that he could hear her breathing. He felt whole. The magic, however, was too good to last as he thought about the reality that awaited him back in Ashland. He closed his eyes hoping to retreat from the truth.

"Angela, I like to still my mind, shut it down to a blank page, after relaxing this way awhile. Then after the first image or thought creeps into my consciousness, I try to figure out why that particular thought or image emerged out of all the possibilities. Consciousness is such an astonishment."

"What a novel thing to do. Let's both try it."

After a few minutes of concerted effort to keep his mind blank, the face of a woman emerged in his consciousness. The memory of the Italian woman on Palatine Hill came to him. Why, he asked himself, would that experience pop into his consciousness here on the top of Mount Mitchell? There must be a connection with Angela, he thought. Beyond their dark-featured attractiveness, he could make no connection between them.

He sensed a dimming of the sun's brightness and opened his eyes and saw grey clouds. He sat up to check the horizons. Darker clouds were drifting in from the west.

"Rain clouds are moving in from the west, Angela, but we have a few more minutes before we have to scramble."

"I'll take them," she said and sat up facing him. "In spite of the tranquility of the moment, I couldn't still my mind. I kept having all these pleasant thoughts. What about you?"

"I had a strange experience and don't know what to make of."

"Was it good or bad?"

"I don't know how to categorize it."

"Is it something you can share?"

"The summer before Hannah was born, I spent two months traveling in Europe all by myself. Debbie had no interest in Europe but insisted that I go without her. Late one afternoon in Rome, I was wandering about on Palatine Hill, totally enchanted by the place. Actually, the experience was so mystical that I don't have the words to describe it. I was in the past and the present at the same time.

"As twilight began to settle over the place, I started up a pathway and met a woman coming down. There was something magnetic in our eye contact that turned me around after we passed. And there she stood, a dark-featured woman looking back at me. I expressed my amazement at the ruins of Palatine Hill, and she responded with something in Italian that I didn't understand. Afraid to face the possibilities of the moment, I turned and walked on up the path. End of story.

"Well, guess what? An image of that woman was the first thing that came into my consciousness after I had stilled my mind. I've had that experience at least twice before but not recently. The last time, I was sitting in my study, thinking about various things and suddenly the memory of that woman surfaced."

"Did you regret the lost possibilities of that moment on Palatine Hill?"

"Truthfully, I don't know. I would not have been unfaithful to Debbie. But there was something unnerving about the experience."

"Like you say, consciousness is such an astonishment."

"We're about to get caught in a heavy downpour. Let's pack up and head for the car."

They gathered their things and made it to the car just as the rain moved in.

CHAPTER TWENTY-FIVE

They left Mount Mitchell and drove south on the Blue Ridge Parkway, the rain sweeping across the road from the West.

"I had planned all along to take this route back, and now with the rain this is definitely the best way out of the mountains. We'll stay on the Parkway until we get to I-26 and take it to Spartanburg. From there we'll head north to Ashland. Before the rain I thought we'd exit at Tunnel Road and drive through Asheville, but now I think we'll save that for another outing."

"How far is it to Ashville?"

"About thirty miles. Would you like to experience a bit of Asheville in spite of the rain? I'm game."

"No, but I would like for you to bring me back. I think of Thomas Wolfe when I think of Asheville. I love his novels."

"Then we'll plan a literary outing later this fall and visit The Old Kentucky Home. It's quite an experience for anyone who likes the big man. The halls and stairs and rooms and crannies of that old boarding house will come alive. You'll think about young Tom taking note of all the people who boarded there. The first time I visited the place the guide read the scene from *Look Homeward, Angel* in which Ben Gantt is dying. We were in the very room where Wolfe's brother Ben died."

"I'd really love to do that, Barsh."

"Then that's what we'll do. We'll also have lunch at Grove Park Inn, which is an amazing place. You won't believe the size of the two fireplaces in the Great Room. An average adult could stand in them without stooping. The logs they burn are at least five feet long. They have several excellent restaurants, but the best for lunch or an early dinner is the Terrace Restaurant. It's like a giant porch, high above the ground, with a panoramic view of the mountains to the west."

"Yes, please take me to lunch at Grove Park Inn. You sure know how to please a woman, my friend."

"We could also visit Connemara, Carl Sandburg's last home at Flat Rock, North Carolina."

"I didn't know Sandburg lived his last days in the South. I assume Flat Rock is near Asheville."

"Not far at all. I'll show you the exit for Flat Rock, which was once known as 'little Charleston of the mountains' because wealthy planters from the Lowcountry had summer homes there early in the nineteenth century. Entire families, along with their house slaves, would spend the summer there escaping the mosquitoes and the oppressive heat of the coast."

"That reminds me of my first visit to Cooper. You told me Old Main was built as a resort hotel catering to Charleston and coastal planters during the summer."

"That's true, and they also built summer homes in Ashland. Flat Rock was more difficult to reach because they had to travel over the Blue Ridge Mountains, but the cooler mountain air was also more desirous. Connemara was built in the 1830's by Christopher Memminger who later became the first Secretary of the Confederate Treasury. He named the place Rock Hill. The next owner changed the name to Connemara to honor his ancestral home in Ireland. Sandburg bought the place in . . . 1945 if I remember correctly."

"How ironic, Barsh, that the biographer of Abraham Lincoln would spend his last days in a house built by a member of the Confederate Cabinet."

"I hadn't thought about that but you're right. The place is now a National Historic Site. I could spend hours just reading the titles of Sandburg's books. I think there are more than ten thousand volumes, carefully arranged in improvised bookshelves for the most part. I once noticed books about the KKK on the same shelf with works by prominent black writers, including Richard Wright and Zora Neale Hurston."

"I'd like to find that shelf," she said. "Was there a copy of Hurston's *Their Eyes Were Watching God*?"

"Yes, and I had to hold it in my hands for a minute before moving on. It was a first edition, which speaks well for Sandburg's reading habits."

"That book was required reading for one of my graduate courses that focused on strong women in novels. I found myself totally engrossed in it. After I got the hang of it, I even enjoyed the Black English everyone spoke. I assume you've read it."

"Yes, and I have nothing but high praise for the novel."

"Before reading the book I had no idea there was an all black town in the South. Eatonville, Florida, was a real place."

"There was also one on Hilton Head named Mitchellville. It was founded during the Civil War after the Union Army captured and occupied the Island. Like Eatonville, which was founded a little later, Mitchellville had its own schools, mayor, and town council."

"Is it still there?"

"No, it gradually disappeared after the Union Army left."

The rain seemed to be falling in sheets as the wind whipped it across the road, the windshield wipers marking the silence that had overtaken them.

"How long will it take us to get back to Ashland?"

"About two hours. You want to talk or listen to music?"

"If you're leaving it to me, I say, let's talk."

"Then talk we will. I even have a subject, your mother. You said things weren't good between you and her. Are you up to talking about that?"

"This is intriguing, coming on the heels of our discussion about Thomas Wolfe and The Old Kentucky Home. Wolfe got it right: *You can't go home again*."

"That may be so, but you can keep in touch with your parents and visit them from time to time. I'm a firm believer in that."

"Even if your mother drives you crazy."

"Yes, as long as you have control of your life. Sometimes you have to be the mature one and cut your parents a little slack. You don't have to like who they are, just understand them and what their needs are. Give them what you can in the way of filial love without emptying yourself for them or letting them control your life. It's the strong ego that can give freely, even go the extra mile without depleting itself."

"You're right, of course, but I'm not there yet. I function best when I'm not around Mother. The problem is primarily a religious one. She's a devout Catholic. When I go home, she always presses me to go to mass with her. Whenever I did attend, I felt so hypocritical. During my last visit, I refused to go to mass and she made the rest of my stay miserable. That was two years ago. Our phone conversations are not much better. As soon as she asks how I am, she wants to know if I've been to mass recently."

"Believe me, I understand the difficulty of the situation," he said.

"But you still think I should go home, right?"

"Only if you can manage it."

"And go to mass with her?"

"Not feeling the way you do."

"So?"

"You know, of course, what underlies her behavior. Fear and love. She believes you'll end up in Purgatory or worse if you don't hold steadfast to your childhood faith. Put yourself in her shoes. She loves you, yet fears for your soul. So forgive her, if you can, for the trouble she causes you."

"But I don't have to go to mass with her?"

"No, the Catholic doctrine of transubstantiation is untenable, like a lot of other church dogmas, both Protestant and Catholic."

"So you couldn't go to mass with your mother if you had grown up Catholic."

"Actually, I could go to mass if I were in your shoes, but I would take my own understanding of the bread and wine. We have an obligation to think for ourselves, regardless of the official doctrines of the church we grew up in. The Catholic Church can ex-communicate you, but it can't burn you at the stake. Fortunately, the Inquisition is over."

"I like the way you think. This could be the solution to my problem with Mother."

A strong wind rocked the Audi as it crested a mountain ridge on the Blue Ridge Parkway.

"Wow. This is a hard wind-driven rain, and it may follow us all the way to Ashland. What about sharing more of your music?"

"I brought a John Denver cassette with 'Rocky Mountain High.' It seemed appropriate for this mountain outing. But from this day forward, I will transpose Mount Mitchell High into the lyrics when I sing along. How's that for a ringing endorsement of this outing?"

"It's pleasing to me."

They drove in the rain, listening to the John Denver cassette. When it got to "Annie's Song," Barsh silently worked out another transposition. Angie for Annie. From him, it was now Angie's Song. He would keep the transposition to himself, however.

She removed the cassette from the player and dropped it in her bag.

"I also brought some classical music. I'm in the mood for Stravinsky's 'The Firebird' if that's okay with you."

"Ah, another good choice. That's one I happen to know."

For the better part of the drive to Ashland, Angela kept them entertained with a wide range of music. In between various cassettes, there was more conversation. They stopped once for coffee and a restroom. He thought about stopping for dinner in Spartanburg but decided against it.

A graceful silence settled over them as he exited I-85 for Ashland. They drove through downtown and were almost back to Angela's house when she broke the silence.

"This has been an extraordinary day in every way. Even the rain seemed to play a role in enhancing the drive back. You certainly know how to pack a lot of good things into an outing. Linville Cavern, my first experience of being inside a cave. And what a thrill it was to watch those hang gliders taking off from Grandfather Mountain, another first for me. But lunch on Mount Mitchell and the conversation there as well as going and coming . . . honestly, I don't have the words to express my true feeling. This was a day like no other for me, and I'll definitely journal about this outing before I go to bed tonight."

"It was an exceptional day for me, too. You know that I have family duties, but whenever we can manage an outing, I want to expose you to the good things around Ashland."

"And you know me. I'll be ready."

He pulled into Angela's backyard and parked beside her car. The sky was still overcast, but the rain had finally stopped.

"You can come in, can't you?"

"I'll take the picnic basket for you, but I can't stay."

He got the basket from the trunk and followed her into the kitchen.

"Could we have a drink before you go?"

"Sorry, but I have to get on home. Hannah will be looking for me to come rolling in any minute now."

"Do you two have something planned?"

"Just our poetry project that I wrote you about. She was a little resentful of the fact that she had to go to church with Debbie while I was free to go to the mountains. I didn't say so, but I let her think I was hiking a long mountain trail today. That's what I usually do when I don't take her. She would've been upset if she had known I was going to Mount Mitchell without her. I encouraged her to work hard on her writing, and I promised her we would have a long session of reading and discussing poetry when I got home."

"Now I feel conflicted that I've infringed on her time with you."

"No, please. Even if I had never known you, I would've gone to the mountains today without Hannah. Of late, I've taken a break from church."

"Can you tell me why?"

"It's a complicated story, and I'd rather not go into it now. I do have a favor to ask you. Could I bring Hannah by your office after she gets out of school on Thursday? I could introduce you and then fiddle in the office for a few minutes while you two talk. If that goes well, I'd like to find a way for you to take a look at a couple of her poems sometime. Maybe you can help me figure out the next step."

"Sure, please bring her by. I'll just ask about her writing and offer to help her with it. If she's interested in my help, I'd like to set up a weekly tutorial for her, perhaps after she gets out of school on Thursdays. That's a good time for me."

"That would be wonderful. Of course, I'll pay you for tutoring her."

"No way. This is something I want to do."

"But it's an infringement on your time and energy and I insist on paying you."

"Please don't mention money to me. We'll call it a tradeoff for fieldtrips like today if you insist on some kind of exchange arrangement."

"Okay, I'll look at it that way."

"Do you mind if I hang on to your jacket. It's been such a comfort; I don't want to pull it off."

"That jacket is one thing I don't need now or ever. Throw it in the truck whenever. A good evening to you," he said and turned to leave.

"And a good evening to you," she said and followed him to the back steps.

"Oh, I almost forgot," he said and turned back. "I plan to work at the farm Wednesday afternoon. I'll bring you back some firewood if you're ready."

"Yes, I'd love that."

"Will you be home around five?"

"I'll be waiting for you. Will you show me how to build a fire?"

"I'll teach you the old fashion way that I learned from my elders. See you tomorrow."

"Yes, tomorrow."

CHAPTER TWENTY-SIX

The new academic year got underway without any significant problems, and the first three weeks rolled by rather quickly. Barsh was lecturing again with his old intellectual vitality, and he admitted to himself that Angela was the force behind the change. Even so, he was still a conflicted man.

Angela got off to an excellent start with students and colleagues who were constantly stopping by her office. She seemed exceptionally happy to be teaching at Cooper. At his maneuvering, Georgette Wingo had included her in a luncheon, and the two of them had hit it off big time as he had hoped they would.

In previous years, Barsh taught his classes in the mornings and spent the afternoons in his office, but now he had cut back significantly on the time he spent on campus. On Mondays, Wednesdays, and Fridays, he typically left the College at noon to work on his earth skills at the farm.

As usual, he drove there that Friday, ate a light lunch, and sat at the kitchen table, thinking about his wilderness sojourn. It occurred to him that he'd need at least a month to achieve his goal of experiencing total dependence on himself and nature. Almost anyone could limp along for two weeks in the wild. But if he could survive a month in the dead of winter, that would prove to his satisfaction that he could survive a year. This new plan would cause him to miss the first two weeks of his sabbatical courses, but that was fine with him. With extra effort, he could catch up.

Finished with lunch, he changed his mind about working on his earth skills. The forest and Pacolet River were calling him. He had promised Angela that he'd be back in his office for tea and discussion at four, but he could make it to the river and back in time to meet her if he hurried. He got his backpack and set out across the pasture for the woods, walking at a fast pace.

There was a hint of fall in the air, and he was happy to be in the forest. On reaching his favorite spot on the river, he climbed on top of the granite ledge and sat watching the currents drift by. Soon the rippling river was calling him to be a boy again. He stripped and dove from the ledge into the river, something he'd done twice back in the summer after testing the depth of the water. He swam up and down the river a few times and climbed back onto the ledge. He didn't have a towel so he dried off with his undershirt and dressed. Checking the time on his watch, he realized he'd likely be late for tea with Angela and so he left in a hurry.

***

Angela's Volvo was the only car left in the Kimberly parking lot when he got back to Cooper. He hurried to her office, twenty minutes late. At the top of the stairs he heard the Dean talking with Angela. Catherine, who was sitting within his view, heard his boots clanking on the wooden floor and turned to face him.

"Speaking of the devil, we were just talking about you, wishing you could join us for dinner. I'm taking Angela out this evening. Any possibility you could join us?"

"Actually, I think I can. Debbie's working late on a special account she manages, and I promised Hannah we'd eat out tonight."

"Then you must join us," Catherine said.

"Okay, but dinner is on me. Where are we going?"

"I had planned to take Angela to the Ashland Hotel which, as you know, has the best restaurant in town. But I'm open to suggestions. Where would you like to go?"

"How about Antoine's in Spartanburg?"

"Oh, that's much better. Is that all right with you, Angela?"

"I'm happy just to be going anywhere with friends on a Friday night."

"Then that's settled," he said. "I'll drive. Is six too early for you ladies?"

"That's fine with me," Angela said.

"Me too," Catherine said. "Now if you two will excuse me, I have phone calls to make before I can leave campus."

He walked with her to the stairs. When he turned back, Angela was standing in the door, smiling.

"Sorry I'm late. I hiked to the Pacolet River and didn't manage the time well."

"You've already made up for being late. I'm excited about dinner. What a happy turn of events. Now tell me about the hike to the river."

"There was a hint of fall in the forest, which was invigorating. When I got to the river, the boy who still hangs out in my soul challenged me to strip bone clean and demonstrate my Tarzan stoke for the keen-eyed vultures circling above the river."

"Bone clean?"

"Well, I used to say butt naked. That's the way I often swam in creeks and rivers as a boy. It was a frivolous thing to do, but I enjoyed it. I do apologize for being late, however. I should've managed my time better."

"Just know I'm glad you're here."

"Okay, I'll get the tea started."

She followed him to his office and sat in her usual chair. He got the water heating on the hotplate and sat facing her.

"I hope Hannah won't be disappointed to learn that we're dining together."

"I assure you that she'll be jubilant over this development. She idolizes you and talks about you all the time. You've made a huge impact on her writing since you started working with her. I can't thank you enough. You're just the mentor she needs."

"That warms my heart. Hannah is special, and you two are so lucky to have each other."

The kettle started whistling and he fixed the tea.

"Just in case you didn't notice," she said, "I had a wonderful time at Georgette's luncheon on Wednesday. She's a fascinating woman. And what an art collection. I've never know anyone who owned a Picasso. Thanks for seeing that I was included."

"It was so obvious to me that you two should meet. And as I expected, Georgette was delighted to meet you. She called me Wednesday evening to tell me so. She'll definitely include you in her circle of friends."

"Oh, I almost forgot something," she said and rushed across the hall.

He watched her striding back, fluid as a silk scarf, and they sat facing each other again. Leaning toward him, she held two silver charms in her open hand.

"While you and Hannah were driving to Alabama my first Sunday in Ashland, I said a prayer for your safe return and decided to order these Saint Christopher medals for you. They came in the mail yesterday. Will you please keep one in the Audi and the other in the Ford pickup? They're my way of saying that I need you to be safe when you're traveling."

"Thank you. From now on I'll travel with Saint Christopher and with an awareness of your concern for my safety."

"Do you know when you and Hannah will be going to Nashville?"

"A week from tomorrow if all goes as planned. I called Susan Monday evening, and we had a long conversation. It's been almost twenty-five years since we last talked. She sounds more sophisticated, but I would have recognized that voice anywhere. She insisted that Hannah and I come as soon as possible, and we settled on next weekend."

"I'll be wishing you a good visit. If your little pal ever comes this way, I'd like to meet her."

"In spite of Susan's apparent enthusiasm about our coming, I'm quite nervous about the trip. Yet it's one I have to make. On a different note, I'm eagerly looking forward to visiting Caesars Head in the morning. I'm taking Hannah there for the annual Hawk Watch. Do you have plans?"

"I have no plans. And the answer is yes if this is an invitation."

"Let's call it the setup for an invitation if you're willing to play along."

"What do I need to do?"

"On our way back to your house from Spartanburg, preferably after we take Catherine home, ask if we have plans for the weekend. I'll tell you that Hannah and I are going to Caesars Head for the annual Hawk Watch, and you can express an interest in doing that sometime. That will give me an opening to invite you to join us."

"Thank you, my dear friend. I've been dying for another outing. Please tell me more. What is a Hawk Watch and where is Caesars Head?"

"Caesars Head is an escarpment on the eastern rim of the Blue Ridge Mountains with a breath-taking view. It's a flyway for hawks this time of the year. They use the thermal drafts of the mountain on their migration to warmer climates for the winter so it's an excellent place to watch them. The Greenville Audubon Society is sponsoring a hawk count there the next two weekends. On a good day, they count hundreds of hawks making the journey south. It's a crude way of trying to keep up with how the hawk populations are doing.

"I usually help with the count, but I wanted to take Hannah this year just to watch them for an hour or so, not all day. And now I'm happy with the prospects of your joining us. Oh, we could also work in a little hiking if you'd like that."

"Great, please pack as much in as you can."

"There are more than fifty miles of trails in Caesars Head State Park. My favorite is the one to Raven Cliff Falls, but I don't think Hannah is ready for this hike yet. I'll save it for another outing with you. I think the Carrick Creek Trail will work out just fine for the three of us. Hannah loves to hike this trail, and I think you will like it, too.

"After we spend a couple of hours on the Trail, we'll drive to Caesars

Head and watch for hawks awhile. Then I'll take you and Hannah to Brevard, North Carolina, and beyond. Who knows, we might make it to Grove Park Inn for an early dinner.

"Wow! What an outing this has shaped up to be. I won't be able to sleep tonight."

"Angela, I have something I've been carrying in my pocket all week trying to decide whether or not to share it with you."

"Out with it. You don't have a choice now that you've mentioned it."

He retrieved an arrowhead from his pocket and leaned toward her with it hidden in his hand.

"You want me to guess what it is?"

"I want to tell you that it's something I made," he said and opened his hand.

"You made this arrowhead?"

"With my own hands."

"Why were you hesitant to share it with me?" she asked taking the arrowhead.

"I was afraid you'd think I was crazy to be making flint arrowheads."

"You've made others?"

"Quite a few. It's part of my project to learn the earth skills of Native Americans. You can have this one as a token of my craziness if you want it."

"If I want it? I'll treasure it. Barsh, you've amazed me once again. This looks like it would be hard to make. How did you learn to do this?"

"I found someone to help. Actually, the lithic technology was all but lost by the beginning of the twentieth century. Here's a story about the last known Native American flint-knapper in California.

"His name was Ishi, and he was thought to be the last of the Yahi tribe. He was still following the Stone Age traditions of his people in California when he was discovered in ... I think it was 1911. An anthropologist from the University of California at Berkeley brought him to the university where he worked as a janitor while teaching them about his culture.

"He made excellent flint arrowheads. When he died a few years after, they said the Stone Age in California came to an end. For most Native Americans, it had ended long before when they started trading for rifles and metal tools. Ishi was a rare relic from the past."

"How interesting. I love your stories."

"I think the story of flint-knapping would have ended with Ishi if it had not been for an archeologist named Don Crabtree. He's credited with reviving this ancient skill. He grew up in Southern Idaho at about the same time Ishi was discovered in California. One of his boyhood interests was looking for arrowheads among the ruined village sites of the Snake River Plain. He later spent time at Berkeley.

"It's my opinion that the anthropologists who had watched Ishi flint-knapping told Crabtree about the technique. Anyway, Crabtree became a proficient flint-knapper and did demonstrations for scholars, students, and museum visitors. He later published a book on the subject. Today, there are quite a few people who make beautiful stone tools, especially arrowheads, as a hobby. I spent a week taking flint-knapping lessons from a park ranger at Ocmulgee National Park."

"You are a different kind of man and I love the different. Thanks again for the arrowhead and the stories about Ishi and Crabtree. Do you know how excited I am about tonight? I have a new dress I'm wearing. You can call me Miss Delighted."

"Then we'd better get moving, Miss Delighted. See you a few minutes after six. I'll get Catherine and then come by for you."

"I'll be ready and waiting with a warm heart."

CHAPTER TWENTY-SEVEN

Barsh and Hannah were up and dressed early Saturday morning, eagerly anticipating their outing with Angela. They prepared breakfast together and ate leisurely. After cleaning up the kitchen, they went to the study to wait until it was time to pick up Angela.

He felt pleased that dinner with Catherine and Angela at Antoine's had gone exceptionally well for Hannah. She had the best time riding in the back seat with Angela. The two of them chatted with ease when the adults were not conversing. His plan to invite Angela to go with them appeared so spontaneous that Hannah had no idea that he had orchestrated it. Then he introduced the idea of adding a hike on Carrick Creek Trail, and Hannah seized the moment to sell Angela on the hike.

"I think we both have time to read a couple of short poems. Did you mark anything to share?"

"I have several new ones. You go first and then I'll pick two from my list.

He read her Henry Reed's "Naming of Parts" and Randall Jarrell's "The Death of the Ball Turret Gunner." She liked both poems and read him "Harlem" and "Dreams Deferred" by Langston Hughes.

"Daddy, I've added Langston Hughes to the list of the poets I want to study."

"Good decision. I'll take your list with me Monday and check to see what we have in the library. What the library doesn't have, I'll order through the college bookstore."

"Daddy, I've been working on a new project that Angela has—"

"Angela? When did you start calling her Angela?"

"Thursday, during my writing session with her. That's what she wants me to call her. You let me call Dean Thompson by her first name so I didn't think you'd object."

"No, that's fine as long as Angela asked you. Tell me about your new project."

"It's called creative non-fiction. She wants me to write short pieces of prose about experiences that have had an emotional impact on me. Things like awe, surprise, compassion, fear, dread, anxiety."

"That does sounds like an interesting project."

"Angela says this type of writing will open up ideas for poems, and I can already see that."

"Well, I'm pleased with your project," he said and looked at his watch. "It's time for us to get on the road. But first, I'll let you in on a little secret. One of the reasons Angela took the position at Cooper was to get a firsthand experience of the South. She's an expert on Southern literature, but she had spent only a few days in the South before moving here. That's why I'm packing a lot into our outing today, to give her a better feel for the culture. Are you with me?"

"Yeah, let's show her a good time."

He chose to drive the Ford pickup so that the three of them could sit together. Angela was sitting on the porch steps with her big cloth bag when he drove up. He got out and opened the door for her. Hannah slid to the middle of the seat and they were off.

"For you information, Angela, we'll be driving south on Highway 11. About ten miles down we'll pass the entrance to Cowpens National Battlefield. You probably don't remember, but I told you about this revolutionary battlefield when you came for the interview."

"Oh, yeah, I remember."

"We don't have time to stop today, but I'll take you later if you're interested."

"I'm definitely interested."

"I want to go, too, Daddy."

"Then we'll make it a threesome."

"Barsh, I know you said it was a significant battle, but I don't remember why."

"It was the second major victory of the Patriots over the British in the South after they invaded Georgia, the first being Kings Mountain. The bottom line is that General Daniel Morgan and his American forces routed Lieutenant Colonel Banastre Tarleton and his British forces there at the Cowpens.

"Before this battle, Tarleton had pursued a savage war against the Patriots in South Carolina. He burned their crops and houses and took no prisoners in battle. The Patriots called him the Butcher. His slaughter of the Patriots after they surrendered at the Battle of the Waxhaus became known as Tarleton's Quarter, which meant no quarter.

"The cocky Tarleton had rushed his men to the Cowpens, with little food and sleep, intent on catching Morgan before he could retreat into North Carolina. Knowing that Tarleton would confidently rush straight into the battle, Morgan devised a brilliant strategy to trap him. The victory was swift, and Tarleton had to flee for his life, along with his men who were not killed or captured on the battlefield.

"This was a great morale and tactical victory for the Patriots because Tarleton's forces were British professionals. If you remember, the British forces at Kings Mountain were American Loyalists, except for their leader, Lieutenant Colonel Patrick Ferguson."

"You seem to admire, or at least respect Ferguson."

"I think respect is the better word to describe my feelings for him. He used his persuasive abilities to gain support for the King, rather than Tarleton's tactics of total war. Oh, here's an idea. Let's take turns talking about different people we admire. I suggest we start with women. Angela, tell us about a woman of national or international fame whom you admire?"

"Okay, give me a moment. So far, I'm thinking only about literary women."

"That's fine. Who was the first woman who came to mind?"

"Emily Dickinson. I definitely admire her."

"And so do I. What specifically do you admire about her?"

"The fact that she stuck with her poetry project with little or no public recognition. Yet, she left us such a splendid collection of poems."

"That's exactly what I admire about Dickinson. But would you trade places with her?"

"I've never thought about that. No, I would not want Dickinson's life for myself, even with the posthumous fame she has received."

"The same here. Although I have tremendous admiration for her, I need more from life than she seems to have gotten."

"Like what?"

"A lot of things but especially a daughter like Hannah who has enriched my life beyond measure."

"Oh, yes, definitely. I'd love to have a daughter like Hannah. But I haven't been as lucky as you. I've made some bad choices in picking men."

"The existentialists are right," he said. "You never know for certain what's inside another person's head, which means there can be no emotional intimacy without trust. And that, of course, makes one vulnerable to disappointments and all kinds of betrayals."

"That's for certain."

"Hannah, do you want to go next?" he asked.

"I don't want to play. I want to listen to you and Angela. This is fun."

"Okay," Angela said, "tell us about a woman of fame whom you admire, but not a poet or novelist."

"Two women come immediately to mind. One is a Southerner, the other a Brit."

"I want to hear about both, but start with the Southerner."

"Coincidently, you share her given name, Angelina Grimké. Do you know about her?"

"Sorry, but I don't."

"I wouldn't either if it weren't for Catherine, whose roots strike deep in historic Charleston. The history books I studied managed to leave the likes of Angelina Grimké out of their story, but she definitely had a national reputation during her day. She was born in antebellum Charleston, the daughter of a wealthy judge and planter who owned several plantations. He was a major slave owner.

"Angelina was deeply disturbed by the slave culture of her native South and eventually moved to Philadelphia, seeking the quiet peace of the Quakers. Later she took to the lecture halls in the North as a forceful abolitionist. Although she's known primarily for her activism against slavery, she was also a strong advocate for women's rights. In fact, she insisted on making women's rights a part of her activism. But guess what?"

"The abolitionists wanted her to focus solely on the abolition of slavery," Angela said.

"You're exactly right."

"My kind of woman. I must learn more about her."

"You should talk with Catherine. She's something of an authority on Grimké and the suffragists."

"Then she probably knows about Matilda Joslyn Gage, one of my favorite suffragists."

"I'm sure she does, but I'll have to plead ignorant about her."

"In one of my courses on women's rights, I had to digest and report on Gage's *Woman, Church and State*, which was published toward the end of the nineteenth century. The book has been out of print for years, but fortunately, the library at Brown has a copy. I'll see if I can find my notes. I can tell you she documented a sad history of how women have been treated by both Church and State through the ages."

"Oh, I'm well aware of that, and it is a horrendous story. Here's an idea. Catherine has me over for Saturday breakfast every three or four weeks, and we always have a lively discussion about something. Would you join us some Saturday morning and share your notes on *Women, Church and State*?"

"I'd love to do that. Just get me an invitation."

"That won't be a problem. Catherine has already said she wants to invite you to join us."

"Daddy, could I come, too?"

"I'm sure Catherine would love to have you."

"Oh, yes, please bring Hannah. Now tell us about the British woman you admire."

"You, no doubt, know about Jane Goodall."

"She studied the chimpanzees in the wilds of Africa for many years. What a courageous and dedicated woman."

There was silence except for the engine noise of the pickup truck pulling the uphill grade of the highway.

"Well, who's going to tell me about her?" Hannah said.

"You're on, Barsh."

"I admire her tenacious determination to discover and record the social life of the chimpanzees under difficult circumstances. I also admire the courage she exhibited in publishing her conclusions, namely that our pre-human ancestors lived social lives similar to the chimpanzees, who are our closest relatives."

"So you accept the theory of evolution with no reservations," Angela said.

"The evidence is overwhelming. You'd have to be ignorant of the facts or have a closed mind not to believe in evolution. In fact, the paleontologists, especially people like Louis Leakey and his second wife Mary, are high on my list of heroes.

"By the way, Leakey played a big role in Jane Goodall's work. He had long envisioned a prolonged study of the chimpanzees in Tanzania, and when Goodall joined his team in Kenya, he talked her into undertaking the study. He also secured the first funds to support the project.

"Angela, I just thought of a Jesuit paleontologist and philosopher that you may know, Pierre Teilhard de Chardin."

"I've heard about him. I think some of his views were censored by the Catholic Church."

"You're correct. He never got permission from the Catholic Church to publish his best philosophical works. His friends advised him to break his vow of obedience and publish them, but he remained faithful to his Jesuit vows. It's my understanding that he took comfort in the fact that his friends planned to publish his manuscripts posthumously. They're now widely read, even in Catholic Universities."

"Then I must read him. What do you recommend?"

"I suggest *The Phenomenon of Man*. Not only does he reconcile his own faith with the facts of evolution, he advances an idea he calls the law of complexification. He believes that matter, by its own fundamental mature, organized itself into more and more complex units until the human mind evolved. Evolution thus moves forward by the law of complexification from the pre-biosphere to the biosphere to the *noos*-sphere, *noos* being the Greek word for mind. As he expresses it, modern man is evolution thinking about evolution."

"And his books are now popular at Catholic Universities?"

"So I've heard. Look, there are the Blue Ridge Mountains."

"Oh, this is so exciting," she said.

"Let's enjoy the scenery while I drive us to Table Rock State Park."

"Good idea," Angela said and pulled Hannah into her arms and hugged her as if she were her own daughter.

***

The hike up the Carrick Creek Trail and back was a huge success. Angela exclaimed over and over how exhilarating it was to be so close to nature. Hannah was excited to be hiking with Angela, and Barsh was delighted to watch his daughter bonding with Angela.

After hiking for about two hours, they were back at the parking lot at the State Park by midday, just as he had planned. They claimed one of the picnic tables and ate a light lunch that he had prepared. Then they were off again, headed for Caesars Head.

The place was crowded with hawk watchers, but he found an open spot with a good view. In less than an hour, the three of them had identified four species of hawks and seen a total of eleven. Angela was effusive in her appreciation for being included in the hawk watch.

They left Caesars Head for Brevard, North Carolina, where they stopped for coffee and hot chocolate. Then he decided to take Angela and Hannah to an art gallery up the street. He had been impressed on previous visits by a regional artist who painted mountain streams and waterfalls.

"Angela, look at this painting of Raven Cliff Falls."

"Wow. Are those the falls in Caesars Head State Park you told me about?"

"Yeah, and I like this artist's work."

"Me, too. What else does he have here?"

They checked out several more paintings of falls, and then he spotted a painting of Carrick Creek that they had just hiked.

"Ah, here's a good one," he said. "Anybody recognize the place?"

"Are those the falls at Carrick Creek?" Angela asked.

"The very ones."

"What a beautiful painting," she said and checked the price. "I'd like to buy this someday for my study at home to commemorate my first hike with you two."

"That's a sweet thought," he said. "It's an excellent painting and would be a wonderful addition to your collection."

They left downtown Brevard for the Blue Ridge Parkway, but he was still thinking about the Carrick Creek painting. If he had followed his heart, he would have purchased the painting on the spot and given it to Angela, but that seemed too inappropriate for his sensibilities. Now he had decided to come back by himself at the earliest opportunity and buy it. He would store it away at the farm until he had an appropriate occasion to give it to her.

"I'm taking a short detour through the campus of Brevard College," he said shifting his mind back to the outing. "We just might see a white squirrel."

"A white squirrel?" Angela said.

"Brevard is known for its population of white squirrels, and they're not albino squirrels."

He drove slowly around the campus a couple of times, but they didn't see a white squirrel, so he headed for U.S. 276 which would take them up the mountain to the Blue Ridge Parkway. Shortly after he began the ascent, he stopped to show Angela and Hannah the well-visited Looking Glass Falls, which were more than sixty feet high.

Walking back to the car from the falls, he told them about Looking Glass Rock, a mammoth ball of exposed granite called a pluton. It was visible from the Blue Ridge parkway, and he promised to show it to them. He also told them about the hiking trail to the place. Angela wanted to know if they could hike the trail sometime. He told her it was on his list of things for the three of them to do next summer. They'd have to train for the hike, however, because it was a challenging trail with lots of steep inclines.

Further up U.S. 276, he stopped to show them a popular recreation spot known as Sliding Rock. A few people had pulled into the parking area by the creek, but on a summer weekend, there'd be a crowd sliding down that rock into the large natural pool.

At the top of the mountain, he drove to a good place on the Parkway to view Looking Glass Rock. Angela and Hannah were most impressed and promised to train hard for the challenging hike. They stopped at three other overlooks before taking the exit for Asheville.

He drove through the downtown area and by The Old Kentucky Home. They had an early dinner at Grove Park Inn, capping off their day in the mountains.

"You were so right in describing this place as a must experience," Angela said as they drove away from the hotel. "Have you ever stayed overnight?"

"No, I've only stopped in for lunch and dinner a few times."

"Well, an over-night stay is now on my list," she said. "Truthfully, it's just a dream. But this day is for real, and it's one I'll remember forever."

"Yeah, I had the best time ever," Hannah said.

"It was an excellent outing," he said.

On the drive back to Ashland, Barsh and Angela engaged in wide-ranging discussions. Hannah spoke up occasionally, with a comment or question, but she was listening intently.

"Did you, perchance, bring music?" Hannah asked.

"I do have music," Angela said. "I brought a range of things, hoping I'd have something you might enjoy. What kind of music do you like?"

"I don't listen to music that much. Play something you like."

"Okay, I'll start with some folk songs that I like."

Angela kept them entertained with a varied selection of music until Barsh parked in her backyard next to the Volvo.

"I can't thank you two enough for inviting me to join you today. The whole day was so exceptional I'll have to journal the varied experiences tonight."

"It was a pleasure to have you along," he said.

"Yeah, it was much more fun having you with us," Hannah said.

"Oh, I hate to see this day end. You can come in for a while, right?"

"We'd enjoy that, but we do have to go. I'll see you to the door."

He stood beside her at the kitchen door as she unlocked it.

"Just so you'll know, I plan to spend as much time as possible working at the farm next week."

"I understand. Is it next weekend that you're visiting Susan in Nashville?"

"That's the plan unless something comes up. Have a good evening," he said and turned to go.

"And a good evening to you, my friend."

Driving away, he looked back, and she was waving from the steps. God, she was special. He smiled at Hannah and gave her a thumbs up.

"This was a fun day, Daddy. I've decided I want to be like Angela with I grow up."

"That's easy to imagine. She's an excellent mentor for you."

He was pleased that the day had gone so well. He thought, what joy to watch Angela and Hannah display such affection for each other. Hopefully, the bond they were forging would hold after Debbie took Hannah to Louisville. She'd need all the affirmation she could get.

CHAPTER TWENTY-EIGHT

Early the next Saturday Barsh pulled out of the driveway, determined to make the trip to Nashville a positive experience for Hannah. She was in high spirits and well stocked with poetry books and writing pads.

"Daddy, are you getting excited about seeing Susan after all these years?"

"I'm glad we're on our way to see her because I need to tell her, face to face, how pleased I am with all her achievements. But truthfully, I'm a little anxious. The last time I saw her was the day of the big move.

"It was early spring of my freshman year and I'd driven home in my old pickup to help with the move. Dad had already sold my horse and all the livestock. He had also sold my Harley. Of course we had no choice but to sell all those things, but it was still a sad time for me when Mother wrote to tell me.

"For some reason I had a hankering to drive our Farmall one more time. I remember looking for it when I turned into our yard late that Friday. It was gone, too. At fifteen, I learned how to plow with the tractor all by myself. Dad grew up on a farm, plowing mules, and to my knowledge, he never so much as cranked it up. Anyway, the happiest days of my youth were woven into the fabric of that farm, but that phase of my life slammed shut that weekend.

"Early Saturday morning, Susan came and stayed to the end. Soon after the moving van left my parents drove away, leaving Susan and me alone. It was time for me to go, and I'd dreaded that moment beyond words.

"Dan, her palomino horse, was in the lot beside the barn. She had removed the saddle, knowing she'd be with us most of the day, and I asked her to let me saddle him for her. That was the last time I saddled a horse. Now I'm wondering if I remember how to tie off the leather straps. There's a certain way you have to do it or the saddle will work loose.

"I led Dan out of the lot, Susan closed the gate, and there we stood facing each other, not knowing how to say goodbye. Tears began trickling down her face and then she started sobbing her heart out. I dropped the reins and held her in my arms for the first and last time. I told her that our riding days were over, but I'd never forget them. I'll never forget the image of her as we cantered our horses side by side. I assured her that if she kept up her studies and love of horses, she'd make a good life for herself.

"That was it. I drove off with her standing there alone, holding the reins of her palomino. If I could have cried, I would have cried all the way back to Birmingham. Not for myself, but for her."

"You two seemed so right for each other."

"At first, she was like a little sister. Later as she began to develop into a woman, I was attracted to her. My heart, however, belonged to April Morehouse."

"You haven't told me about her. I didn't know you had a sweetheart in high school."

"Only in my dreams. She did come to see me at the farm a couple of time one summer, but we never had a single date. Yet, I loved her above every other girl. I dreamed about her every day for almost five years. Otherwise, I might have fallen for Susan as we grew older. Anyway, I'm a one-woman man when it comes to romance.

"By the time my parents sold the farm and moved, I knew I wanted to be a college professor. With that goal, I realized I'd have to wing it alone if I expected to complete the long course of formal education I'd need in order to live my dream.

"If I remember correctly, I began to give up on April on the way back to Birmingham that day. I immersed myself in academics. Do you remember what I told you about romantic love?"

"Yeah, I remember. It's something we have to manage or it will manage us. What if Susan is still in love with you? Have you thought about that?"

"I can't imagine that being true. Not after twenty-five years. I trust she's passionately in love with her husband."

"You could be in for a big surprise. You could even have some buried feeling for April Morehouse."

"No, I was crazy about her at the time, but looking back, I'm glad things didn't work out for us. Hannah, my dear, do you plan to read or write?"

"I plan to read. Angela says my writing should grow out of my own experiences as a young girl, the way I feel and interact with everything. Reading other poets will help me explore the things I experience for insights and meaning."

"Sounds like a good plan to me."

"She's the best, Daddy. I can't believe I'm so lucky. I have you to help me think and Angela to help me write."

"But I'm luckier than you because I have this amazing daughter named Hannah."

"Don't be silly, Daddy. Guess who else feels lucky?"

"Sorry, but I don't have a clue."

"Angela. She feels lucky to have you to tutor her. During our writing session Thursday, she told me you've already helped her work through one major problem that was bugging her big time. We talked a lot about our outing last Saturday. She said it was one of the best days of her life."

"Angela is an impressive woman, and I'm delighted to have her for a friend. Now if you'll read, I'll focus on getting us to Susan's. It's a six-hour drive, but we'll break it up with at least two stops."

CHAPTER TWENTY-NINE

They were in horse country, one rolling estate after another. Hannah read aloud the last of Susan's directions. Then Barsh saw the gateway to Halford Farm, turned up the lane, and drove toward the big house.

"This is too rich for my taste," he said.

"I'm with you, Daddy."

He rang the doorbell and took a deep breath. The maid answered and let them in. Susan, dressed in a riding outfit, came running down the hall and threw herself into his arms.

"Oh, my dear Barsh!"

"What a joy to see you, Susan," he said pulling back from her tight embrace to look into her big brown eyes.

"God, I thought you'd never get here. I've been wild to see you ever since you called. I tried several times to tell Terry what our days together in Alabama mean to me, but they're really beyond words. Finally, he said, 'I get it. Please calm down.' But I couldn't as you can see."

"It's been a long time, Susan, far too long."

"And this is Hannah. You are just beautiful, my dear. I love your long black hair. Do you know the last time I saw your father he had a flattop? But I like his ponytail, don't you."

"I like everything about my daddy."

"That doesn't surprise me one bit. I liked everything about him when I was your age. Lord, I can't believe you're here. I'm dying to show you my horses, but they can wait. The spotlight will be on you two this evening. I can't wait to show you off at the Country Club. Barsh, I'm counting on you to dance with me."

"Well, yes, but I'll undoubtedly embarrass you. I've never been much of a dancer."

"There's no way that will ever happen. I know two snobs who will be green with envy when they see me on the dance floor with you. Come on. I want y'all to meet Terry."

The distinguished man rose to greet them as they entered the huge den. A good twenty years older than Susan, Terry Halford looked rather delicate compared to Susan's vigor, but he was confident and self-assured without a hint of arrogance. Barsh liked him immediately for his wit and grace. Terry took orders and left to fix the drinks. The maid brought in a tray of hors d'oeuvres.

Frederick W. Bassett

***

Late Saturday night, Barsh and Susan sat in the den alone for the first time since he and Hannah had arrived. Terry had excused himself and retired for the evening after Hannah went to bed well past her usual bedtime. Susan had just made coffee and insisted that they stay up late.

Barsh thought that without a hint of phony airs, she had added a lot of hard-earned polish to the girl he had known back in Alabama, and she was definitely the queen of Halford Farm. Terry seemed to adore her, and she clearly honored and respected him.

"Barsh, you filled me with joy and pride at the country club tonight. And don't ever tell me again that you're not much of a dancer. Those snobbish lady friends of Terry's ex-wife are still trying to find out who you are and what our connection is."

"It was a delightful evening, and you should know that if we had been dancing back in Ashland, you'd have doubled my status as a man in that little town."

"You're sweet to say that. I can't thank you enough for coming. I hate to think where I might have ended up if you hadn't come into my life all those years ago. I owe you so much for everything I've accomplished."

"Susan, you're giving me way too much credit. You had the right stuff, as they say. I've always believed in you. Do you remember the last thing I told you that day we parted?"

"Those parting words kept me alive during the hard years. I still hold them close to my heart."

"Just know that vision of you riding alongside of me has never faded. I truly regret that it has taken so long for this day to come. I've thought of you so often through the years. You were, and still are, the most beautiful woman I have known. But more importantly, you've always had grit and determination and integrity. I never doubted that you'd do well. I was so pleased when your mother told me that you were a successful veterinarian, trophy-winning horsewoman, and breeder of champion Tennessee Walkers. My little pal has become quite a woman."

"Barsh, we never talked, boy to girl, but I knew we were close. You made me feel special. And, oh God, were you special to me. From the day I met you, I looked up to you. By the time y'all moved away, I was desperately in love with you, and I thought I would die without you.

"Eventually, I came to understand that being your little pal, as you called me, was something to cherish and that you were destined to move on without me. That realization was finally enough for me. I treasure those days even more, knowing that you could have taken advantage of me. I would never have said *no* to you about anything, whatever the consequences might have been."

"Don't think I wasn't tempted. I probably would've made a move on you if you had only been looking for a roll in the hay. But I sensed that you were in love with me, and I knew my conscience would give me hell if I'd tried to take advantage of you. You knew, of course, that I was in love with April Morehouse. I didn't get her out of my system until I was halfway through Samford."

"I probably shouldn't tell you this, but John Marshall did try to have his way with me after you moved. I kicked him in the balls and that was the end of that. You taught me to set the bar high."

"Susan, I was just thinking about how Mother loved you so. I wish she could have seen what you have accomplished. She would have been as proud of you as I am. Now please tell me about yourself."

"Terry and I have been married eleven years. He has two daughters and a son by his first wife. They were divorced when I met him. This is my first marriage. I had just started doctoring his horses when he invited me out for dinner. That went well so we quickly moved toward marriage, which has worked well for us both. I've never wanted children, and that suited Terry just fine because he already had three. We all get along, although his ex-wife seems a bit on the wild side. She had already remarried when I met Terry, and the rumors are that she's running around again."

"Terry seems like a good man. I like him a lot."

"He is so good to me. Barsh, I'm amazed when I look at Hannah. She reminds me so much of your mother, the sweetest and kindest woman I've ever known. I so admired your parents and couldn't believe Mother didn't tell me about their funeral. God, I flew into a rage when she finally told me. I would have been there to honor them and to see you. I trust you know that."

"Honestly, I was afraid you wouldn't want to see me. I felt like I had failed you. I did wonder, however, if you'd be there, and I was disappointed because I needed to see you."

"I finally figured out why Mother didn't tell me about the funeral. She was afraid that if I saw you, it would send me to my knees again. She never could understand me because she was always looking for a good time, not love. You know who my father was, don't you? He's dead now, bless his soul."

"I know what people said."

"Then you know. John Marshall told me that you beat the devil out of Howard Bowen for calling me a bastard. Tell me about that."

"I'd never wronged Howard to my knowledge, but he resented me for some reason. One day he was accusing me of ... I can't say it. Anyway, he ended up referring to you as that little bastard. I demanded that he take it back. Otherwise, I was going to make him wish he had never said it. So that's how it happened."

"Well, it made me feel good when I heard about it. Tell me about your wife. Where did you meet her? What kind of woman is she?"

"During my studies at the seminary in Louisville, I was the student pastor of a country church about fifty miles away, and Debbie's parents were members there. We met one weekend while she was home visiting her parents. The rest is history."

"And you're now a professor at Cooper College. That's impressive."

"A professorship at Cooper is far from an academic prize, but I'm proud to be a part of any institution devoted to higher learning."

"I'll bet your students love you."

"They seem to like me. They're always telling me how much I've helped them."

"I couldn't believe it when Mother told me that Thunder was the only horse you ever owned. Why? I can't imagine you without a horse."

"First, there was college, seminary, and graduate school. After getting a professorship, I wanted a place in the country where I could own horses, but Debbie wouldn't consider it. This past summer I did buy a farm, just for myself, and it's been a wonderful place for me to get away. I'm thinking about buying horses for Hannah and me, but I need to wait until next June."

"Oh, please let me help you with that. I'd love to fix you up with horses if you're interested in Tennessee Walkers."

"I've wanted to own a Tennessee Walker ever since I first saw one. After Mother and Dad moved to Georgia, I lived on campus at Samford during the school year and with Uncle Edward in Birmingham during the summers. That first summer, he took me to the horse country of Tennessee and Kentucky. I don't remember where, but somewhere on that trip, I got to see Midnight Sun, the most amazing saddle horse I'd ever seen. I think he was the Grand Champion at one time."

"He was the World Grand Champion twice, 1945 and 1946. My stallion is out of his line from the Harlinsdale Farm in Franklin, Tennessee. Barsh, I have five colts and six fillies. After I break them in the spring, I'll keep two for myself. You and Hannah can have your pick of the rest. Then I'll put the others on the market."

"I love your horses, Susan, but I'm not sure we should invest in championship type horses. We're just interested in riding them around the farm, not competing in shows."

"Barsh, I want to give you and Hannah each a horse. That's the least I can do after all you've given me. And I don't expect you to get into competition."

"I can't let you give us each a horse, but I'll consider buying two when you put them on the market."

"No, I'm giving them to you. You can't deprive me of this joy. You and Hannah come back in June to pick them out, and I'll bring them down for you. I can haul four in my trailer. Do you know what I'm dying to do?"

"What's that?"

"I'd like to jump in some jeans and go for a ride, just me and you riding through the night, once more, like we did in the good old days."

"You think we could pull that off?"

"Give me two minutes to change, and I'll lead the way."

"Okay, I'll change clothes, too."

***

Wide awake, Barsh lay on his back staring into the darkness from the four-poster mahogany bed that Susan had all but tucked him in. He thought how good it felt to connect with her again on such a wholesome footing of mutual admiration. He had never dreamed that the two of them would get a chance to ride together in the night or to talk alone about how they felt about each other growing up in Alabama.

The day had gone so well for everyone, but he wondered what the future held for him. His thoughts shifted, inevitably, to Hannah. The trip had definitely been good for her. He couldn't wait to tell her that Susan was giving them both a horse next June. That would give Hannah something else in Ashland to connect with. He felt like he'd soon be able to tell her about the separation. Then he'd have to tell Angela everything.

It was late, and he had to get to sleep. Susan was getting him up early so that they could spend time with her horses. Then he and Hannah were leaving after lunch for the long ride home. He tried every method he knew to still his mind until sleep finally took him down.

CHAPTER THIRTY

Angela's car was parked in her usual place beside Kimberly Hall when he got there a little before eight Monday morning. He hurried upstairs with briefcase in hand and stopped at her office door.

"Welcome back," she said. "I've been waiting for the sound of those boots coming down the hall."

"It's good to be back."

"What time did you and Hannah get home last night?"

"It was almost ten. We didn't leave Susan's until late afternoon. Sleep deprived and weary, I went straight to bed so I'm ill prepared for my class next period. But, it won't be the first time I've had to fly by the seat of my pants."

"How did the visit with Susan go?"

"Wonderfully well. I'll give you a full report later. How was your weekend?"

"Friday evening I built my first fire, just like you taught me, and sat on the couch with a glass of wine, reading. I toasted you as if you were sitting in the big chair. Saturday and Sunday, I wrote my heart out on the novel. It is the best writing I've ever done."

"You can't imagine how deeply moved I was by the opening chapters you sent me back in the summer. I'd love to see more whenever you feel like sharing."

"I want to share everything with you, but I prefer to wait until I get deeper into the story."

"That's fine. I'm especially intrigued that the novel is somewhat autobiographical."

"The problem with that is you won't know what's fact and what's fiction. Here's another teaser for you. You'll appear as a major character as the story unfolds? Thinly disguised, I should add."

"That would be hard for me to imagine."

"Anything is possible in fiction."

"If that's the case, I may have to revise my judgment that you're on your way to writing a best seller. How could you base a major character on me?"

"I'll show you before I'm done."

"Well, with that bit of startling news, I'd better see if I can get focused for my class."

"Could we have tea this afternoon? I'm eager to hear about your visit with Susan."

"Sure. How about four o'clock. I've decided not to go to the farm today. I have to catch up on some work, and Catherine wants to talk to me about something."

"Then I'll see you at four," she said and looked at her watch. "I'm off to my eight o'clock class."

***

Just before tea time, Laura Buck came sashaying into Barsh's office and closed the door. Since they last talked, she had filed for divorce and wanted to bring him up to date. There was no residue of love for the surgeon, who had swept her off her feet when she was a young nurse. That was a discarded chapter of her life, and she was moving on in high gear.

It was obvious that she was making a play for him, but he had no interest in any kind of intimacy with her and tried to signal that in a professional way without being rude. Still, she lingered far too long for his comfort before leaving. As soon as she cleared his space, he hurried from the office with kettle in hand and stopped at Angela's office door.

"Sorry that I got delayed by Laura Buck. Do you still have time for tea?"

"It would make me happier if you would stop by the house for a drink. I need to talk to you about something."

"Uh … what time?"

"What about now?"

"Let me go to the hardware store before it closes, and I'll stop on my way back. It shouldn't take more than thirty minute."

He took the kettle back to his office, grabbed his brief case, and left for the hardware store, a bit unsettled. What did she need to talk to him about?

***

Angela opened the back door with a bright smile. She had changed into a soft lavender dress that hugged her body, curve by curve. Sleeveless, the dress had a plunging neck line and hem that fell short of her knees.

"Thanks for coming. What can I fix you?
"What are you drinking?"
"Vodka and tonic."
"I'll have the same."
"As soon as I fix the drinks, I want to show you my office. I've finally got it fixed to my satisfaction."

With drinks in hand, she led him to the study.

"It looks so you. I love it. Please sit at the desk for a moment if you will. I need a visual to store in my memory."

"You want me to pretend I'm working on the novel?"

"Yes, I'd like that," he said and she struck a pose with her fingers on the typewriter.

"Let's move into the living room," she said.

He took the stuffed chair at her gesture. She sat next to him on the couch, her dress riding up her thighs.

"First off, my dear friend, what's the story with that Laura Buck? I've never seen you close your office door before."

"Angie, I didn't close the door. Laura—"

"Do you realize you just called me Angie?

"No, I wasn't aware of that."

"You did and I love it. Please call me Angie. Okay, Laura Buck closed the door. What did she want?"

"Have you met her?"

"No, but you obviously know her well."

"She's taken two of my courses as electives and has stopped by the office on several occasions."

"She's not a traditional student. Who is she?"

"A nurse from Spartanburg who's working on her bachelor's degree. Cooper has an excellent program for nurses like her."

"And what did she need today?"

The question put him on the spot. As a rule, he didn't discuss a student's personal conversation with anyone. Always perceptive, she immediately noticed his reticence.

"I'm sorry," she said. "My curiosity got the better of me. I know you're a true professional."

"That's okay. I can tell you that she's just filed for divorce and wanted to give me an update."

"Looks like she wants to get her claws in you. I saw the way she looked at you as she left."

"That will never happen."

"Are you sure? She looked rather seductive. I've heard that men have a special weakness for red hair."

"You can bet your virtue and your fortune on my word here."

"Okay, but I'll still have to watch her closing your office door, right?"

"Possibly. I'm empathetic with students who share their personal problems. But I keep my distance. I've never gotten romantically or sexually involved with a student."

"Then you're different from most of the professors I've known."

"I won't deny that Laura would be fun, but with my conscience, the buck wouldn't be worth the entanglement. I have a hard time walking away from connections."

"Buck . . . entanglement . . . connections . . . you're giving me new connotations for those words."

"Sorry, I did get a bit carried away."

"Don't be. Now please tell me about your trip."

"It was a remarkable visit. I couldn't have asked for a better outcome. Susan and I had a chance to talk by ourselves about things we had never discussed."

"Does she still love you?"

"No, she's obviously in love with her husband, who's a great guy. Susan and I are both happy to be friends once more, and we don't intend to lose contact again."

"How did Hannah and Susan get along?"

"Just fine. Hannah was taken with Susan and her horses as I had hoped she would be. My plan was to explore the possibility of buying Hannah and me each a horse next June. Now Susan is determined to give each of us a Tennessee Walker."

"Susan is giving you two horses?"

"She wouldn't even let me discuss money. She has five colts and six fillies that she plans to break next spring. From those she'll pick two for herself, and then Hannah and I get our pick before she sells the others."

"Do you think I could learn to ride a horse?"

"Sure, I'll teach you."

"Are you serious?"

"Well, yes, I'll teach you to ride."

"That would be wonderful. Let me fix you another drink."

"Thanks, but that one settled me down. Today was unusually hectic for me. I noticed you also had a flood of traffic dropping by."

"Dr. Jacobs came by, again, trying to connect with me. But you had warned me about him. You were also right about the students. They do like me, and it's a joy to have them stop by. They're all excited about the school dance that's coming up. What's it like to chaperone dances here? They said they always count on you, and now they've asked me."

"It's not too bad. We have a large faculty table to ourselves and try to make the best of the evening, although it can be vexing for me at times. One of the coeds usually drags me onto the floor at least once when there's a slow number. Thankfully, they keep cutting in on each other so it doesn't get too embarrassing for me. It's a joke they play on me, and everyone knows it. Now it's like a Cooper tradition."

"So the co-eds make a game out of dancing with you. How did that come about?"

"During my first year here, a moon-struck coed from Charleston asked me to dance with her. I was embarrassed but took it in stride. Then it became obvious to me and everyone that she had lost her senses when she came back, asking for a second dance. The laugh was on me, and I knew it. But how do you say *no* to a girl who asks you to dance? One of my all-time favorite students saved me by cutting in on her during the second dance and that started a chain reaction. Now the coeds do it just for fun."

"I can't wait to see the show. Can I join in the fun this year?"

"If you don't mind getting your toes stepped on. Unfortunately, I had a boyhood aversion to dancing so I never advanced beyond the two-step they taught us in junior high."

"You had a boyhood aversion to dancing?"

"For some reason, dancing didn't fit my notion of rugged manhood in my youth so don't expect much from me as a dancer."

"I'll take my chance."

An easy silence settled over them. The evening traffic buzzed by on the street. He looked at his watch.

"Do you have to go so soon?"

"Before long. You said you needed to talk with me about something."

"I'll tell you later. I've lost my courage."

"That's okay. Trust your feelings."

"Thanks. I wish we could do like this every week?"

"I'd like that, too, but it's more than I can manage. If I came again next week, twenty people would know about it before sunup. The gossip would be—"

"I'm sorry. I'm not sensitive enough yet to small-town life. I hope this doesn't mean we can't do any more fieldtrips."

"I promised that I'd help you get a Southern experience, and I intend to keep my word. I even have an idea that will make it easier for me to take you on fieldtrips if you approve."

"That's a relief. Out with it."

"Truthfully, I'm afraid you'll think it unacceptable."

"Either I don't know you or you don't know me. Please tell me."

"Would you be willing to meet me at the farm for our outings? We can leave your car there and be off in the Ford pickup or Audi."

"You should know that's acceptable. I don't care what the neighbors think about me, but I will do anything to protect your image. Just give me directions and a time and I'll be there."

"Could you meet me at the farm Sunday morning? I have a historical outing in mind for you."

"I'll be there, but keep the details a surprise."

"I'll give you directions to the farm tomorrow. Can you manage a full day's outing?"

"Oh, yes, make it a full day."

"Dress for a little hiking. But I also have other things in mind. Thanks for the drink. I do have to go now."

"I know, I know," she said as they stood. "Sorry to be so shaky today, but I need to feel the strength of your arms before you go."

She walked into his arms and they held each other tight until he pulled back.

"Thanks, my dear friend. I needed that more than you can know."

"I'll see you at school tomorrow."

"Yes, tomorrow."

She followed him into the screened porch and stood at the steps. When he started the engine and looked back, she waved and blew him a kiss. Saluting her, he drove home, most unsettled about the way forward. He needed Angela's friendship, something he thought he could manage. In truth, he needed her love, something he knew he could not manage. Even so, he knew he was already in over his head.

CHAPTER THIRTY-ONE

Barsh sat at the kitchen table in the old farmhouse, drinking coffee and worrying that he didn't have a backup plan in case Angela couldn't find the place. There was still time to call before she left her house. He dialed the number for the first time.

"Good morning, Angie—"

"Oh, I hope nothing's wrong."

"No, it just occurred to me that we don't have a backup plan in case you have trouble finding the farm."

"Don't worry. I drove out there yesterday. Your directions are perfect. Can I come now?"

"Sure."

"I'll be right there."

He hung up, relieved that she had already tested his directions. Deciding that he'd show her the house when they returned, he packed a midmorning snack, locked the door, stashed the backpack in the truck, and ambled about in the yard.

Blue jays owned the old white oak, squawking back and forth. They could mimic the sweet cry of a hawk. At the thought of a hawk, he lifted his eyes toward the Pacolet River where he often saw them soaring above the forest. Nothing there but a turkey vulture drifting high on the wind currents. Restless, he moved to the north side of the yard where he spotted a red-tail hawk circling above the pasture.

It pleased him that he knew the swift-winged predator was searching for a field rat scurrying about or a cottontail rabbit that had foolishly bedded down for the day beside a clump of tall grass or even a snake slithering along in the grass. As a boy in Alabama, he had seen them swoop down from the sky and take such prey from open pastures. He watched the hawk until it drifted over the forest.

Back in the front yard, he sat on the porch steps. The blue jays had vacated the white oak. Now *he* was the jittery one. The sound of a car. Angela parked beside his truck, and he hurried to open the door for her.

"Welcome to the farm."

"I love this place," she said and gave him a high five.

"I was afraid it would be too isolated for you."

"No, I love its privacy."

"If you don't mind, I'll wait until we get back to show you the old farmhouse."

"That suits me just fine. Wow, this is a huge tree. What kind is it?"

"A white oak. I'd say it's at least three hundred years old."

"It certainly has character. You're making a tree-hugger out of me."

"This white oak is the sole survivor of the old-growth forest that surrounded the log cabin that Jeremiah Keeble built here in 1792 before he started clearing the land to plant his crops. Those old fields have since been turned into pastures. He left this oak for shade. As you can see, the previous owners made good use of the rest of the land around the house. There are pecan trees on the north side of the yard, and on the south and west sides, there are peach, apple, and pear trees. The pecans will start falling soon. You can have as many as you want. I'll gather them for you or you can do it yourself."

"I want to gather my own. Something I've never done before."

"There are probably some on the ground already. Would you like to check and see? We could take some to leave along the forest trail we'll be hiking. The squirrels will love them."

"Good idea."

He stopped before they got to the pecan trees, having spotted a bird on the ground. He pointed to it, and they watched it foraging in the leaves until it flew away.

"I've never seen a bird like that. Such a beauty. What was it?"

"Peterson's field guide calls it a rufous-sided towhee. Others call it an eastern towhee. They like to feed on the ground."

"I saw a brown-backed bird running around in the backyard last week. It had a white breast with brown spots. I tried to find it in Peterson's but couldn't."

"Did it have a long or short tail?"

"I think it was kind of long."

"It was probably a brown thrasher," he said, and led her to the first pecan tree. "Good, they're already falling."

They picked up enough pecans to fill their hiking vest pockets and walked to the backside of the house.

"Barsh, I truly love this place."

"I wish you could've seen the blooming shrubs around the house this summer. I'm especially fond of the hollyhocks and the hydrangeas. They bloom all summer, as do the crape myrtles at the edge of the front yard."

"I've been dying to get out here ever since you wrote me about it. Which way is the Pacolet River?"

"South," he said pointing that way. "As soon as the temperature drops about ten degrees, I'll take you to my favorite place on that river."

"And I'll be jumping to go. What's first on the agenda today? You did say you were planning a full day, right?"

"Yes, and I'm afraid you'll be drooping by the time we get back. The first stop is Musgrove Mill Revolutionary War Battle Site less than an hour's drive from here. Wilfred Roberts, from whom I am directly descended, rode with Colonel Elijah Clark's Georgia Militia during the Revolutionary War. The British shot his horse from under him at the Battle of Musgrove Mill. Fortunately, he wasn't injured.

"The story was handed down to me by Uncle Edward. He heard it from Paw-Paw Roberts. When I was a boy, Musgrove Mill was just a mythical place somewhere in South Carolina. I never dreamed I would someday walk that battle ground.

"Wilfred Roberts was Paw-Paw's grandfather. Before the Revolutionary War, he was an indentured servant to a man near Augusta, Georgia. I like to think it was the lure of the vast wilderness beyond the settlements of Georgia that enticed him to sell his services for several years in order to secure passage from England. We don't know the number of years he had to serve because they varied from contract to contract. After the Revolutionary War, he traveled west from Augusta deep into Creek Indian Territory, eventually taking a Creek wife and settling down at the foot of Talladega Mountain in what is now Alabama."

"What an interesting family you have. How did you find Musgrove Mill?"

"As I told you, Aubrey Morrison is an expert on the Revolutionary War. I told him the story my first year at Cooper, and the next week he took me to Musgrove Mill. I've been back several times. To my delight, Hannah came with me the last time I was there.

"Angie, there's nothing extraordinary about the Musgrove Mill Battle Site. It's special to me because Wilfred Roberts was a part of the battle."

"That's reason enough. I promise you I'll enjoy visiting the place."

"On the trail to the battle site, we'll pass Horseshoe Falls on Cedar Shoals Creek. Hannah and I ate a picnic lunch on the exposed bedrock above the falls. I thought you and I would have a midmorning snack there after we explored the battle site."

"Good plan. Did you pack us some dried fruit and roasted nuts?"

"That I did. As a rule, I'm very predictable."

"Then I assume you have a canteen of water. But today I want to drink straight from the canteen, no paper cups."

"As the woman wishes. Let's get on the road.

***

He stopped at the gate to lock it, and they were on the way. Their conversation was spirited and wide-ranging as he drove through the countryside.

He parked at the trail head, and they hiked through the forest to the battle site on the north side of the Enoree River. Angela seemed genuinely interested in his narration as they walked about the grounds. On the way back, they stopped at Horseshoe Falls, and she was delighted with the place. They bantered playfully as they sat on the flat bedrock above the falls, eating dried figs, roasted pecans and drinking water from his canteen.

As they stood to leave, she wanted to turn the pool below the falls into a wishing well. He fished a coin from his pocket and gave it to her. She insisted that he make a wish, too, so he played along. What could he wish for? He could not see a happy ending to their friendship. Even so, he silently wished for an enduring friendship with Angela that would include Hannah. They each tossed their coins into the pool and hiked back up the trail to the parking area.

"That was fun," she said as they drove away."

"The place is not as enchanting as the mountains, but I enjoyed sharing it with you."

"If you only knew the joy I felt at Horseshoe Falls. I don't suppose you could share your wish with me. I'm obviously curious."

"I thought a wish had to remain a secret in order to come true."

"Then I will hold mine within my heart forever."

"And so will I. Angie, I'd like to show you the British Star Fort at Ninety Six while we're down this way."

"Now that's an interesting designation for a place."

"The little town of Ninety Six was originally a trading post. Some say it got its name because it was located ninety-six miles from Keowee, the nearest Cherokee town. During the Revolutionary War, the British built a fort there in the shape of a star and thus its name.

"General Nathanael Greene and his Continental Army lay siege to the fort in 1781. They had completed the parallel trenches and were digging a tunnel to blow a hole in the wall when they got word that British reinforcements were on the way from Charleston. Knowing that he didn't have time to complete the tunnel, General Greene ordered a frontal assault on the fort. The assault was a bloody failure, and Green ordered a retreat before the British reinforcements could arrive. Ironically, the British almost immediately abandoned the fort. The grounds and what's left of the fort is now a National Historical Site. Are you with me?"

"All the way. And I hope there's more on the agenda after Star Fort."

"There's more. Something quite different, I might add. The Greenville County Museum of Art with lunch somewhere in between."

"I repeat myself. You really know how to plan an outing."

"I think you'll enjoy the museum. In my opinion, it's exceptionally good for a place no larger than Greenville. It has a fine Southern Collection, a major Andrew Wyeth Collection, and a strong Contemporary Collection. Among works by other nationally known contemporary artists, the museum has paintings by Jasper Johns who, as far as I know, is the only South Carolina artist with paintings in New York's Museum of Modern Art. I've seen his paintings of the American flag there. You may have seen them, too. I'm sure you've visited many time."

"I don't remember that name, but yes, I've visited MoMA many times. My friends and I would take the commuter train from Peekskill early Saturday morning and spend most of the day there. I was fascinated early on by the expressionist and surrealists, and now you're making a naturalist of me."

"Well, you can still love the expressionist and surrealists. Believe it or not, I appreciate them. I've only visited MoMA once. A return visit is on my bucket list."

"Then I'm adding that to my dream list of place I want to take you."

"Well, I'm fond of dreaming myself."

"Can you share one with me?"

"I dream of taking you to Charleston, but given the driving time involved, we wouldn't be able to do much in one day. And I can't manage an overnight outing."

"I understand. Just know it pleases me that you'd like to take me to Charleston."

"Would you consider going with Catherine some weekend? She'd love to show you her old city, and you must visit the place."

"Catherine would love to show me Charleston?"

"When I told her I'd promised to introduce you to the Carolina Mountains, she said that she would love to introduce you to Charleston. And believe me, she's the one to do it. Her sister still lives in the family house where the old aristocrats lived. Catherine would love to take you some weekend. You'd be staying with her sister in their wonderful antebellum house. It's what they call a row house with an enclosed garden. Hannah and I once drove up for Hilton Head Island for lunch when we were vacationing there during spring break."

"Then please tell her I'd like an invitation."

"Will do. I can assure you it will be a good experience for you. Okay, we'll be at the Star Fort in about forty minutes. What about a little music."

"I have just the music for my exuberant mood."

***

They both enjoyed the trails and battlefield of the British Star Fort at Ninety Six. Angela found it especially enchanting to walk with him down the old sunken roadbed that was once the Cherokee Path. It came down from the lower Cherokee town of Keowee to Ninety Six and ultimately made its way to Charleston.

At the site of the old stockade near the Star Fort, he told her about General Henry "Light-Horse Harry" Lee, his favorite hero of the Revolutionary War. How Lee and his forces, known as Lee's Legion, captured the stockade while General Green's forces attacked the Star Fort. How Lee had later written his memoirs of the Revolutionary War in debtor's prison after his post-war land speculations failed. How his famous son Robert E. Lee had edited the memoirs.

Finally, they explored an authentic two-story log house and left. It was well past noon.

"We'll be in Greenwood in about fifteen minutes," he said. "I suggest we eat lunch there. We're more than an hour from Greenville."

"Lunch in Greenwood is fine with me."

"Have you gotten to know Jackie Love yet?"

"Yes, and she's a trip. I find her delightful."

"She told me last week that she'll have a painting on exhibit at the Greenwood Arts Center during the month of December. It's a state-wide juried competition, and she's excited about making the show. One of her former students is a member of the Greenwood Artist Guild, and she raves about the talent of the local artists and the status of this annual exhibit.

"Jackie has invited me to the reception and awards ceremony, which will be held the first Friday in December. She also asked if I would bring Catherine. I'm very fond of Jacky and her art. I usually attend her exhibits with Catherine. If you're interested, you can join us."

"Well, yes, I would like to go."

"I was in Greenwood with Catherine about four years ago, but I don't know anything about the restaurants. You'll have to help me look for a suitable place to eat as we drive through."

"Why were you and Catherine down this way, if I may ask?"

"For the inauguration of Larry Jackson as the new president of Lander University. She was the official representative from Cooper College and participated in the academic procession. I was there to meet Benjamin Mays, who was receiving an honorary doctorate. Catherine predicts good things for Lander under Dr. Jackson's leadership. She also claims that Dr. Mays is the most significant man to come out of Greenwood County. I can't speak to that, but I can say that I hold him in highest esteem for his leadership in higher education for blacks.

"Sorry, but I don't recognize the name."

"I learned about him from Catherine who knows most of the prominent people with ties to South Carolina. She recommended Mays' autobiography, *Born to Rebel*, and I found his story most interesting.

"Both of his parents were born in slavery. It's hard for me to believe that the parents of someone living today were born in slavery."

"That is definitely chilling."

"Well, Mays was born on a tenant farm in Greenwood County just before the turn of the century. When he was four years old, a mob of armed white men on horseback rode into their yard and humiliated his father. They cursed him and made him bow down to them, repeatedly. That mob scene was Mays' earliest memory."

"What an awful first memory. Why did they do that to his father?"

"He had no idea at the time, but later learned that those men were one of several white mobs roaming the county after an incident knows at the Phoenix Riot. In those days, blacks outnumbered whites three to one in the county, and the whites were trying to disenfranchise them with new restrictions on who could vote.

"A Mr. Tolbert, a wealthy landowner and Republican in the community of Phoenix, had controlled the Negro vote since Reconstruction and intended to keep them voting Republican. During an election, there was an altercation between Tolbert and a Mr. Ethridge, a well respected Democrat. Someone from the crowd shot and killed Ethridge. A little later, several white men were fired upon from the woods as they were walking down a dirt road.

"The next day, mobs of armed white men on horseback were riding over that part of Greenwood County, searching for any black man who was at the murder scene. They rounded up eleven men, took them to a nearby church for a kind of hearing, and determined that four of them were present when Ethridge was killed. The other seven were told they could run, although one was shot in the back as he did. The four black men were taken to the edge of the churchyard and killed. Before things settled down, several other black people were killed."

"What a horrendous story," Angela said.

"Yeah, and I find it all the more astonishing that Benjamin Mays escaped from a predestined life of poverty and humiliation in such a place. There was something within him that drove him to find a better life. Fortunately, the culture down here has changed dramatically since Benjamin Mays' childhood. Catherine claims that Greenwood is now one of the most progressive towns in South Carolina, and I take her word for that.

"I do know that Greenwood boasts the Nation's first independent genetic center. The fact that the founders, who are not South Carolinians, chose to locate the facility in Greenwood speaks well for the town. Catherine and I were recently invited to sit in on a presentation they made to the Wingo Foundation for a major grant. I was most impressed.

"Okay, we're coming into Greenwood. Help me look for a place to eat lunch."

"I've got my eyes wide open."

CHAPTER THIRTY-TWO

"Barsh, I've been reveling in our experience at the Greenville County Museum of Art. I especially enjoyed the Wyeth exhibit."

"I never tire of seeing his work. I only wish 'Soaring' was a part of the collection. It's an aerial view of three turkey vultures soaring high above a farmhouse and an outbuilding. You're looking down on the vultures that are looking down on the farm. I bought a large print of it at the gift shop back in the spring and had it framed."

"Ah, vultures. I haven't even seen the print, but I can understand why you'd like it."

"When I bought the print, I didn't have a place for it. But guess where it's hanging now?"

"The farmhouse, of course. So I'll get to see it, right?"

"That you will. Angela, the house is a patchwork of additions that have been built onto a log cabin, which now serves as the den. I've made several improvements, starting with a new tin roof. The only structural change I made was to the bathroom. I had the old one torn out and a larger one built. The floors are all made of pine boards, which I had sanded and finished with a clear sealer. Then I replaced all the kitchen appliances and had a central heating and cooling system installed. Even with the improvements, it's still an old farmhouse."

"If you're worried about me, I assure you I'll love the house."

"It's like I enter a different time zone when I come out here, and I'm not talking about measuring the time of day in different parts of the world. One of the happiest days of my life was when we moved back to the country the summer I turned fifteen. Twenty-nine years later, I have my own place in the country, and I'm delighted with it."

From the front porch, they entered the big room, which served as kitchen, dining, and living area. She exclaimed about its country charm and examined some of the old furnishings. Next he showed her the view from the screened porch off the west side of the big room.

"I love this double swing," she said. "Come, let's swing together."

As they sat side by side, swinging gently, a bird landed at one of the feeders beside the porch.

"What bird is that?"

"A purple finch."

"I do so enjoy watching the birds in my backyard, but I haven't seen that one yet. I want to become a good birder like you. That was such fun trying to identify the hawks at Caesars Head."

"Hannah and I enjoyed that, too. She's pushing me to plan the Cowpens Battlefield outing.

"You should know by now that all you have to do is mention the word go and I'm ready."

"Here's a proposal. After visiting Cowpens Battlefield, we could work in the literary outing I promised you."

"Connemara, the Wolfe House, and lunch at Grove Park Inn?" she said.

"That was my promise."

"Yes, yes, yes," she said and he led her back through the big room to the den.

"Angie, we're standing in the middle of what used to be Jeremiah Keeble's one-room log cabin. Look how the logs have weathered to this pewter shade of gray. I just have to touch them occasionally. The stories they could tell if they could talk. And look at this old fireplace. The original mortar between these fieldstones was clay, not the concrete you see. You can also tell that the hearth was raised when they added the wooden floor. The original floor was dirt."

"I dearly love this room, Barsh."

"Let me show you the Wyeth's print."

"Wow. Now I understand why it is so special to you. That's quite an artistic conceit, and Wyeth executed it perfectly."

"The original is on the list of paintings I'd like to see. According to the information on the back of the print, it's in the Shelburne Museum in Shelburne, Vermont."

"I'd like to be with you when you check it off the list."

"I'd like that, too, but I can't imagine it happening."

"But a woman can dream, right?"

"Dreams are good as long as we control our expectations."

"That's a good point. Did some of this furniture come with the farm?"

"This is my old stereo. The couch is new. The rest of the stuff came with the house."

"What kind of records do you have?"

"Just a hodgepodge of this and that. No serious collection of anything. Well, I guess I do have a decent collection of bluegrass and early Mississippi blues records. Uncle Edward gave me most of them. I never had much time for music, but I did enjoy some of these old records during lunch when I was working here this summer."

"Can I see the bedrooms?"

"Sure. There are only two," he said and led the way.

"Hannah has claimed this room, although she hasn't spent the night here. We call it the blue bedroom. I left all the old furniture. Of course, I replaced the mattress."

"Wouldn't it be interesting to know the people who have slept in this room?"

"Or maybe died in this bed. Forgive me. That's too somber. Or made love in it."

"That's better," she said.

He opened the door to the green bedroom and motioned for her to enter.

"This room had an iron bedstead that I knew Debbie wouldn't like so I put it in the tool shed and built a box frame for a queen-size mattress set just to keep things simple. Everything else is the same. I'm fond of this antique armoire, and this cedar chest is full of hand-sewn quilts. Some of them are quite handsome. I've no Idea why the heirs didn't take them. I feel certain their mother sewed some of these quilts."

"I'm intrigued by the composite nature of this farmhouse, and I know what it means to you."

"Let's get something to drink," he said and led her back to the kitchen area. "I have bourbon, gin, wine, and sodas. I can also make coffee."

"What are you having?"

"Gin and tonic."

"I'll take that, too."

She went to the bathroom while he fixed the drinks. Then they settled in the den, she on the couch and he in the old rocker angled toward her.

"How can I tell you what you mean to me?" she said. "I was thinking last night about how miserable I'd be if I had taken the position at Bennington. I'd be right back in the same old rut in spite of all my good intentions to take a different path. You're so different from the men I have known."

"Can I take that as a compliment?"

"I would walk through fire for a man like you."

"If I were a free man, I'd walk through fire for a woman like you."

"Do you want to be a free man?"

"I can't go there, Angie."

"I'm sorry."

"It's okay. I trust you know that I treasure your friendship."

"I do know that, but you probably don't know that your friendship is better than any love I've ever known."

"That makes me sad."

"Let's forget the sad and focus on the happy because I am a happy person these days."

"Okay, Happy Person, I have something good in mind for us. How would you feel about hiking the Chattooga River Trail two weeks from today?" That would mean back to back outings on Saturday and Sunday. Is that too much for your schedule?"

"I'm free and ever so eager for both."

"Then Hannah and I will pick you up at your house for our Cowpens and literary outing. But I'd like for you to meet me here for our Chattooga River trip."

"Just let me know what time."

"I'm thinking eight o'clock for both outings."

"I love the way you take care of all the details. Barsh, do you remember promising to tell me the story of how you got from a boy who loved the wilds of Alabama to the most distinguished professor at Cooper College. Would you please share your story with me?"

"I'm not sure I know all the forces behind that transformation, but some of them were traumatic. The year I turned fifteen, several disturbing things happened that caused me to raise some challenging existential questions, even though I had never heard the word existential. I think the most troubling was the death of my neighbor and friend, Becky Wade. She was only thirteen when she was killed by lightning. A lesson in the tenuous nature of life and what, I would learn later, a Spanish philosopher called *the tragic sense of life*.

"To make matters worse for me, Becky was killed in the tepee that I had built in the meadow below our house. I had outgrown the tepee as a plaything, but I'd go there at night just to think about things. Unfortunately, Becky had fallen for me, which was troubling enough because I wasn't in *love* with her. Knowing my habit of spending a lot of time in the tepee at night, she would slip off occasionally, hoping to fine me in there. If she did, we'd talk about things until I made her go home. I warned her that it was dangerous for her to be there by herself, but she wouldn't listen to me.

"One night during a thunderstorm, she was there by herself when lightning struck the tepee and killed her. As soon as I knew what had happened, I realized that I had played a role in her death. If it had not been for me and my tepee, she wouldn't have died that night. Consequently, I experienced unrelenting guilt."

"Barsh, your penchant for philosophy and theology was already manifesting itself when you were only fifteen?"

"I'd say so. I had a lot of deep questions and no answers. I also wanted to get out of that neighborhood for good. Dad knew it. He bought his grandfather's old farm and moved us back to the country in late August of that year. It was the best thing that happened to me growing up. That's what some philosophers call the coincidence of opposites.

"Of course, you know that by the time I was seventeen, I was sexually involved with a married woman, an experience that shattered what was left of my innocence. The guilt I experienced was not over what I had done with the woman. It was what I had done to her husband. He was my neighbor and friend, and I had betrayed his trust and violated my own sense of honor."

"I remember you said she was lonely. Because her husband had volunteered to fight in Korea, I think that makes him responsible for her loneliness. Maybe you did him a good deed by keeping her out of a relationship with someone who would not have been as caring as you."

"She said I had saved her, but that didn't relieve me of the guilt."

"Barsh, would you share with me your ideas about sex?"

"Personal or general philosophy?"

"Your personal ideas."

"My first experiences would fall under the concept of pleasure fairly exchanged for pleasure with no other expectation. But oddly enough, I have evolved into a hopeless romantic. Sex is intrinsically tied to my need for intimacy with the woman of my heart. The desire or lack of desire for children is a totally separate issue. Thus my heart is my guide for sex."

"Then whoever holds your heart is one lucky woman."

"That statement is highly debatable."

"I'd like to take that debate up sometime, but that's another day. Please take me back to your youth in Alabama, and I'll try not to sidetrack you."

"Are you sure you want to hear this?"

"I need the rest of the story."

"The summer after the affair ended, Dad got me a job with a logging company. The workers were all black men, except the truck driver, Echols, and me. Within a month, I watched a black man, named Knox, slam a double-bladed ax into Echols' chest, killing him instantly. Knox actually killed him in self-defense. Echols had shot him three times with an automatic .22 rifle before Knox threw the ax."

"What a horror. I can't picture you working with such violent men.

Were you ever in personal danger?"

"I got along well with all the men, and I desperately wanted to defuse the situation with Echols and Knox as the tensions kept building day by day. I didn't have a clue, however, about how to head off the impending fight that I knew would be deadly. Wanting to save them both, I was unable to save either, and that left me reeling."

"Of course, it would leave you reeling. What happened between them that led to such violence?"

"Here's the back story. Echols had previously worked for my father, and I had known him since I was fifteen. Aside from his womanizing and racism, there was a kind of primitive honor about the man. He was as good as his word, and he actually got along just fine with all the black men in our logging crew except Knox. That was because they never challenged him with their blackness. He was even kind and generous to them and often went out of his way to help them.

"Knox was an angry black man in his late twenties. He had been stationed in France at the end of World War II and, according to him, the French women were happy he was there. He loved to talk to me about the French women. After experiencing France, he had a difficult time accepting the place that had been assigned to him in the segregated South. I understood his anger, but I could see he was headed for trouble with Echols.

"About mid-morning that day, Echols drove back into the woods for another load of logs, and we all stopped what we were doing to load the truck. We were a small crew. It took us all to roll the logs onto the truck using skid poles. The two antagonists were sparring verbally when Knox began bragging about his success with the French women. That was more than Echols could take. He told Knox that he'd kill him if he ever saw him so much as looking at a white woman. Knox came back saying he'd do it to Echols' wife if he got a chance.

"Without another word, Echols went for the rifle he kept behind the seat of the truck. With gun in hand, he walked within ten feet of Knox, who had picked up a double-bladed ax. Echols raised the rifle and started shooting. In response, Knox threw the ax into his chest, severing the main artery from his heart. I knew he was dead but I checked his pulse anyway. I then drove Knox to the hospital and the doctor was able to save him.

"In spite of my explanation of what had happened, Knox was charged with first-degree murder, convicted, and executed. I was a witness for the defense, but the jury refused to believe my testimony. The prosecutor badgered the black men who were on the scene into admitting that Knox had first threatened Echols with the ax. It was a horrible miscarriage of justice."

"I can't believe you had to endure such a horrible experience. You of all people, who are so caring and compassionate."

"I have to admit I had a hard time dealing with it. The racial violence, bigotry, and legal injustice that I experienced firsthand that summer had shattered my trust in people and our social system. I started thinking seriously about going to Alaska and living in the wild.

"In late August of that year when footfall practice started, one of our star players came strutting out of the shower, bragging about how he had gotten this girl's cherry on their first date, calling out her name for everyone to hear. He said she clawed him like a wild cat, but he had his way with her. He was a prominent town boy, she a shy country girl, a rising junior in our school.

"I was stunned by his arrogant gloating over such a dastardly violation of the girl. The other boys were laughing and teasing with him, but I took it upon myself to take him down. I called him a stupid rapist and told him that I hoped her father would castrate him, that I certainly would if I were her father. I embarrassed him and proved him a coward because he didn't attack me for calling him a stupid rapist. But he never admitted his error.

"I told the coach what had happened and that I was quitting the team. How could I play on a team with a rapist? The coach eventually talked me out of quitting, saying that it probably didn't even happen, that the boy was likely bragging, and that I would be letting the rest of the team down. I stuck it out, but during practice, I plowed through that boy with every ounce of energy I could muster every time I got a chance. Finally, he chickened out and quit the team.

"Until my senior year, I had counted on going to college on a football scholarship, something the coach had assured me I could do. But I was through with football. So Dad and I worked out a plan for me to go to Auburn University and major in civil engineering, something that would keep me working outdoors. But my heart wasn't in it.

"I limped through my senior year, confused and bewildered, not knowing what I wanted to do with my life. Then that summer, I had a profound religious awakening. I don't know how to explain it, but one night I experienced the mystical presence of God and felt a clear sense of calling. From that experience, I realized that I could be a voice for justice and righteousness and a servant to broken humanity.

"The next morning, I shared the experience with my parents and later with our minister. With their guidance and support, I enrolled at Samford University that fall to study religion, and thus began the formal part of my spiritual and intellectual journey."

"What a powerful story, Barsh."

"This is the first time I've ever tried to explain the story behind my sense of calling. I now know a lot more about the cultural dynamics of the human psyche and could explain the experience in totally secular terms. Even so, I've accepted the calling as my authentic mission in life. Soon after I entered college, I realized that I could best fulfill my mission as a professor of religious studies, not a parish minister."

"Well, that development turned out to my advantage. Otherwise, I'd have never known you. Our paths would never have converged if you had become a parish minister."

"That's statistically true, although one never knows what the future holds. At the time of our birth, the odds that we would ever meet were staggering. But here we are sharing this day. One is lucky to stumble into such a friendship."

"You are absolutely right."

"Angie, this has been a good day, but it's time for me to head home."

"Truthfully, I need to get home, too. I have a ton of work to do before classes tomorrow. But what a day. What a day."

CHAPTER THIRTY-THREE

The next week rolled by with no major challenges for Barsh. He spent as little time on campus as possible. He told Catherine about Angela's interest in spending some time with her in Charleston, and she took her that weekend.

The following Saturday, he took Hannah and Angela on a day-long outing, which could not have gone better. The three of them had a joyous time together.

It was Sunday morning, time for him to take Angela hiking along the Chattooga River Trail. He had promised her such an outing the first day they met, never dreaming that he would fall so deeply in love with her. He had felt a strong affinity with her immediately, but he had no intention of letting her get so close to him.

He drove to the farm, checked out the house, locked it, and waited for Angela in the front yard. The weather was perfect for their long anticipated hike. The last time on that trail he was all by himself with no thought of what it would feel like to have a special woman with him.

He sat beneath the huge white oak in a homemade chair someone had fashioned from hickory limbs. A mockingbird held forth with a joyful song from the top of a crape myrtle. How poorer the world would be without birds and their songs, he thought. He mused about the studies of Charles Hartshorne. How amazing that a renowned process philosopher like Hartshorne would devote years of his life to the study of bird song.

The rumble of a car caught his ear, and there was Angela easing up the lane in her Volvo. He stood to greet her, his heart beating faster. She parked beside his truck and came running to him.

"Catch me," she yelled and jumped, locking her arms and legs around him.

"Wow. There must be something extraordinary in this country air today."

"I love the privacy this place affords us," she said still clinging to him.

"I do like your zestful spirit."

"That's good to hear. I'm so excited about hiking today that I thought I might get away with such a stunt. I saw someone do it once and have wanted to do it ever since. Hope that tells you how special you are to me."

"You did take me by surprise. Be assured that I'll not forget the experience. And please know how much I appreciate the special attention you gave Hannah yesterday. You're so good for her. She quotes you every time we have a poetry discussion."

"Yesterday with you two was extraordinary. This is going to be another wonderful day. I can feel it in my bones. I've dreamed about this day since I flew home from Charlotte after the interview. Did your ears burn on the drive from the airport? I relived every moment of my time with you."

"No, but my heart soared higher than an osprey."

"You're kidding me, aren't you?"

"Actually, I was a bit depressed. You were the most interesting woman I had ever met, and I left the airport thinking it unlikely that I'd ever see you again."

"But here I am, headed into the wild with you."

"I hope the outing lives up to your expectation."

"Have no doubt. I'm going to enjoy this day."

She got her big cloth bag from the Volvo, and they left in his Ford pickup.

"Barsh, you promised to tell me about William Bartram this morning."

"I had planned to hike a section of the Chattooga River Trail that intersects the Bartram Trail. That's what made me think about him, but I've decided to take you to a different section of the Chattooga. I'll tell you about Bartram anyway. He's one of my heroes.

"He was born in Philadelphia in the early eighteenth century. I don't remember the exact date. A naturalist with a special interest in botany, he's best known for his book *Travels,* which recounts his journeys into the wilderness areas of the South over a period of four years. His primary interest was in studying the flora, but his accounts of the various Indian tribes he visited are the most interesting parts of the book to me. In general, he had a high opinion of the indigenous people he met, including the Cherokee.

"We'll be traveling through sections of South Carolina that were once the tribal lands of the Cherokee. Somewhere along the trail today, I thought you might like to join me in a silent homage to them. They were overwhelmed by the advancing whites, who first pushed them out of South Carolina, and finally removed most of them to Oklahoma. The Trail of Tears.

"There were a few who managed to stay in the mountains of North Carolina. They're now known as the Eastern Band of the Cherokee. I'd like to take you to their reservation sometime."

"Yes, please take me. And yes, I would like to pay homage to them somewhere along the trail today. You're getting to know me quite well."

"Then I trust you brought music to share with me."

"You're right on the money, again."

"Then enlighten and entertain me while I get us to our trail. The last two miles are over a narrow gravel road, but I've never had any trouble making it. You may hear the underbody of the truck hit the gravel occasionally, but have no fear."

"I have no doubt you will get us there and back safely."

***

From the small parking lot at the end of Nicholson Ford Road, they took the Foothills Trail west and were totally enveloped by a mixed forest of evergreens and hardwoods after hiking only a few hundred yards. They stopped and silently surveyed their surroundings.

"What is this tall tree?" she asked and stretched out her hand to touch its trunk.

"That's a white pine and there are lots of them in this forest. Look how the top of its roots are exposed on the trail. Best to look out for them or they'll trip you up. But it pleases me that they've left the trail as natural as possible."

He caught a glimpse of a bird out of the corner of his eye and turned to watch it sail into a deciduous tree below the trail on the last wave of its bouncy flight. He pointed to the bird and gave Angela his field glasses. She watched it work its way up the tree trunk and fly away.

"Was that a woodpecker?" she said.

"You got it. That one was a male yellow-bellied sapsucker. See those holes in the bark. They drill those so the sap will seep out."

"So that's how they got their name."

She gave him a big smile, and they were off again. Soon they could hear Licklog Creek rushing down the hollow below them. About a half mile down the trail, they crossed the creek on a narrow wooden bridge and followed it until they came to the intersection of the Chattooga River Trail.

"We're turning left on the trail which will take us down the river. The next time, we'll take the right. The Foothills Trail merges with the Chattooga Trail, going up river, and then brakes off on its own, following the Blue Ridge escarpment all the way to Table Rock State Park about eight miles from here."

"Eight miles? Have you hiked the whole trail?"

"No, but there are access points along the way, and I've traveled several sections of the trail."

"I never imagined how much fun this would be before I met you. You know what these hikes mean to me now, don't you?"

"Your joy is obvious. It's essential for me to get back into the wild for a good walk periodically, and now your presence makes them all the more enjoyable."

She gave him a high five, and they were off on the Chattooga River Trail, which quickly dropped down to Licklog Creek just below a waterfall. They crossed back to the other side on another wooden bridge and followed the trail to Licklog Falls, which dropped down in two tiers some eight feet.

"This is so enchanting," she said.

"It gets even better. The trail takes a sharp left just ahead of us, and we'll be looking down through the trees on the Chattooga River far below us."

"Then lead the way," she said and they were off again eager to get to the river.

"There it is," he said.

"What a beautiful sight. You were right about *far below us,* and this bank is almost straight down. It looks impossible to access the river from here?"

"We might be able to make it, but it wouldn't be worth the effort. Further down the trail, we can get to the river's edge with less effort. When we do, I suggest that you baptize yourself as a communicant with this wild place by pouring a handful of river water over your head. I did it the first time I hiked this trail."

"Then I shall do the same."

They continued down the trail until he found a place where they could sit by the river. He helped her down the bank onto a flat rock. They sat there, silently watching the currents dance down the riverbed.

"Would you perform the water ritual for me?" she said.

He dripped a cupped handful of river water on the top of her head.

"Peace to the river and peace to you," he said. "You are now one of us."

"Yes, I definitely feel the connection."

"Angie, at Licklog Falls, I thought about Whitewater Falls, which are the highest falls east of the Mississippi River, more than four-hundred feet. They are within easy driving distance. Would you like to go by there when we leave here?

"Most certainly."

"There's a good observational deck not far from the parking lot. From there, we could also hike down into the gorge if you'd like. Or we could save the gorge for another outing. You can make that decision when we get there."

"Sounds great."

"Okay, we'll have a late lunch in Walhalla and head that way. I know a place that serves good pulled-pork barbecue. Or we can look for something else if you're not in the mood for barbecue."

"Barbecue suits me just fine."

"From Whitewater Falls we could drive to Brevard. You said you'd like to go back sometime. We'll be taking a different route, but it's a good scenic drive. We could then ascend the mountain to the Blue Ridge Parkway and take it back to I-26 and leave the mountain for home that way. I'll let you decide."

"You know the answer. I want to stretch this day out as long as possible. Could we have coffee in Brevard and look for white squirrels again?"

"Of course. Are you ready to extend our hike down the Chattooga River Trail?"

"Ready."

They climbed back up the river bank and turned down the trail, stopping from time to time to enjoy some specific feature of the landscape. Angela followed his preference of hiking with little conversation in order to be totally alert to the sights, sounds, and smells of the wild. After about another mile, he began looking for a suitable place away from the trail to take a break.

"Angie, that bluff ahead looks like a good place for us to eat our snack. If we take the angle from here, I think we can make it up there."

"Lead the way. I'll be right behind you."

They made the climb and sat, side by side, on a thick bed of leaves at the edge of the bluff. They silently ate dried cranberries and roasted almonds and took turns drinking water from his canteen.

A Carolina chickadee settled in the top a bush below them. Angela whispered its name and he nodded with an approving smile. She gave him a high five and the bird flew away.

"I hope your thoughts are good ones," he said after they finished their snack.

"I was thinking about Mother. I plan to call her tonight and tell her how happy I am here at Cooper. I wish I could tell her about you, but there's no way she could understand the nature of our friendship. I don't have a good track record with men, and she'd immediately think, Oh, there you go again."

Barsh reflected on that comment for a moment. He wanted to know what she would like to tell her mother about him but would never ask.

"Well," he said, "you know how I feel about keeping in touch with your parents. It pleases me to hear you plan to call your mother tonight."

"I'll say hello to Daddy before I hang up. He's always understood me better than mother, although we were never very close. He was too obsessed with his career. I'm so impressed with your devotion to Hannah. She's so lucky to have you for a father."

"Sometimes I doubt the wisdom of my parenting."

"Please, no doubts. You are the perfect father."

"Back to your parents. The Dean and I will make sure they get a royal reception if you want to invite them for a visit. We'll make a special effort to show them how pleased we are to have you on the faculty."

"I hadn't thought about that, but yes, I might invite them next summer."

"Please know that I'll be available to help you show them the area if you need me."

"I'll definitely need your help. Would you consider bringing Daddy and me back here? He's an insurance executive, and the golf course is as close to nature as he has ever been."

"It'll be my pleasure."

His thoughts leaped to the coming year when Debbie and Hannah would be in Louisville and he'd be on sabbatical somewhere. Had he just mislead Angela about entertaining her parent next summer? No, he'd be back in Ashland for the summer no matter where he decided to study. Still, he dreaded telling her about the sabbatical.

"I'm positive Daddy will be most impressed with you. I wish you knew how at peace I am with myself this moment. Just sitting here with you amid the awe-inspiring beauty of this place is deeply satisfying."

"So the Chattooga River Trail has lived up to your expectations?"

"In every way."

"Can you imagine what this whole region must have been like when the Cherokee lived here in an almost perfect balance with nature before the whites came? The abundant wildlife has long since been decimated. Much of the forest has been cleared. Most of the rivers have been dammed. The Chattooga is the exception. At least, we can be grateful to Congress for designating it a Wild and Scenic River before it was too late."

"It's truly a national treasure."

"Let's make our silent homage to the Cherokee before we head back up the trail for the truck."

"I'm ready. Then we're off to other good things. What a special day."

***

They left Whitewater Falls for Brevard, North Carolina, both delighted that he had thought about adding the falls to the outing.

"Well, I hope the hike down into the gorge and back didn't leave you totally exhausted," he said.

"I made it fine. I've never felt so energized. I've been walking the college track four or five time a week, usually with a student or two. I'm now up to three miles without stopping."

"You're a good trouper. No more hiking today. But other good stuff. I just thought of something that might interest you if you are around next summer."

"I assure you I'll be around."

"The Brevard Music Center presents dozens of concerts every summer, and they are excellent. Much of the orchestra is made up of talented high school and college students who come from all over to study at the Center and perform in the concerts. They perform with regional professionals and guest artists under the direction of nationally know conductors."

"The auditorium seats about fifteen-hundred. It has a roof but no sides. It's not quite like being outdoors, but I love its openness. You can even buy a ticket to sit in your own chair on the lawn."

"Yes, I'm most definitely interested. How often have you attended?"

"I've gone to one or more concerts for the past eight summers. Hannah has gone with me the last two times. We take a picnic supper and eat on the grounds down by a lake. Perhaps you could join us next summer."

"I'm counting on it."

"Three years ago, they had a guest cellist who had me enthralled with her performance. She walked on the stage to much applause and embraced the cello as if it were her beloved. Then she attacked the cello with the kind of passion I once longed for a girl to shower on me. The conductor, the orchestra be damned. She was the show and one of the best I've ever seen."

"How interesting. You did say *the kind of passion I once longed for*, right?"

"Those were my words."

"You're telling me you sat through that performance without a single passionate yearning."

"Uh … my statement told only half the story. In my youth I had longed for this one girl to love me with such passion. It never happened. That night at Brevard, I felt only the yearning. I didn't have a specific woman in mind."

"I understand what you're saying. I, too, have known such yearning." There was a heavy silence between them.

"Barsh, I sometimes wonder what would have happened if we had met earlier in our lives. Do you think we would have connected?"

"Truthfully, I don't think you'd have found me interesting," he said.

"That's what I was thinking about myself. I don't think you'd have taken an interest in me if we had met earlier."

"Oh, I would've been fascinated with you, but I'm also rather certain that I'd have been wary of you, the big city woman."

"Now you're teaching me how to be a naturalist. I'm loving every minute of it. Oh, I have a good piece of music for this moment. Are you ready?"

He gave her a thumbs up and a big smile.

***

Barsh exited the Blue Ridge Parkway and followed the signs to I-26 where he took the eastbound ramp for Ashland by way of Spartanburg. The whole outing had gone so well. They even saw a white squirrel in Brevard. Angela bought matching coffee mugs for them from a local potter. He thought about stopping in Spartanburg for an early dinner, but decided against it. The line between the friendship he wanted to maintain with her and the love he felt in his heart had already blurred too much for comfort.

"Is something wrong?" she said. "You look worried."

"I was just thinking about Hannah," he said shifting his thoughts quickly. "Sometimes I wish she were more like other girls her age."

"She's definitely exceptional. I know you're anxious to get home to spend time with her. I remember what you said that first day we met, about being a parent. That it was the greatest joy and the most horrific responsibility. I know there are heavy demands on you, and I hope I'm not too much of a burden to you. Just know that I'll take whatever slice of your life you can give me."

"I'm eager to get home because I know Hannah will be waiting for me. But this has been a good day for me. Your friendship is very dear to me."

"If you only knew, my friend."

Traffic on the Interstate was light. They listened to Angela's cassettes and talked from time to time about various subjects as the miles rolled by. When they exited for the farm, she took his hand from the stick-shift and pulled it into her lap until he stopped at the farm gate to unlock it.

He apologized for not inviting her in, using Hannah as an excuse. She raved again about how wonderful the day had been as he walked her to her car.

"See you tomorrow," he said.

"Yes, tomorrow," she said and drove away.

CHAPTER THIRTY-FOUR

Debbie was reading a magazine when he got home. He knew immediately that she was in a bad mood when she tossed it on the coffee table.

"I guess you had a good time in the mountains."

"I enjoyed the mountains very much. How was your day?"

"It couldn't have been more depressing."

"I'm sorry. Would you like to go out for dinner?"

"Not really, but you can take Hannah. She wants to go."

"Daddy," Hanna said rushing into the room, "I'm glad you're home. How were the mountains?"

"The mountains were happy to see me. They made me feel right at home."

"The next time you go, I want you to take me, even if it is Sunday."

"Okay. Debbie said you'd like to eat out. She's not going so I'll let you choose. Where shall we go?"

"What about Jackson's Steak House?"

"Good call, my sweet girl."

They drove to the restaurant with Hannah talking all the way. She had had a good afternoon with her writing. The meal and the conversation at the restaurant were good, but they were both happy to get back home. It was soon Hannah's bedtime, and she turned in without his having to remind her. Debbie was already in her bedroom with the door closed.

He went to the study and began reading Angela's copy of Denise Levertov's *Here and Now*. Although he was weary from the day's activities, he was soon pulled into Levertov's world by her poetry. Again and again, he felt the power of her poems. Finishing the book late that night, he sat thinking about his own aspiration of becoming a poet.

Something stirred his memory of a James Dickey poem, and he retrieved *Buckdancer's Choice* from the bookcase. Before opening it, he saw himself sitting in James Dickey's class at the University of South Carolina, studying contemporary poetry. "Eureka," he whispered.

Finally, he knew where he would spend his sabbatical. He'd enroll as a post-doctoral student in the graduate school at the University of South Carolina and begin a formal study of contemporary poetry and fiction. If he limited his classes to Tuesdays and Thursdays, he could live at the farm and commute to Columbia.

The house was quiet, except for the humming of the refrigerator, and he was thinking about Angela. He no longer dreaded telling her about the sabbatical now that he could keep his promise to befriend her. He'd be even more vulnerable, however, with Debbie and Hannah in Louisville.

Her earlier confession was hot in his mind. *I would walk through fire for a man like you.* Then the looming question was on his tongue. Could he follow his heart and still fulfill his responsibilities to Hannah? He tried to approach it rationally, but here were too many unknowns for his analytical mind. Yet he had raised the question. This, in itself, was a major development, and he realized the question would keep coming back until he found the answer.

It was well past his bedtime, but he dreaded facing the inevitable tossing and turning that the bed would produce. He toyed with the idea of going for a walk in the neighborhood. Then he had a better idea: self-induced exhaustion by running around the athletic track at the college. He left a note on his desk just in case Hannah should wake up and come looking for him.

Driving by Angela's house on the way to Cooper, he noticed that the light was on in her bedroom. Was something wrong? He remembered her saying that she was usually asleep by eleven most nights. He parked beside Kimberly Hall and walked to the athletic field and ran the track until he could run no further.

PART III

CHAPTER THIRTY-FIVE

In the dream, Hannah was calling his name from some dense forest, but when he woke, Debbie was standing in the bedroom door, calling him.

"What's wrong?" he asked and sat up trying to read her face.

"It's seven-thirty. I let you sleep because I knew you left around midnight and were gone a long time. I saw your note to Hannah."

"Sorry. Can you take her to school?"

"She's waiting in the car. Barsh, you must tell her about the separation. It's not going to get any easier."

"Okay, I'm ready. I'll pick her up after school and tell her at the farm."

"Don't forget to emphasize the fact that you can visit her anytime and she gets to stay with you during holidays and summers."

"I'll do my best."

"While you two are at the farm, I'm coming home to talk with Davis. I have a job offer for her as a live-in maid."

"That will be a relief to me if she accepts your proposal. Do you think she will?"

"I don't know. I'm offering her a good salary with a big bonus if she stays one year. Please tell Hannah about my plan. She and Davis have always gotten along so well."

"I'll tell her."

"I'm sending Davis home early, and I'd like to talk with Hannah without you when you bring her home."

"I'll drop her off and go to the office."

"I'll be praying that it goes well," she said and left him sitting on the side of the bed.

After going to the bathroom, he went to the kitchen, poured a cup of coffee, and sat in the study. The dreaded day was upon him, and he didn't feel like being around anyone, not even Angela. Fortunately, he had no meetings or appointments. He'd go to the farm after his eleven o'clock class and hang out there until it was time to pick up Hannah.

***

He eased the truck away from Hannah's school and headed for the farm. His pulse was beating hard and the solemnity of the occasion showed on his face in spite of his effort to hide it.

"What's up, Daddy? You look worried."

"I have to talk to you about a most unsettling matter."

"You don't have some dreaded disease, do you?"

"No, I'm not aware of any health problems."

"Is it about Mother?"

"It's about all three of us. If you don't mind, I'd like to wait until we get to the farm. Davis is at the house so we can't talk there. As serious as this is, I can assure you that we'll all get through it."

"You're scaring me, but I can wait."

"You are one in a million, my sweet girl."

They rode in silence to the farm, Barsh trying to reassure her with a forced smile from time to time. Inside the old farmhouse, he poured two glasses of cranberry juice and led the way to the den.

"You know Debbie was despondent most of last year and still has bouts of depression. You know I've been sleeping in the guest bedroom since spring. You also know Debbie hates living in Ashland. Do you remember what city she likes best of all?"

"You told me Louisville."

"That's right. Last April, her old boss there called and offered her a partnership in his accounting firm."

"Daddy, I think I can see where this is going."

"Okay, tell me."

"She's moving to Louisville."

"Yes, and without me. She wants a separation for a year to see how things work out. I have only one problem with her plan, and it a big one because it involves you. Do you know what it is?"

"She's taking me to Louisville," she said and began crying.

He stood and pulled her up into his arms, letting her cry as he held her tight.

"I want to live with you, Daddy."

"I want you to live with me, too, but that would destroy Debbie's self-image of being a good mother. When people separate or divorce in our culture, the mother usually takes the children. There are cases in which the mother actually wants the children to live with their father, but they are rare exceptions. Sometimes fathers take the matter to court, but judges usually rule in favor of the mother unless she's totally incompetent or morally unfit.

"There's no happy solution to our problem. Debbie wants you to live with her, and I want you to live with me. You can't be in two places at once. But you can be in two places, alternately. Debbie had promised me that I can visit you at any time, and you can spend holidays and summers with me. Believe me, there's no way that I will not be a major part of your life."

"I know that, Daddy. When is she moving?"

"Sometime before January."

"I don't like this one bit, but I can see I don't have a choice."

"You do have a choice, Hannah. You can rebel and make us both miserable or you can make the best of it."

"I'll make the best of it. After all, I'm your daughter. What did you teach me about facing the inevitable?"

"My dear sweet girl, you are the joy of my life. I've dreaded this day since April. I do hope you can understand why I waited as long as possible before telling you the bad news."

"I knew something was troubling you and now I understand."

"All I needed to know is that you can handle the separation. Here's my strategy. I'm going to treat this as if you were away at a boarding school. I'll be counting the days until you come home for holidays and the summer. I'll also look forward to visiting you in Louisville. We'll talk often by phone, and you can read me your poems. We can also correspond."

"I like it."

"I also plan to ask Angela if she'll continue working with you on your writing by correspondence."

"Do you think she will?"

"I'm confident she will. Angela knows nothing about this, however. So please wait until I get a chance to tell her before you bring it up."

"Does anybody else know?"

"Catherine. I had to tell her because I'm taking a sabbatical starting in January."

"A sabbatical?"

"It's like a year-long leave of absence. Professors get to take one every seven years so they can do research or study somewhere."

"What will you do?"

"I'll be commuting to Columbia twice a week to study contemporary poetry and fiction at USC. I think this will be good for me."

"I think so, too."

"I'm glad you approve. Here's something else that I think you'll approve if Debbie can pull it off. She was going home early today to ask Davis to go to Louisville as a live-in maid. That will be a great relief to me if she accepts. Davis would take you to school and pick you up, and she would always be there with you when Debbie is at work."

"I'd like that very much, but I'll be okay either way."

"I'm sorry, Hannah. I wish we could have done better by you. This is not what I wanted, and yet I'm morally bound to support Debbie's decision."

"I know."

"Would you do something for me before we leave?"

"What?"

"I want you to pick out a stall for the horse Susan is giving you. I plan to tear out the old partitions and build new ones, and I have something special in mind for the stable you choose."

"I'm still getting a horse?"

"Most definitely. I'm building a riding arena, and Susan is coming to give you lessons."

"Let's go," she said and they left for the barn.

"Susan's horses are all registered, which means they already have official names. But I intend to give mine an unofficial name; something that I think matches the horse. That'll be the name I call the horse by."

"Then I'll do the same."

***

Hannah had taken the bad news on the chin. It staggered her, but she managed to stay on her feet. She was definitely mature for her age, and Barsh could not have been more proud of his daughter. He left her at home with Debbie, and drove to the college.

Angela's car was still there. They had hardly spoken all day, just one brief exchange on the stairs of Kimberly Hall as he was leaving for his nine o'clock class and she was returning from her first period class. He hurried up the stairs and stopped at her door.

"What a surprise to find you here this late," he said.

"Please have a seat and catch me up on your day. I had given up hope of getting to talk with you."

"There's not much I can report. I spent most of the afternoon at the farm. How was your day?"

"Quite troubling, to tell you the truth, and it started last night. You have no idea what our trip to the mountains yesterday meant to me. I reveled in every aspect of it until I fell asleep. Then I woke up a little after midnight with a strong premonition that something was wrong with you and started shaking uncontrollably. I had a hard time settling down and getting back to sleep. And then when we met on the stairs this morning, you were not your usual self. Please tell me nothing is wrong."

"I did have a bad case of insomnia last night. After Debbie and Hannah went to bed, I worked out as usual and then read until midnight. But even then, I knew it would be foolish to go to bed so I resorted to an old tactics of inducing exhaustion. I ran around the college track until I could run no more. And it worked. As soon as I crawled into bed, I went down into that nether region of deep sleep."

"But something was worrying you, right?"

"I can't deny that I had a troublesome evening that extended into this day."

"Then my vibes were right."

"I don't know about vibes, but I am sorry that you suffered such anxiety."

"You're worth it, my friend. I don't suppose we could talk about your troubles."

"Not now but soon."

"Soon?"

"Yes, soon."

"Oh, I wanted to tell you that I called Mother last night. It was the best conversation we've ever had. I told her that I love everything about being at Cooper and that I had been to mass at the Catholic Church here. Mother was ecstatic."

"Obviously, I'm pleased to hear that."

They sat quietly studying each other.

"Angie, are you ready for our hike to the Pacolet River?"

"When can we go?"

"Can you meet me at the farm Sunday around ten o'clock? I'll grill beef kabobs for lunch and then we'll hike to my favorite place on the river."

"I am eager to make that hike with you. But first we have the dance Saturday night."

"Truthfully, I'm a little anxious about the dance. Sorry to rush off, but I have to see Catherine before she leaves for the day."

"Can you swing by on your way back?"

"I should be back in … twenty minutes."

***

Catherine listened intently as Barsh gave her a detailed report on his trip to the farm to tell Hannah about the separation. The concern etched on her face gradually relaxed as his narrative moved toward a hopeful summation.

"I can't tell you how relieved I am just to know that part is over for you," she said. "Hannah is going to be all right and so are you. Not that it's going to be easy for either of you, but you'll find a way to make the best of this."

"I trust you're right about both of us. Catherine, I now know where I want to study during my sabbatical."

"That's progress. Please tell me."

"I'd like to study contemporary poetry and fiction at the University of South Carolina. Maybe limit my classes to Tuesdays and Thursdays so that I can commute."

"How wonderful. I enthusiastically support your plan."

"Thanks you. Now I have to tell Angela. She's meeting me at the farm Sunday. I don't know how it'll go."

"I don't think the sabbatical will be a problem for her now that you have changed your plan."

That was all the Dean said, although he knew she was worried that he could be facing a whole new set of problems. He thought about putting the matter on the table but decided to wait until after he told Angela about the separation.

"Catherine, I don't have time today, but I need to talk with you soon about when to go public with all of this."

"I've already given it a lot of thought as I'm sure you have. We'll work it out together. Just let me know when you can meet with me."

He embraced her, lovingly. She seemed so fragile in his arms that he was suddenly alarmed. He had burdened her too much with his troubles. He should be relieving her load as Dean, not compounding it.

His stride quickened as he walked toward Kimberly Hall. The place seemed deserted as he took the stairs to Angela's office.

"How was your meeting with Catherine?" she asked.

"It was productive," he said as her exotic perfume found his nostrils. "Angie, I'd like to tell you one of my little secrets."

"Please, out with it."

"I love your perfume. I've wanted to tell you since the day I met you but didn't have the courage."

"How dear of you. I wish you had told me. Now this gives the matter more gravity."

"I have to go, but there's a good chance I'll be back with Hannah to pick up a book. If you're still here, I'll invite you to join us for dinner."

"Now you've got me buzzing with expectation. Hurry back, please."

She rose to give him a high five. This time, they stood their ground for a brief moment, drinking in the other with their eyes. She followed him to the stairwell, but he did not look back.

CHAPTER THIRTY-SIX

Somewhere between Cooper College and Fern Meadows, Angela slipped from his consciousness and the dreadful anticipation of entering his own house settled upon him. What dark mood would he find there? He parked and entered the den. Debbie, already in her pajamas, sat in her chair, eating a sandwich.

"Barsh, come sit with me a minute."

"Where's Hannah?"

"In her room. Believe me, she's going to be all right. I am so relieved. Whatever you told her seems to be working. It would have been horrible without your support. Don't think I'm not aware of that and grateful, too. You are an honorable man."

"What did Davis say? Is she going to Louisville with you?"

"She needs to think about it, but I think she'll accept my offer."

"What can I do to help get her on board?"

"Just tell her how important it is to you. She respects you. I don't feel like cooking or going out. I'm emotionally exhausted."

"That's okay. I'm taking Hannah out for dinner."

He left the den for her room. She was lying on the bed, holding an open book on her stomach. He sat on the side of the bed.

"It's been a bad day for you, my sweet girl. Please know how much I admire the way you're dealing with this. You are far beyond your age in maturity, but that doesn't take away the hurt. You know I'm hurting, too."

She crawled into his arms and began to cry. He held her until the crying ran its course.

"Let's go out for dinner," he said.

"I'm ready as soon as I wash my face."

She left for the bathroom, and he went to the den to wait for her. Too nervous to sit down, he stood by the door to the garage.

"We may go to Spartanburg and could be late getting home."

"That's fine, but thanks for telling me. I'll probably be in bed when you get back."

Hannah joined him in the study and they left in the pickup, glad to be leaving Debbie at home.

"Tell me how it went between you and Debbie. She seems to be satisfied with your response."

"I did what you expected me to do. I listened to her and told her I'd be all right as long as she kept her word about you and me."

"That's one thing you don't have to worry about. She'll keep her word about that. I had a good idea while I was waiting for you. If Davis decides to live with you in Louisville, I can occasionally fly you two down for the weekend. That will be in addition to holidays and my trips up there."

"You can fly us home?"

"I can and I will. You and Davis can fly out of Louisville after school on Friday. I'll pick you up in Charlotte, and you can fly back to Louisville Sunday afternoon. That'll give us two nights and a day and a half together."

"I'd like that a lot, Daddy."

"I'll talk to Davis tomorrow. I think she'll like my idea, too. It could be a dealmaker. I need to go by the office for a book I intend to read tonight."

They rode the short distance to the college without further conversation. In spite of his forced smiles, she remained somber. Given the mood that hung over them, he was pleased with his decision to invite Angela to join them for dinner. If anyone could distract Hannah from the reality of the separation for an hour or so, she could.

"Hannah, that's Angela's car. You want to say hello to her while I get my book?"

"Yeah."

They were standing in the middle of Angela's office waiting for him with big smiles.

"Well, Barsh, do I need to say how surprised I was to see Hannah standing in my office door just now? She says you came by for a book."

"What keeps you here so late?"

"Too tired to get up and go home. It's been a rough day."

"Sorry about that. Hannah and I are going out for dinner. Why don't you join us?"

"Yeah, Angela, why don't you go with us?"

"I'd love to join you. Do I have time to change clothes?"

"Of course."

"Give me ten minutes. Oh, this is so wonderful. I didn't feel like cooking, and I didn't want to go out by myself."

***

Angela eased down the steps as soon as Barsh pulled into the backyard. He got out of the pickup and opened the door for her. Hannah slid to the middle of the seat.

"Daddy, where are we going," Hannah asked as he bucked up.

"What would you two think about Antoine's Restaurant in Spartanburg?"

"You have my vote," Angela said and Hannah agreed.

"Daddy, we don't have to be in a hurry, do we? I'd like to stay out until midnight."

"Ah, my kind of girl," Angela said and pulled her into her arms with tender affection. "Hannah, think of some place we can go after dinner, and we'll gang up on your father. Two against one always wins, right?"

"Unless it's a school night," he said. "But if you two want a midnight outing, I can make that happen some weekend."

"I'm ready to put it on my calendar," Angela said.

"Me too, Daddy."

"Do you want the three of us to plan the outing? Or do you want me to surprise you with something?"

"What do you want, Angela?"

"I'd like for Barsh to surprise us."

"Okay, Daddy, plan us a midnight outing."

"I'll try not to disappoint you."

Pleased with the turn of events, he smiled at Angela, and she winked at him, something she had never done before. She caught the quizzical look on his face and flared her eyes wide open.

"I'm so delighted to be going out that I feel like a silly girl," she said.

"Me, too, Angela."

"Hannah, I hear you and Barsh are getting horses."

"We're getting them next June. I've already picked out my stable at the barn. Daddy's going to tear out the old partitions and build new ones."

"I'm so envious of you two. I've wanted a horse since I was twelve-years old, but that was never in the cards for me."

"It's not too late," Barsh said. "We have six stables and pasture enough for twenty horses."

"Are you saying that I could keep a horse at your place?"

"Yes, that's what he's saying," Hannah said. "The three of us could ride together."

"Is that right, Barsh?"

"Right as right can be."

"I can't believe this. I have a chance to own a horse."

"I'm sure Susan will give you a good deal if you'd like one of her Tennessee Walkers."

"Yes, I'd like that if I can afford one."

"Susan will work something out with you. I'll give her a call."

It was a good evening for the three of them. During the outing, Hannah had sublimated her anxiety about the move to Louisville. And as he expected, she carefully studied all the exchanges between Angela and him.

Late that night as he sat in the study, the question of the day was back in his mind. Could he follow his heart and still fulfill his responsibility to Hannah? This time he found the answer.

CHAPTER THIRTY-SEVEN

Sunday morning, Barsh left home to meet Angela at the farm. In the solitude of the pickup, he relived their one dance Saturday evening. Sally McCarter, one of his majors, had pulled him onto the floor for the first slow dance, and other co-eds started cutting in until Angela ended their game. She pressed herself against him as if they were lovers. He found himself leading her with a grace he did not realized he possessed.

He parked the pickup, checked out the house, and ambled about the yard, killing time. A few minutes before ten o'clock he walked to the gate to wait for her. Precisely on time, she turned off the highway, waving and smiling, and drove though the gate. He locked it and got in the car.

"Good morning, my friend," she said. "Don't ever tell me again that you're not much of a dancer. That was a moment of pure magic."

"Well, I don't have to tell you that I enjoyed it."

She laughed and gave him a high five.

"I'm looking forward to another good day with you," she said.

"I hope it turns out to be a good day," he said with less than a confident face. "I don't want to spoil it, but I need to share some things with you."

"I hope they are not as ominous as the vibes I'm feeling."

"Let's get coffee, and I'll tell you in the den."

"While the coffee's making, I'd like to show you some of the things I've made using my newly acquired earth skills."

She followed him to the green bedroom.

"Oh my, you made all these things?"

"I made the buckskin shirt, trousers, moccasins, shoulder bag, and quiver from deer hides that I tanned myself. You know about the arrowheads. The bow and the arrow shafts were easy to make. I was making them when I was a boy."

"I'm astonished. If I didn't know you so well, I'd have a hard time believing this. But you are uniquely Barsh."

He led her back to the kitchen where he poured coffee and then ushered her into the den.

"Angie, you know that Hannah and I often do things without Debbie."

"Yes, and I've assumed things between you and Debbie were not ideal, although you have never complained about your marriage like other men I've known."

"Your assumption is correct. Debbie has asked for a trial separation for a year and plans to move to Louisville. She doesn't want a divorce, just a trial separation to see how things work out for her in Louisville."

"I don't know what to say, except that I'm stunned. Why?"

"Let me tell you the back-story, and I think you'll understand Debbie's decision. You know she's a successful accountant with her own firm, but we haven't talked about her beyond that.

"She and her parents were members of the little country church I served as student minister during my theological studies in Louisville. I'd drive the fifty miles there every Sunday, conduct the morning and evening services, and then drive back to Louisville.

"Most of the people in the community lived on upland farms with small tobacco allotments. The tobacco they raised was the major source of their modest income. Debbie's family, however, owned a big bottomland farm along the Kentucky River with a large tobacco allotment. They were well off by local standards.

"Debbie had finished college and was working at a prominent accounting firm in Louisville when I arrived on the scene. One weekend when she was home, her mother invited me for Sunday dinner. Soon Debbie was coming home almost every weekend. Then she started riding with me every Sunday. It wasn't long before her mother insisted that we come on Saturday. So I started spend Saturday nights with the Whalens.

"Everyone assumed we planned to get married, although we weren't engaged. Actually, we never talked about marriage until my final year at the theological seminary. That summer we got married, moved to Atlanta, and I begin a Ph.D. program at Emory."

"So it was not passionate love at first sight for either of you," she said.

"That's a fair statement."

"Do you think Debbie's mother pushed you into this relationship?"

"I'm rather certain that we wouldn't have started dating if Mrs. Whalen hadn't been involved. She definitely wanted to get us together. She was exuberant when we finally announced our engagement. But I was happy. Truthfully, I don't know how Debbie feels about her mother's involvement.

"Those years in Atlanta were extraordinary for me. My courses at Emory were excellent, and I had a teaching assistantship, which included tuition and a stipend. The first year I was an assistant to a brilliant archeology professor from Israel who had participated in numerous excavations there. The second year, I taught an introductory course to the

207

Bible in the College of Liberal Arts. The last two years, I taught Biblical Hebrew in the School of Theology. I couldn't have asked for a better experience.

"Debbie hated living in Atlanta even though she had a good-paying job with a reputable accounting firm. She was the major breadwinner, and I managed to earn a Ph.D. without taking out a single student loan. I'll always honor her for supporting me during those years."

"You were lucky. You'd be shocked at the amount of student loan debt I have."

"Angie, you've hardly touched your coffee. Can I get you something else to drink?"

"No, what I need is the rest of your story."

"Here's the problem as I see it. Over the years, I became more liberal while Debbie remained conservative and traditional. I was eager to share my intellectual and spiritual journey with her, but she wasn't interested. In fact, she was frightened by my critical Biblical studies, liberal theology, and modern scientific worldview. Please understand that I'm not putting Debbie down. She's a good woman. I honor and respect her. But she's always been miserable around intellectuals.

"Back in April, she got a call from her old boss in Louisville, inviting her to become a partner in his accounting firm. By the time she shared that conversation with me, she had decided to give it a try. In support of her, I agreed to move to Louisville, but she wanted a trial separation. She's taking Hannah with her, and that's the thing that's been worrying me crazy. You know how close the two of us are. Nevertheless, I've supported Debbie's plan from the first."

"Why haven't you told me?"

"I couldn't tell you until I told Hannah. Knowing the news would be devastating to her, I've been trying, in various ways, to prepare her for the harsh reality of the separation. Finally, I was able to get the whole story out Monday afternoon—"

"Before you took us to dinner?"

"We both needed to get out of the house so I decided we'd have dinner somewhere. After seeing you at Cooper, I thought it would be good for us if you joined us, and I was right. Having you along was good for Hannah and me."

"That's kind of you. How's she taking the news? She did seem more subdued than usual."

"In spite of her maturity, she's having a hard time dealing with this."

"Is there anything I can do to help her make the adjustment?"

"You can be a big help. Writing is so important to her, and you are such a good mentor. She idolizes you and needs your affirmation."

"Affirming her is such a joy to me. I'm with you all the way on this. Tell Hannah I'll continue to work with her by correspondence as well as by phone, if that's permitted."

"She'll be pleased to hear that. Things have finally fallen in place that'll make the move easier for her. I'll tell you about them later."

"When is Debbie moving?"

"Sometime before the end of the year."

"What's behind this move? Is she looking for more money or something else?"

"She has a profitable business and has built up significant savings and investment accounts so I don't think money is her motive. But truthfully, I don't know what she's looking for. I do know that she has been despondently unhappy living with me in Ashland and that she wants to live in Louisville for a year to see how that works out. If things go well for her, I firmly believe she'll stay there."

"And you're willing to let it play out either way."

"What else could I do? She has a right to happiness. She certainly isn't happy here with me. Anyway, I immediately realized I had two problems. Hannah was obviously my major concern. I had to find a way to prepare her for the separation. I think I did a decent job easing her along. I also knew that I wouldn't be able to teach at Cooper after Debbie left."

"Why? I don't understand that."

"Perhaps it has something to do with pride. You know the male ego that's shaken by the words *she left him*. But I think it's more a matter of integrity. How could I teach about spiritual matters with my own household torn asunder? Moreover, I'm also feeling rather vulnerable now. My critics will see this as justification for their attacks on me and my liberal views. I can already hear them saying, *His own wife couldn't live with him*."

"What will you do?"

"I've asked for a sabbatical starting in January, and Catherine has gotten it approved."

"Please don't tell me that you'll be going away for a sabbatical."

"No, I'll be living right here at the farm. I plan to commute to Columbia two days a week to study contemporary poetry and fiction at the University of South Carolina."

"Now that is a wonderful plan."

"Unfortunately, it took me too long to come up with it. At first I lost my way, trying to figure out how to deal with the separation. I came up with a crazy scheme that would deceive Hannah about the move to Louisville. I'll tell you about it later if you're interested."

"Sure. And you say Catherine supports this?"

"I had to tell her because of my original plan. Her goal is to get me reappointed as Professor of Humanities. If this happens, I will probably stay at Cooper. But there's no guarantee that Catherine can pull this off."

"Just know that I'll be desperately hoping that she will achieve her goal."

"I can deal with my own destiny. If I have to resign, I'll find something to do. But you have no idea how devastated I was when Debbie told me her plan. I immediately moved into the guest bedroom and started trying to figure out how I could prepare Hannah for the separation."

"May I ask a personal question?"

"Ask me whatever you wish."

"What happens if things don't work out for Debbie and she comes home? Will you move back into the bedroom with her?"

"No. If she comes back, she'll be retreating from some failure or rejection, seeking sanctuary for Hannah. She'll not be coming back to me. I have no expectation of restoring an intimate relationship with her. That aspect of our marriage is dead."

"Surely you know that I love you."

The silence was heavy as he studied how to answer.

"What about your vow never to get involved with another married man?"

"I made that vow last winter before I met you."

"Angie, I'm in a strange place right now. Until Debbie physically moves, I'm frozen at the level of friendship. There's nothing certain about Debbie's move. Henry Dugan could die or withdraw his offer. Should something like that happen, I don't think Debbie would move to Louisville. Then duty would prevail over everything else. But you must know how deeply I care about you."

"What if Debbie follows through with her plan and moves to Louisville?"

"Then I'll no longer be frozen at the level of friendship. But truthfully, I'm not a good risk for you. I'll still be a married man and any intimacy we could establish would likely fail you in the end."

"I'm a strong woman, and I want us to move beyond friendship with all my being. I'll be happy with you even if we aren't married."

"Before I can respond, I need to tell you about a plan I've been working on for months. If Debbie leaves for Louisville by the end of this semester, I intend to spend a month in the wild, living off the land, relying completely on my strength and the things I have made with my own hands. I want to experience what it's like to live in a state of total dependence on myself and nature, and I've promised myself this journey."

"My dear Barsh, only you could envision such a journey. Now I understand your focus on the old earth skills. What a unique vision. I applaud your plan and will be right here in Ashland, waiting for your return."

"I suppose I should tell you that I've been at war with myself since the day I met you. I kept hoping you didn't share what I was experiencing even though I knew Debbie planned to leave me and would not likely return once she got to Louisville."

"Why would you hope for such a thing?"

"I knew I wouldn't divorce Debbie and wasn't prepared, at the time, for an intimate relationship outside of marriage."

"And now?"

"When I return from the wild, which assumes that Debbie will be living in Louisville, I'll offer you my heart and all that goes with it."

He rose to meet her as she rushed into his arms. This time she kissed him passionately until he pulled back.

"You did understand the waiting part?"

"Yes, but even a conditional promise needs an appropriate response."

"Just know that I love your passion. I also love commitment and openness. If our day comes, I'll commit myself to you totally. I want us to live together openly as if we were legally married. Is that what you want?"

"With all my heart," she said and stepping into his arms, she nestled her head against his chest as they held each other tight.

"Angie, I was afraid this day would not go well for us. But now you've given me new hope."

"And you've given me my heart's desire. This is the most wonderful day of my life."

"I'm confident our day will come, but confidence doesn't guarantee the future. Meantime, we can enjoy being together in our own special ways."

"And I love them even more now that I know you want me just as much as I want you."

"Can I assume you're still interested in hiking to the Pacolet River?"

"I'm dressed for hiking and ready to go."

"Then let's get lunch started. We'll eat a little early. I don't want us to be pressed for time. Would you like to fix the salad while I'm grilling the beef kabobs?"

"With a heart overflowing with love."

CHAPTER THIRTY-EIGHT

They sat on a granite ledge overlooking the Pacolet River. Barsh had shared with Angela his practice of musing on whatever entered his mind as he watched the currents drift by. She wanted to try it. The silence held for a good spell as they sat side by side.

"I love this place," she said. "Sitting beside you here is like being in paradise."

"The first time I sat on this ledge, I dreamed about bringing you here."

"Ah, how dear of you to share that. Now please tell me about your thoughts."

"Would you believe that I paddled a canoe, with you in the bow, all the way down this river system to the Hampton Plantation beside the Santee River in Coastal South Carolina? It was a fantasy trip, but it was symbolic of the fact that I long to travel widely with you."

"I like the sound of that. So narrate for me our journey. I don't know this river system."

"I pushed off from the bank, and we rode the Pacolet currents to the Broad River. Then I paddled down to Columbia where it joins forces with the Saluda River to form the Congaree. About twenty miles below Columbia, we drifted by the Congaree Swamp National Monument, the largest track of old-growth bottomland forest in the United State."

"The Congaree Swamp National Monument?" she said emphasizing the word swamp.

"That's the designation Congress gave the place, but swamp is misleading. The river occasionally floods the huge bottomland but then drains, leaving most of the land dry most of the year. The biodiversity of the place is amazing. The significant thing is that it is now protected as a wilderness area. They're still developing the trails and have plans for a welcome center. There's also an effort underway to make it South Carolina's first National Park. I believe that'll happen someday soon. It's on my list of places to take you hiking, but I don't wish to take you any place where you're uncomfortable."

"The word *swamp* shot a jolt of anxiety through me, but as long as we're not wading through snake infested water, I'm good to go."

"Okay, this would be a good trip for us in late winter or early spring after I return from my sojourn in the wild. We could leave Friday afternoon after your classes are over and spend the weekend in Columbia. There are lots of good things for us to do there. I'll have to show you the bronze stars on the State House, which mark the places where Sherman's cannon balls stuck the building. Unfortunately, you'll see the Confederate flag still flying."

"Sounds like a good trip to me. Now take me back to our river voyage."

"After passing the monument, I paddled hard to the confluence of the Congaree and Wateree, happy at last that we were moving down the Santee. Then we landed at the Hampton Plantation, the birthplace of Archibald Rutledge, the first Poet Laureate of South Carolina. Well, so much for fantasy, but this plantation is on my list of places to take you. We'll travel by car, however."

"When can we go?"

"I'm not sure when we'll be able to make it, but when we do, we'll stay in the Charleston Place Hotel, which is a wonderful experience in itself. Then sometime during our stay in the old city, we'll drive up the coast about forty miles to the Hampton Plantation.

"The big house has been restored, but the rice fields are all in ruin. I'm amazed at the physical feat of the West African slaves who built those rice fields, dyke by dyke, and the technique they used to flood the fields. When the ocean tides came in, pushing the fresh water of the Santee River to the surface, the slaves would open the trunks to the dikes and flood the fields. Then they'd close the trunks and the fields would stay flooded after the tide ebbed. As you know, it takes a lot of water to grow rice. The place is now a State Park.

"Angie, I love Coastal Carolina almost as much as I do the Carolina Mountains, and I've a long list of things for us to do in the Lowcountry. For me, it's a wonderland filled with natural and cultural riches. In addition to Charleston and the smaller coastal towns, there are the Sea Islands. I've been visiting the Lowcountry for years and have not exhausted my list of places I want to experience. Oh, I just thought of a place near Charleston to take you that will please your mother."

"What could that possibly be?"

"Mepkin Abby. Have you heard about it?"

"No, but it sounds Catholic."

"You're right. It's a monastery. A group of trappist monks from the Gethsemane Abby in Kentucky built it on the Cooper River in the late 1940s. I think Clair Boothe Luce gave them the land which was part of historic Mepkin Plantation.

"The grounds of the place alone are worth a visit, but I thought we might attend the noon prayer service with the monks. They welcome visitors. Are you interested?"

"It's already on my list. And speaking of Mother, I called her again Friday. It really feels good to be in touch with her. She hasn't changed, but I can deal with her so much better. Thanks to you, I'm learning the value of tolerance as well as patience."

"You just reminded me of something I've been thinking about. A trip north."

"New York?"

"You nailed it. Do you know how often I've thought about being in New York City with you as my guide?"

"Tell me."

"I can't count the times."

She took his hand, kissed it, and clasped it to her breast as they absorbed the beauty of the day.

"I hate to say so but we should head back," he said.

"I love this spot by the river. Thanks for bringing me and thanks for sharing your dreams of traveling with me."

He helped her down from the ledge, and they left for the farmhouse.

"Do you realize you haven't shown me the pottery you've made?"

"It's in the barn. I thought we'd swing by on the way back."

"Yes, please, I'm eager to see it and to explore the barn with you. Does it have a hayloft?"

"It has a fine loft with some hay leftover from the previous owner."

"That gives me an image to get excited about."

"The feed room is the best place in a barn for that."

"Uh … how does that work?"

"On top of several sacks of crushed grain."

"Okay, I'm game. I'll dream about it, too. Lead us to the barn. I promise to be a good girl. Oh, have you had a chance to talk to Susan about a horse for me?"

"I called her Saturday morning. We worked out a deal."

"But what if I can't afford one of her horses? I'll probably have to borrow the money."

"The money part is between Susan and me. All you have to do is pick a horse that you like. Susan has invited you, Hannah, and me to spend a few days with her next June. We'll each get to choose the horse we want from a group of seven horses."

"I'm totally at a loss as to what to say."

"There's nothing to say. Oh, you can pick out a stable while we're at the barn."

***

They sat in the den of the old farmhouse, mellowed by wine, as the day slipped away.

"Angie, I hate to part ways, but it's time for me to head home."

"I understand your situation. I wish I could tell you how much I love you. But you want me to hold on to the unspoken words that swell in my heart, don't you?"

"For the time being, yes. As long as Debbie is living with me, I want us to be caring but restrained. On campus, I may seem distant, distracted, or even aloof at times. Just know I'm wearing a public face until our day comes.

"When we're together with Hannah, you can be playful, even a bit flirtatious if you want. I'll be attentive but somewhat reserved. I want her to see that we're special friends, who just might be well suited for a deeper relationship down the road. She's perceptive and will discover this on her own. When this happens, we'll share our plans with her."

"I'll try to strike the right balance, but you know how I tend to get carried away."

"I have a surprise for you, Angie. I'm sending you home with a gift that I think you will like."

"A gift for me?"

"I'll be right back."

He retrieved the Carrick Creek painting from the blue bedroom and returned to the den, holding it before him with its back to her.

"Do you want to guess what it is?"

"A painting?"

"But not just any painting," he said and turned it around.

"Oh, my God, you bought me the Carrick Creek painting," she said jumping to her feet and taking the painting in her hands. "I love it. Thank you, my dear man. You are one in a million. When did you purchase it?"

"On Wednesday after we saw it. I've been waiting for an appropriate occasion to give it to you."

"I could not be more surprised and yet it so you. I mean, your thoughtfulness."

"Just know that it's from my heart. Now I need to get you on the road. I'll ride with you and unlock the gate. Then I'll walk back and clean up the kitchen."

"Please let me help you. I loved the way we prepared lunch together."

"Thanks, but this will give me something to do while you put a little distance between us."

"So that's why you've been sending me off first. You always think of everything."

She said her goodbyes to the house, and they left in the Volvo, Angela holding his hand as she drove slowly down the lane. She stopped at the locked gate and faced him.

"Today has been wonderful beyond word," she said, "and I'll cherish it forever. My heart is overflowing."

"It was indeed a special day. I'm more at ease with myself than I have been in a long time. And you … you're so special I couldn't be more amazed if you had fallen from the night sky."

"That is the dearest thing anyone has ever said to me."

"I'll see you at Cooper tomorrow," he said.

"Yes, tomorrow, my dearest Barsh."

He kissed her hand and got out to unlock the gate.

CHAPTER THIRTY-NINE

The whole house was disturbingly quiet when Barsh got home from the farm. He found Hannah bent over his desk, writing.

"I'm glad you're home, Daddy. As soon as I finish making this change, I want us to do something together."

"Okay. Is Debbie taking a nap?"

"I don't know. She turned off the TV and went to her room a few minutes ago."

"I'll wait for you in the den."

Settled in his chair, he began reading the Sunday paper. Soon he heard Debbie coming down the hall.

"We need to talk," she said.

"Okay," he said and laid the paper on the coffee table.

"Hannah, please join us," she called in a voice that carried to the study.

"I'm coming," she answered and left the study running, but slowed to a hesitant walk as she entered the den.

"What do you want, Mother?"

"Come sit beside me on the couch. I need to talk to you and your father about my plans. A week from this Wednesday, I'm leaving for Louisville and won't be back until I have a contract to buy a house. I also plan to spend the weekend with Mother so it'll be sometime the following week before I get back. I'll keep you updated by phone."

"When will we move?" Hannah asked.

"My target date to close on a house is Friday after Thanksgiving. I want you to go to Mother's with me for Thanksgiving. If I do close that Friday, I plan to move the next week, but I've decided that you can stay with your father until you're out of school for Christmas. Is that okay with you, Barsh?"

"Yes, of course, and you're wise not to make Hannah change schools before January."

"It took me all week to reach that conclusion, and I'm glad we're in agreement. Hannah, when I worked in Louisville, I used to dream about owning a house in this wonderful neighborhood with such fine houses. If it's still like I remember it, I hope to buy a house there. It was zoned for the best schools in the whole city. I want nothing but the best for you. If you're not happy with the public schools, I'll find a private one that suits you."

"I'm not worrying about school. Whatever you decide will be all right with me."

"Barsh, will you take care of supper? I'm going to bed early. Oh, don't forget Davis is off this week. You have to pick up Hannah after school and stay at home with her or take her to the farm."

"I won't forget."

Hannah had managed to keep a straight face until Debbie was well down the hall. Then she began to cry. He stretched his arms to her and she ran for his embrace.

"Can we go out to eat, Daddy?"

"Sure. Where would you like to go?"

"I don't care. You choose something."

"We could eat in Spartanburg and then check out the movies?"

"I'm not in the mood for a movie. Let's get a hamburger here. I'd like to work on my writing until bedtime."

Barsh drove away from the house, trying to decide what to say that might comfort Hannah. The reality had undeniably set in. Debbie was taking her to Louisville.

"Hannah, you deserve to grow up in the same household with both your parents, but it's not going to happen. I keep coming back to the analogy of a boarding school. I'm going to act like you're away at school getting a good education. If I look at it this way, I can manage your absence."

"I like the analogy, too, and I've been using it ever since you first mentioned it."

"Truthfully, your new school will be much more challenging and much better for you."

"I hope so. Anyway, I'm not worried about school. But how can I keep from worrying about you? I'll have Mother and Davis, and you'll be living all by yourself at the farm."

"No, please, I don't want you worrying about me. You know how I enjoy being out there. And I'll have Catherine. She would have me over for breakfast every Saturday if I'd let her. And there's Georgette Wingo. She always invites me to her luncheons and parties. Actually, I have lots of friends."

"Do you know who you didn't mention?"

"Jackie Love?"

"Daddy, you know who I'm talking about."

"I do and Angela is definitely on my list of closest friends."

"Have you told her about the separation?"

"I did this morning."

"I thought you were at the farm today."

"I invited her to meet me there, and I told her in the same place I told you. Then we hiked to the Pacolet River this afternoon."

"What was her reaction?"

"She was shocked. But there's good news for you. She's committed to working with you on your writing by correspondence. It's okay now if you want to talk with her about the move. Tell me about the poem you're writing. What's it about?"

"Soot Cave, Creek Indians, and a boy."

"Well, you've got my interest. Can you read it to me when we get home?"

"That's my plan."

CHAPTER FORTY

Barsh woke from a dream, the bedroom still bathed in darkness. He and Angela were on a blanket beside a creek, but he couldn't identify the place. He wished that he could will himself back into the exhilaration of the dream, but it was gone, leaving only fragments of memory.

He lay there in the comfort of his solitary bed, marveling at the ability of the brain to create dream experiences capable of sending such powerful emotions throbbing through his body. How did the mental apparatus of dreams do that? His sexual fantasies were never as emotionally charged as erotic dreams. Did that mean dreams were closer replications of physical experience than imagination? If so, what were the philosophical implications for the mind-body problem? He'd have to think about that later.

It was twenty minutes before his usual time to get up, but he left the comfort of the bed and headed for the bathroom. Then he eased into the kitchen where he found Debbie eating breakfast.

"I hope I didn't wake you," she said. "I'll be going to the office early and staying late this week. I have tons of work to complete before I leave for Louisville next week. I'm sorry Davis has the week off."

"Don't worry. She's excited about visiting her sister in Columbia. I'll take care of Hannah. We had a good talk last night. She's going to be okay."

He got a cup of coffee and sat down across the table.

"I plan to live at the farm after you and Hannah move, but I think we should keep this house in case things don't work out for you in Louisville."

"This is your house," she said. "You paid for it with funds from your parent's estate, and you can do whatever you want with it. I'll never live in this house or this town again. If things don't work out at Dugan, Johnson and Bennett, I'll start my own accounting firm in Louisville. That's the only place I've ever been happy. I think my emotional health will improve once I get settled there."

"I assume you've thought through this carefully, and there's no turning back."

"That's right."

"Then I wish you well, now and always. Do you want a divorce?"

"No, when I was growing up, all our ministers taught that divorce was against God's law of holy matrimony. Please don't force a divorce on me. I can't deal with that now."

"I'll not force a divorce on you, but you know that I believe divorce is definitely the best solution to some marital problems."

"Yes, and I thank you for respecting my feelings. I did talk to a lawyer last week, and I think we should execute a permanent separation. It should include our agreement about Hannah. Beyond that, what I want is my accounting firm, which I now plan to sell, my savings and investment accounts, my personal things, and the furniture I told you I'm taking. You can have this house, the farm, and your savings and investment accounts. And of course, you have control of the trust you established from the insurance settlement to take care of Hannah and me. You should modify the trust document so that Hannah is now the sole beneficiary. We'll also need to change our wills to reflect the separation agreement. I'm making Hannah my sole beneficiary."

"That seems fair to me. We'll both be responsible for Hannah and her education."

"I suggest we use Jack Kelly to handle the legal aspect of the separation," she said.

"That's fine with me."

"I'll call him this morning and get him started. I want this done before I close on a house. I can't thank you enough for your support and cooperation."

"Debbie, I will always love you as Hannah's mother even if I take up with another woman."

"Wouldn't that be committing adultery?"

"Not in my book. The permanent separation will annul our vows. The only thing left will be the legal record that prohibits us from marrying someone else. No, I wouldn't call it adultery."

"Then I'll leave that between you and God. Whatever you do, I want you to be happy," she said and left for work.

Barsh got a second cup of coffee and sat in the study. His assumption about Debbie's plan had just been confirmed. She had known, all along, that she'd never return to Ashland once she got to Louisville. The good news for him was that she had finally leveled with him. He'd be ethically free to follow his heart as soon as the separation agreement was legally executed.

The toilet flushed. Hannah was up. When should he tell her that the separation would be permanent? Certainly not now. He'd have to play it by ear, he thought.

***

After dropping Hannah at school, he drove to Cooper and parked in his regular place. Angela's car was parked in her usual place. Could they act in public as though the developments on Sunday hadn't happened? He hurried upstairs and stopped at her door.

"Good morning," she said with a big smile. "I trust you had a good weekend."

"Oh, yes, and you?"

"Super special. Someone slipped a letter under your door this morning. Well, I'm off to class. See you later."

He unlocked the office door and picked up the letter which Angela had hand addressed to *Dr. Roberts*. Settled at his desk, he read the most passionate words that had ever been addressed to him. She concluded the letter by stating that she had carefully considered all aspects of their future together and she was ready to consummate their relationship without any expectation of marriage. There was nothing holding her back, but she respected his need to wait until he returned from the wild and would patiently wait for that blessed day.

He folded the letter and locked it in the file cabinet. He was now prepared to move beyond friendship to intimacy before leaving for the wild, even before Debbie moved to Louisville. But he would wait until there was a firm date to execute the separation agreement before telling Angela. No more *if* and *when*. He was ready to follow his heart as soon as the permanent separation was legally executed. Meantime, he would teach his classes, take care of Hannah, and mark the days.

CHAPTER FORTY-ONE

Early the next Monday morning, Barsh sat in the study with his first cup of black coffee. Davis was back in town and would be picking up Hannah after school. The papers for a permanent separation had been prepared and approved. Debbie and he were signing them at three o'clock on Tuesday. She was leaving for Louisville early Wednesday to buy a house. His first priority of the day was to let Angela know that he'd be free to follow his heart after Tuesday.

Debbie and Hannah were up following their usual morning routine. Then Debbie left for work with plans to stay late. Hannah joined him in the study, dressed for school.

"What do you think of your new book, Daddy?" she said pointing to E. O. Wilson's *On Human Nature*.

"It's very special. Have you been reading it?"

"I read the preface and part of the first chapter."

"He's one of my heroes. And guess what? He was born in Alabama and loved to explore the wild as a boy. We have those two things in common, although our interests in nature were different. I was interested in living in the wild: hunting, fishing, camping. Wilson was more interested in studying nature and soon focused his attention on ants. Now he is a highly respected professor at Harvard and the world's foremost authorities on ants."

"But the tile is *On Human Nature*."

"Yes, and I think Wilson has a lot to say about human nature. Changing the subject, I'm thinking this Saturday might be a good time for the midnight outing I promised you and Angela. Debbie will be in Kentucky. Are you still interested?"

"I'm ready. Have you asked Angela?"

"No, but I will today. I just needed to check with you first. Well, my dear, we're running late. Let's go."

He dropped her at school and drove to the college. Angela was descending the front steps of Kimberly Hall on the way to her first class when he rounded the corner from the parking lot. She stopped to wait for him.

"Good morning," she said."

He stepped closer and whispered, "I have a major update to share."

"Will it make me happy or sad?"

"Debbie and I are signing a permanent separation agreement tomorrow at three o'clock. After that I will be on your side of the fence. Would you like to meet me at the farm Wednesday afternoon at two?"

"I'll be there with a jubilant heart."

"Bring music for dancing and be prepared for whatever the afternoon may bring."

"I'm packed and ready."

"Debbie's leaving early Wednesday for Louisville to buy a house and won't be back until next week. That means I'll have Hannah this weekend. Could we do the midnight outing I promised you two?"

"That would be perfect for me."

"Then plan to meet us at the farm Saturday morning around eight. We'll have breakfast there. By the way, Hannah knows I've told you about the separation."

"I'll give her a lot of attention and love."

"Thanks. She needs it. You probably won't see a lot of me before Wednesday."

"Just two more days. I couldn't be happier."

She left for class, and he hurried to his office where he found another love letter from her. He read it eagerly and locked it in the file cabinet. It was time to bring Dean Thompson up to date. He dialed her direct line. She answered on the second ring.

"Catherine Thompson."

"Catherine—"

"I was hoping you'd call. How are you?"

"Actually, I'm doing much better. Could you see me between ten and eleven?"

"No, but I can see you now."

"I'm on my way."

The Dean welcomed him in her tender way, and they sat facing each other in their usual chairs. He shared with her Debbie's latest plans, and they agreed that he should wait until she actually moved before he started telling his colleagues.

She inquired about Hannah and was pleased with his report that she seemed to be taking the new reality reasonably well. Then she asked about Angela. He talked freely about their changing relationship. Sensing the Dean's anxiety, he assured her they would not live together openly before he returned from his sojourn in the wild. She commended him for the wisdom of his decision, noting that such restraint would make it easier for her to defend them.

"Catherine, you've had to defend me too many times over the years. Maybe I don't belong in this conservative community. The last thing I want to do is to cause you more trouble."

"Don't say that, Barsh. You are the best Cooper has."

"That's kind of you, but most people couldn't care less if I left."

"Please promise me you won't do anything rash. Focus on your sabbatical and stay in touch with me. I'm determined to get you appointed Professor of Humanities, one way or another."

"Okay, but don't burden yourself on my behalf."

He left the Dean's Office, picked up his mail at the college post office, and went back to his office to await his nine o'clock class. His mind was tending to business, but his heart was counting the hours until his rendezvous with Angela on Wednesday.

CHAPTER FORTY-TWO

Dressed in a white silk shirt and black pants, he waited for Angela in the farmhouse yard at the appointed hour that Wednesday. She parked and ran for his embrace.

"I love you," he said releasing the words from his heart for the first time, and then he kissed her long.

"My dearest Barsh, I thought this day would never come."

"That makes two of us. Ride with me to lock the gate."

"I do like the privacy that gate gives us. I've never longed for it more than today."

He kissed her again and they left in his Audi.

"God, I love your strong arms," she said.

"That's good because they now belong to you. I'm yours, body and heart. The permanent separation was legally executed yesterday. I've champagne and a cozy fire waiting for us. Did you bring music?"

"Have music. Will dance."

"You look stunning in that lavender dress and white jacket. I assume you know the dress holds a special place in my memory."

"I see you dressed for the occasion, too. The clothes you wore to the school dance, except for that royal blue velvet jacket that looked so handsome on you."

"There's another difference. I wore my dancing shoes for this occasion."

"I understood your dilemma last night. I knew you wanted to dance with me, and that was what mattered most. Regarding my dress, yes, I thought you might remember it. That's why I chose it."

"I was tempted to the limits of my willpower with its soft fabric caressing your body, to say nothing of its plunging neckline and short skirt that kept riding up your thighs as I waited for you to tell me whatever it was that you decided not to tell me. And then the press of your body as you embraced me as I was leaving. Walking away from your arms that evening was one of the hardest things I've had to do."

"Ah, did I ever want you to stay. I knew, all along, you liked me as a person, but that was the first *hard* evidence I had that you liked me as a woman.

"When you pulled back and left, I was confused and disappointed. Believe me I'm learning the value of patience. Now I'm honored by the route you have taken to get us to this day. I know you want me, the whole me, not just my body."

"Yes, I want you, the whole you."

"I'm all yours, my dearest. How long can we stay?"

"Three hours. Davis will pick up Hannah at school and stay with her until five."

"Then let us make haste."

He locked the gate, and they headed back to the farmhouse, filled with love and buoyed by anticipation. Back in the yard, she got her big cloth bag from the Volvo, and they walked, hand in hand, into the den where he had the champagne chilling. She draped her jacket over the back of the couch and exclaimed about the log fire. He popped the cork and handed her a glass of champagne as she moved to his side. Then filling his glass, he lifted it to her.

"To love as true as the North Star," he said and they drank.

"To love as true as the sun and moon," she said and they drank again.

He set their glasses on the coffee table, and taking her hands in his, he looked into her eyes.

"My dearest Angie, I love you truly and commit myself to you and you alone."

"My dearest Barsh, I love you truly and commit myself to you and you alone."

They moved into each other's arms. There was passionate kissing and slow dancing in the old den as love's magic pulled them toward one flesh. He lifted her in his arms and carried her to the green bedroom, where they stripped before the others eyes, one garment at a time.

***

They lay naked on the bed with their hearts slowing to a normal rhythm.

"Barsh, you are the best lover ever—"

"Wait, that's what I was going to tell you. Your passion ... you have given me a new understanding of ecstasy."

"Oh, but you were the captain of this voyage. So gentle and yet so strong. I felt your love in every touch, in every move you made. I have never felt so totally loved."

He took her hand and kissed it, and she rolled against him.

"I assume you still want us to keep our new relationship to ourselves until you return from the wild," she said.

"I think that'll be better for us in the long run, but I'll not deny our relationship even before Debbie vacates the house if the need arises. Just know that I am, as of this day, totally committed to you in every way. There will be negative fallout for us, but with you I can weather anything."

"And so can I with you by my side. When will you tell Hannah?"

"I haven't figured that out yet. I want her to conclude on her own that there's more to our relationship than friendship. She's very observant and will soon reach that conclusion if she hasn't already. As soon as I suspect she's on to us, I'll have an honest talk with her."

"I think she's already on to us."

"You're probably right. If she isn't, she likely will be before the weekend is over. I have a special plan for our midnight outing this Saturday that'll certainly have her thinking about our relationship big time."

"I do like the sound of that, my man. Changing the subject, do you intend to keep wearing your wedding ring?"

"This ring is coming off."

"Can I give you one?"

"Yes, and I'm giving you a ring. Here's an idea. We could buy the rings, go to Charlotte, and exchange them at the airport where we first met. Then we could have dinner at Emile's Bistro where we ate before you flew back to Providence."

"I love your plan. You are such a romantic."

"I used to take pride in thinking I was a romantic. Then I read a biography of Faulkner and discovered the depth of the malady in his love letters. For the first time, I realized it's a sickness."

"Only if you never find your true lover."

"That's a good observation. I guess I had lost faith in romantic love."

"My faith was dead, dead. Then I stumbled into you at the only time in your life when you would've been open to me. How is that for miraculous wonder?"

"I feel that same wonder."

"Back to the rings," she said. "Do you have a preference?"

"Just a simple band of gold. But I'm thinking diamonds for you, maybe with rubies or sapphires. I'll pick out your ring, but I would like to know your preference on some options."

"Then I *would* like diamonds with sapphires."

"Do you know that in medieval times all a couple had to do to be considered married by ecclesiastical law was to exchange vows and rings?"

"No, I've never heard that."

"Just a point of interest. No law, ecclesiastical or secular, could make me feel more bound to you than I already do."

"I feel the same way, and I trust you implicitly to work out the details of where we'll live when that day comes."

"That'll be a joint decision. We're now partners in life, and we do have some options there. But today, we are running out of time. Let's dress and talk by the fire until we have to part ways for a while. If you don't mind, I'll take the bathroom first. I can be out in five minutes or less."

"Then jump to it."

"I'll have to change back into my usual attire. I'd have a hard time explaining to Hannah why I had changed into my fancy clothes in the middle of the day."

"I do love the way you take care of the details."

He stood and looked lovingly at her naked body.

"You remind me of a refrain from the Song of Solomon."

"Then out with it," she said.

How beautiful you are, my love. Oh, how beautiful you are.

She beckoned him with her arms and he eagerly filled them again.

***

They sat by the flickering fire in the old den, finishing the champagne, as the minutes ticked toward their time of departure. He was trying to plan ahead.

"Do you have commitments for Thanksgiving?" he asked.

"No, but I'm hoping we can find a way to be together."

"Debbie and Hannah will be in Kentucky visiting the Whalens. Debbie's goal is to close on a house Friday after Thanksgiving and move the next week. Then I'll have Hannah until Christmas break. But you and I will have the Thanksgiving break to ourselves. Four full days and nights."

"I like the sound of that."

"Would you like to go to Hilton Head Island? We can consider it a mini honeymoon."

"Oh, yes, take me to Hilton Head Island. I've heard it's a wonderful resort."

"True, but the Island has also a growing population of permanent residents, which means the new developments are overwhelming the old Gullah culture there. The general consensus is that it's just a matter of time before all the coastal islands will be developed, and the Gullah way of "making do" will be doomed. Have you read Pat Conroy's *The Water Is Wide?*"

"I've only read a review, which was very positive. I think he also has a new novel."

Yes, and it's very good."

"Then I must start reading him. Is there any chance we could visit Daufuskie Island?"

"A very good chance. There is no bridge to Daufuskie, thus the title *The Water is Wide.* Conroy was astonished to learn that some of the children he taught had never left the Island, and he took it upon himself to take them to Beaufort and beyond on various fieldtrips. And now it will be my pleasure to find someone to take us to Daufuskie by boat. It's a good experience with dolphin sightings on the ride over.

"I'll also take you to Beaufort and show you the antebellum homes in the historic section of town. We'll have lunch at Plumbs overlooking the Beaufort River. Then we'll visit Penn Center, a special place on St. Helena Island. It began as a school for freed slaves during the Civil War."

"It all sounds wonderful. Where will we stay?"

"We can rent an oceanfront condo, or we can stay at a beachside hotel."

"Do you have a preference?"

"I like the idea of an oceanfront condo. It'll be like having our own apartment."

"Then I'm voting for a condo."

"I know the perfect place. And here's something I think you'll like about the location. The Tiki Hut, a beach bar with live music, is just a short walk up the beach from where we'll be staying. It's a favorite with locals and tourists."

"I can't wait. How's the beach there?"

"Great. When the tide is out, there are twelve miles of packed sand to walk or ride a bike on. We can rent beach bikes if you like biking."

"I'd love to."

"I like to walk the beach early in the morning and late afternoon. I also like to walk the beach at night. There's one stretch of oceanfront that hasn't been developed. It's a good place to sit against the sand dunes and watch the starry sky, especially when you can catch the moon rising out of the ocean.

"Once, I saw an unbelievable display of heat lightning. From horizon to horizon, there was a constant barrage that lasted for the longest time. The only thing missing that night was someone to share the experience as it was truly ineffable. I didn't know it at the time, but I was longing for you as I sat there all alone."

"You'll take me to those dunes one night, right?"

"You can count on it and a lot of other good things: Harbor Town, the tabby ruins of Stoney-Baynard Plantation, Sea Pines Forest Preserve, the mud flats at Port Royal Sound, Pinckney Island National Wildlife Refuge, and the list goes on. More than we could ever experience in a single visit. So if you like our Thanksgiving visit, we'll go back for more."

"Then you'll be taking me back because I'll love every minute of our stay."

"Meantime, we'll meet here whenever we can."

"What wonderful music to my ears."

"If only I could stretch out this day. It's time for me to head home."

"How I wish I had the words to express my love for you."

"All I need is a hug and a kiss. Then I need to get you on the road. I'll straighten up things here while you put some distance between us."

CHAPTER FORTY-THREE

He left the farm and somewhere between there and Fern Meadows his thoughts turned from Angela to Hannah. It was time to tell her that the separation would be permanent. He parked and entered the den where Davis was waiting for him. They exchanged greeting and she left. He called Hannah and she answered from the study.

"I'm glad you're home," she said looking up at him from the desk.

"I hope you had a good day, my sweet girl."

"It was okay. I've been working on a new poem since I got home."

"That's good. Did you have any bad moments at school today?"

"Not really. I tried not to think about the move to Louisville. I'm glad I get to stay with you until Christmas break."

"I don't think I could make it otherwise. Has Debbie called?"

"About an hour ago. She made it to Louisville fine and will start looking for a house in the morning."

"I'm sure she'll find a suitable place in a good neighborhood."

"Whatever she does will be okay with me."

"Hannah, I hate to tell you, but this is going to be a permanent move. Debbie told me last week that she plans to start her own accounting firm in Louisville if things don't work out at Dugan, Johnson and Bennett. She said categorically that she will never live with me again."

"Why didn't you tell me then?"

"I thought it best to wait until we were alone today," he said and extended his arms to hug her.

"I guess I've been preparing myself for this," she said without crying.

"Okay, let's sit down and talk about this latest development. At Debbie's request, we got a lawyer to draw up a permanent separation agreement. We both signed it yesterday."

He retrieved the document from the file cabinet and laid it on the desk.

"Here it is. You can read it anytime. The things I told you about us are now legally binding. You can spend holidays and summers with me. I can visit you at any time during the school year, and I can occasionally fly you and Davis down for the weekend.

"Meantime, you and I have lots of good things to do before I have to take you to Louisville, including our outing with Angela this Saturday. We can make the best of a bad situation if we keep the right attitude."

"I'm trying to keep a good attitude."

"Trust me. This move will not keep us apart for long at a time. And here's something I want you to remember. If at any time something goes wrong in Louisville, call me and I'll be there to take care of whatever the trouble happens to be."

"What do you mean?"

"Well, suppose Debbie starts seeing someone who's unkind to you."

"Do you think Mother might start seeing someone?"

"Not really. You know her theology. She'd think God would punish her for dating someone while she was still married to me even though the separation agreement has abolished our marriage vows. We are husband and wife only by law. It's a sham of legality. But truthfully, I don't know what Debbie might do. She could change her mind about divorce and marry someone for all I know. Here's my point. If things should change in any way that would make life with your mother miserable, I'll intervene and fight to get custody of you."

"That's good to know," she said and studies him as if she wanted to ask him something.

"What are you thinking about?"

"You and Angela."

"As you know, she and I enjoy a lot of the same things. We've been friends from the first, and now we're very close. We're good for each other. But whatever the future holds for us, it'll not change my relationship with you.

"I've been an integral part of your life since the day you were born. I fed you, changed your dippers, bathed and dressed you, rocked you to sleep, comforted you in the night when you cried ... and the list goes one. Now you're eleven years old, soon to be living with your mother in Louisville, soon to be charting your own course toward independence from us. And whatever happens, I'll continue to love and support you in every possible way until my last breath."

"I know that. But do you love Angela? It's obvious that she loves you ... the way she looks at you."

"Truthfully, I do love her. Over the years, there have been women who have shown a interest in me even though they knew I was married, but I never let any of them get close to me. I didn't intend for it to happen with Angela, but it did."

"Are you going to marry her?"

"Your mother says she doesn't believe in divorce. She thinks it goes against God's will. I've promised that I will not force a divorce on her."

"But you believe in divorce, don't you?"

"Yes, and a divorce would be better for me than a permanent separation, but I'll keep my promise to your mother as long as your wellbeing isn't an issue. So marrying Angela is not a current option."

"Does she know this?"

"I've been totally honest with her. Without a divorce, there are three options for us. We can accept the fact that we can't get married and go our separate ways. We can keep our relationship as it is, and live separately. Or we can live together openly, which is what I hope will happen when I return from the wild. I don't wish to live out my life alone."

"Is Angela with you on this?"

"That's what she says. Here's a question for you. Are you okay with this?"

"I don't want you to live out your life alone, either. You know I think Angela is the best, and like you said, you're good for each other. I could see that from the first. I like your preference."

"Well, that's a relief. Let's keep this to ourselves until I get back from my wilderness sojourn. Then, if Angela wants to live with me, we'll go public. This will cause us some problems, but I'm confident we can handle them."

"Daddy, can we spend the night at the farm Friday? Then we'll just get up and wait for Angela."

"Good idea. Now help me fix dinner and then you can share your new poem with me or we can just talk."

CHAPTER FORTY-FOUR

Barsh, thinking about Debbie, sat in the farmhouse den with his first cup of black coffee. She sounded so elated when he talked with her on the phone last evening. She had found the perfect house in the neighborhood where she had dreamed of living ever since her first job in Louisville. The closing date was set for Friday after Thanksgiving, only three weeks away. Once more, he had wished her success and happiness in Louisville. She thanked him, again, for supporting her in the move.

He looked at his watch and decided on a second cup of coffee before waking Hannah. Back in his rocker, he reviewed his plans for the day, wondering if he should cut something.

Hannah's feet pattered to the bathroom. The commode soon flushed.

"Daddy?" she called.

"I'm in the den. Good morning."

"How long have you been up?"

"Not long. Did you sleep well?"

"Finally. I was so excited about our outing with Angela I couldn't go to sleep."

"I'm sorry. Take a pillow and you can take a nap while we're traveling."

"I don't want to miss out on anything you two might say. How am I supposed to act now, Daddy?"

"Just like you always have. I'm thinking about inviting Angela to spend the night with us here at the farm. I'd hate to send her home after midnight."

"Nobody will know but us."

"Okay, I'll invite her. If she accepts, she can have the green bedroom. I'll sleep on the couch. We better get moving. I'll go unlock the gate while you get dressed. Then you can help me in the kitchen."

The morning sky was clear; a good day for hiking. He hurried to the gate, unlocked it, and headed back to the house. Hannah was waiting for him at the kitchen table.

"You look good in your new hiking outfit," he said.

"Thank you. I like it."

"If you'll set the table, I'll cut up a bowl of fruit. Angela should be here any minute."

"Daddy, she praises you for connecting her with nature, and she loves our outings. That's mostly what we talked about when we met Thursday. Not writing."

"Well, I trust our outing today will live up to her expectations."

"Don't worry. Whatever we do, we'll be together. And that's always fun."

"Listen, I think I hear her car."

They got to the front porch as Angela parked. Hannah hurried to meet her, and Angela embraced her with sweet affection.

"Good morning," he said and kissed her lightly on the cheek.

"This is the day of our big outing. I was so excited last night I had a hard time getting to sleep."

"I had the same problem," Hannah said.

"Well, my dear ladies, let's eat breakfast so we can get on the road."

He opened the door and followed them into the house, Hannah leading the way to the kitchen. While they helped their plates, he poured milk for Hannah and coffee for Angela and himself.

"Angie, please sit here at the end of the table so Hannah and I can both sit beside you."

"My, aren't you two sweet," she said as he held her chair.

"Okay," he said after taking his seat, "I have a full day planned for us. Anybody want to guess what's on the agenda?"

"A hike in the mountains," Hannah said. "You did say dress for a hike."

"Yes, but where in the mountains will we be hiking? That's the question."

"Give us a clue," Angela said.

"The place is named for an American poet."

"Oh, you're taking us to the Joyce Kilmer Memorial Forest."

"I'm honoring the promise I made when you came down for the job interview. I'm eager to show you two this old-growth forest. You're going to be amazed at how big the hemlocks and yellow poplars are."

"Hannah, can I give your father a hug? I've been begging him to keep that promise ever since I moved to Ashland, and he's been putting me off."

"Let's both give him a hug. I've wanted to go, too."

He stood as they rushed to him, hugging and praising him. Then they all settled down, eating with more delight in each other than the food itself.

"What else have you planned for us, Daddy?"

"Our first scheduled stop will be Highlands, North Carolina, about a three hour drive and much of that in the Carolina Mountains. We'll have an early lunch at the Old Edwards Inn, maybe explore some of the art galleries. Then we'll drive to the Joyce Kilmer Forest with at least one stop along the way. Not far from Highlands, we'll stop beside the Chullasaja River and do something I think you both will enjoy. I know it will be a first for you, Hannah, and possibly for you, Angie."

"So you've done it before," Angela said.

"Once, but it'll be more fun today with you two."

"Whitewater rafting?" Angela asked.

"No, but it involves whitewater."

"Give us a hint," Hannah said.

"I'll just tell you we're going to experience a special place on the Chullasaja River called Dry Falls. Here's the fun part. We can walk behind this thundering waterfall to the other side of the river without getting wet."

"You're right. That'll be a first for me. This is shaping up to be a great day. And it can't end before midnight, right Hannah?"

"That was Daddy's promise."

"Don't worry. I have plans that'll get us well past midnight. Angie, we'd like for you to spend the night with us. I know it's a late invitation, but I hope you can stay over. You can have the bedroom and I'll take the couch."

"I'd love to stay here tonight. Do you have an extra shirt I could sleep in?"

"I have extra shirts, but we can swing by your place for sleepwear."

"Thanks, but I'll make do with whatever. I don't want to waste any time going by the house."

"Let me share this," he said. "After we leave the Kilmer Memorial Forest, the most distant point on our outing, we'll take a different route back by way of Asheville—"

"Any chance we could dine again at Grove Park Inn?" Angela asked.

"Please, Daddy, let's eat there?"

"Just what I was planning. Then we'll celebrate the midnight hour here. But I'm not sharing the details until we get back. Don't mean to rush anyone, but we have things to do. Hannah, remember to get your pillow just in case you need to take a nap on the way home this evening."

***

The outing in the Carolina Mountains had gone exceedingly well, and they were fast closing the distance back to the farm. Hannah, who was curled up with her pillow in the backseat, hadn't spoken for some time, and Barsh assumed she was asleep.

"Angie, I know you must be tired. I'm afraid my plan for today was too ambitious. I thought we would be back at the farm by nine, and it's already after ten."

"Your plan was excellent. The whole outing was marvelous. I wouldn't have missed anything we experienced."

"Daddy, I agree with Angela," Hannah said and sat up. "Are we almost home?"

"Twenty minutes at the most. Have you been asleep?

"I've been listening to you two."

"Well, I hope we didn't bore you," Angela said.

"Listening to you two was the best part of the day to me. Daddy talks to me some when we're on a long trip, but mostly he just drives and thinks about things. You two talk about the most interesting things."

Barsh knew she was contrasting the outing with those long trips to Kentucky when there was no interesting conversation between Debbie and him.

"Well, my dear daughter, Angie and I have limited time for good conversations at Cooper. All the driving time has made this a good day for talking, and don't be surprised if we stay up most of the night, talking."

"Hannah, you can count on that if I have my way. Time after time, I've thought of something I wanted to ask your father, but he'd be in class or in a meeting or with a student or gone for the day. Barsh, I would love to talk the whole night through. Is that possible?"

"I'm game," he said. "Was there a favorite part of the day for you?"

"I enjoyed everything. But I'd have to put the Kilmer Forest at the top of the list if I had to choose. That is such an enchanting place. How fortunate we are that Kilmer's admirers saved that wilderness. But judging the day as a whole, each part complemented the others. Now I'm looking forward to your plan for the midnight hour and then more talking."

"What is your plan for the midnight hour, Daddy?"

"I'm holding on to my surprise until the last minute. When we get to the farm, we'll relax around a log fire. It's all made so all I have to do is strike a match. There'll be hot chocolate for you. Angie and I will have coffee laced with a good helping of Baileys."

A deep hush settled over them, except for the tires whining on the rough asphalt road. Angela reached for his hand and held it in her lap.

CHAPTER FORTY-FIVE

They sat in the den with half-green hickory logs sizzling and flaming in the fieldstone fireplace. Barsh sipped his Baileys, pleased that the day had gone so well. Angela, who had been talking with Hannah, set her cup on the coffee table and embraced her with tender affection.

"I hope you don't mind my hugs," she said.

"You can hug me anytime. I told Daddy that I want to be like you when I grow up."

"You are so dear to say that, but you'll exceed me in every way: beauty, charm, intellect, creativity."

"I'll be happy just to be like you."

"Oh, you'll be like me and more. In the meantime, I plan to hang on to my friendship with you two. Hannah, can we talk about Louisville or is that off limits?"

"No, it's not off limits."

"I know how unhappy you are about the move. I also know you're going to make the best of it, just like your father. You both have grit, and that's one of the many things I admire so about you two.

"Here's my advice. As soon as you start school there, begin searching for a girl who loves to write. She'll probably be a quiet girl who has no interest in winning the Miss Popularity title. When you find this girl, go out of your way to befriend her. You know that your father will be here for you, and so will I. Your mother and Davis will be there for you, but you'll also need a Louisville girlfriend, someone your own age who shares your love of writing."

"That's good advice, Hannah. I wish I'd thought of it."

"I like the advice. But I'll make it with or without a girlfriend."

"Yes, you *will* make it," Angela said and embraced her again.

"Okay," he said, "let me get things underway for the midnight hour. And no critical remarks please."

"So what are we doing, Daddy?"

"First, I'm taking all the quilts form the cedar chest and making a thick pallet in the corner of the backyard away from the house and trees. Then the three of us are going to huddle there and let the wonders of the night sky dazzle us. I don't know if you noticed, but this is a perfect night for stargazing. Moreover, this is a perfect setting. There are no city lights out here to interfere with our view of the heavens. And I have blankets to keep us warm."

"You have the neatest ideas," Angela said. "I can tell you right now, I'm going to love it."

"It does sound like fun. I don't have to go to bed at midnight, do I?"

"There is no set bedtime for you tonight. But I think you should change into your pajamas. Then I can just tuck you in your bed if you fall asleep under the stars."

"Can I change now?"

"Yes, but keep on your socks. Those wool hiking socks will keep your feet warm. Oh, and bring your clothes. I'm putting on a wash so we'll have something fresh to wear in the morning. Angie, I have a sweat suit you could change into if you'd like to wash your clothes, too."

"Good idea."

Hannah left and Barsh led Angela into the green bedroom. He pulled two sweat suits from the armoire, one navy and the other maroon. She took the maroon pants and held them up to her.

"They're way too big for you," he said, "but they do have a drawstring."

"These will work just fine."

"Then I'll wear the navy. Actually, they should work well for huddling under a blanket. Who knows what the night may bring for you and me when the stargazing is done."

She rushed into his arms, and they kissed with an eager passion that had tugged at them all day.

***

He stretched out on the pallet of quilts to test it for comfort. Not too bad, he thought, his mind racing ahead.

Back in the den, Angela and Hannah were sitting on the couch, engaged in a lively conversation. He walked past them and stood with his back to the fire, admiring Angela in his baggy sweat suit.

"Is the pallet ready?" she asked.

"All is ready. The blankets are on the kitchen table. You and Hannah take your pick while I change."

In the bedroom he noticed that Angela had stripped down to skin for the sweat suit. Her bra and panties were scattered on the bed with her hiking outfit. He stripped likewise and clothed his nakedness with the navy sweat suit. Then he let down his ponytail.

"Angie," he called from the hall, "let's put your clothes on to wash."

HONEY FROM A LION

"Coming," she said and joined him in the bedroom.

"Oh, my goodness," she whispered, "I can't wait to get my hands in your hair."

He smiled at her and nodded his head in affirmation of what they were both thinking.

"Shall we do a separate wash for your delicate things?"

"No, let's throw everything in together."

They gathered up the clothes and he started the wash. Then he turned off all the lights and led the way to the pallet of quilts, where they stood gazing into the heavens, each cloaked with a blanket.

"This is truly breathtaking," Angela said. "I don't think I've ever seen a more brilliant night sky. What a perfect way to celebrate our first midnight together."

"Okay, let's see if you two can find the North Star," he said.

"I think you have to find the Little Dipper first," Angela said. "But I've forgotten what you do after that."

"I know," Hannah said. "Daddy taught me. He used to read me a bedtime story, every night, and one of my favorite books was *The Freedom Star*. That's what the slaves used to call the North Star because they followed it to freedom in the North when they ran away. I didn't know about slavery before that book. I couldn't believe people used to own other people like they were cattle. Do you know that the old laws in the Bible allowed parents to sell their children into slavery? The girls for life. The boys for six years, then they could go free."

"No, that's news to me. I need to take your father's course on the Bible."

"Back to the star quest, my ladies," he said.

"I've found the Little Dipper," Angela said.

"Good for you. Let's give Hannah time to find it."

"I've found it. Angela, see the bright star at the end of the handle? That's it."

"Hello, North Star," Angela said.

"Here's an idea," Barsh said. "Let's slowly rotate clockwise, observing as much of the sky above the horizon as possible. When we get back to the Little Dipper, we can stretch out on our backs and study the sky above us."

"Good plan. Will you point out some of the constellations for us? I can only identify a few."

"I'm not even an amateur here, Angie. My studies of the heavens are primarily ones of mystical wonder. But I'll share the little I do know.

Orion, the hunter, was my favorite as a boy and has remained so across the years. I spotted him as soon as I came out to make the pallet."

"Show me."

After he showed her Orion, they turned again to the North Star and followed his suggestion, punctuating their observations with a lot of *wows*. Completing the rotation, they stretched out on the pallet with Hannah in the middle. Within minutes, she complained that she was getting sleepy.

"That's okay, sweetie," Angela said. "We've had a wonderful time together. Come snuggle up with me and go to sleep."

"Is it midnight, Daddy?"

"Midnight has come and gone. Hannah, if I'm still asleep on the couch when you get up in the morning, that'll mean Angie and I probably stayed up all night. In that case, fix breakfast for yourself and then wake me at ten o'clock."

"Okay, I promise not to wake you before ten."

Angela pulled Hannah into her arms and she was soon fast asleep.

"Time to put her to bed," Barsh whispered.

He carried her to the bedroom and tucked her in. Then he made more Baileys. They sat by the fire, waiting to make sure that Hannah would stay asleep.

"Angie, I need to update you on a significant conversation I had with Hannah. When I got home Wednesday after our rendezvous, I told her about the permanent separation papers Debbie and I had signed. She was upset, but we talked until she calmed down. At one point, she asked about us, and I told her that we loved each other and that I wanted us to live together when I returned from the wild."

"And what was her response?"

"Very favorable."

"That pleases me, but you made a special effort today to shield her from the fact that our relationship has already moved to one of intimacy."

"I think it's too early to spring that on her. But it'll happen in due course, probably before she leaves for Louisville."

"You know I love her, don't you?"

"Yes, and she loves you. I'm not concerned about the relationship of the three of us, but part of our responsibility will be to help Hannah love, honor, and respect her mother."

"Oh, I'm with you there a hundred percent."

"I had no doubt that you'd be with me on this. Guess what I'm thinking about."

"I hope it's the same thing I'm thinking. Making the quilt pallet into a love nest."

He stood, pulled her into his arms, kissed her, and led her from the house.

***

They lay side by side, recovering their equilibrium, a blanket holding the warmth of their naked bodies, the heavens smiling down upon them.

"Barsh, only you could have envisioned the possibilities of this night, such romantic ecstasy on a pallet with the stars winking at us. I repeat myself, you are the best lover ever."

"And I repeat myself, the title belongs to you."

"Everything is so easy for me with you," she said. "Not just lovemaking, but whatever we're doing, I'm never anxious when I'm with you."

He pulled her hand to his lips, and she crawled on top of him.

"Hold me tight," she said and he rocked her in his arms.

"Ah, I like the feel of things from up here."

"Then you'll have the privilege of steering the ship from there on our next voyage."

"And just when might that be?"

"It depends on whether you're hungry or not. I can scramble eggs now or later."

"I'm not hungry yet, but I do want black coffee soon. I intend to stay up all night if you'll hang with me."

"I'll be right with you when the sun breaks the horizon. I've been planning this outing for some time. I'm pleased with the way it has gone."

"I love the way you take care of everything."

"I guess I do have a crazy mind for details."

"Does that mean you have a plan for the three of us tomorrow? Even though I never dreamed I might spend the night with you, I worked hard Friday evening grading papers and doing lesson plans so I'd be free just in case you had something in mind for tomorrow. Well, I suppose I should say today."

"At sun up I'm tucking you in bed. Hannah is waking me at ten. She and I'll prepare brunch and wake you around eleven if that's okay."

"Please wake me when you get up. I want to help."

"Okay, I'll wake you as soon as I get dressed. I have two possibilities in mind for us after brunch. We can drive to Charlotte, take in the Mint Museum of Art, maybe a movie, and have dinner there. Or we can go to Chimney Rock, do some hiking, and have dinner in Spartanburg on our way back here. Your choice."

"Do you have a preference?"

"Not really. They're both on my list of places to take you. Wait and see how you feel after just a few hours sleep before you decide. We could even stay here. Maybe hike to the Pacolet River again."

She kissed him long and the voyage was under way.

***

Barsh stood with his back to the fire, waiting for Angela to return from the bathroom. The toilet flushed and then she was back in the den.

"Coffee is ready," he said. "Come stand by the fire and I'll bring you a cup."

"I'll go with you as soon as I warm myself. Do you realize this'll be the first time I've ever stayed up all night? I'll bet you can't say the same."

"When I was sixteen, I stayed up all night at a wake."

"Who was dead?"

"One of my father's friends. They had grown up together. The wake was totally different from what I had imagined it would be like. The women huddled around the kitchen table, and the men sat in the front room with the open casket, talking about their experiences growing up together. I learned a lot of interesting things about my father's youth from their stories.

"The next morning I helped an old man dig the grave as a labor of compassion. It was a slow go with a pick and shovel. That red clay was so hard, but we finished digging the grave before noon. I attended the funeral that afternoon, and didn't sleep until my regular bedtime that evening. That was the longest time I have gone without sleep. It was a good experience for me. But there's nothing in my life comparable to this night."

"I could not agree more. It is by far the best night of my life."

They got black coffee and returned to the den where they sat side by side on the couch.

"Barsh, we haven't had a chance to talk about your plan for a month-long sojourn in the wild. I don't even know where you'll be. But first, tell me how you come up with a plan for such an adventure. I can't imagine another man in the civilized world who'd deliberately decide to return to the stone-age for an interim."

"The plan grew out of my struggle to deal with Debbie's decision to move to Louisville for the trial separation. As I told you earlier, I was totally unprepared for that. It challenged my perception of who I was and what I should be doing with my life. I could no longer see myself teaching at Cooper after the separation. Yet I had no idea what I'd do. Then several things converged in a way that got me thinking about how, as a boy, I had found strength and grace in the wild, living off the land by my own hunting and fishing skills.

"From there, I came up with the idea of taking a sabbatical and living in the wild for all the seasons of one year, solely dependent upon myself and nature. This, of course, would require me to learn the old skills of Native Americans, which I was eager to do."

"I didn't know you originally planned to stay a year."

"That was the original plan: a journey from our modern technological world back into the natural world of the forest where I would live alone. Cut off from the civilized world, I'd examine the foundations upon which human societies were first constructed as well as the philosophy upon which I had built my life, and hopefully, I'd return with a new understanding of my place in the modern world.

"So what caused you to shorten your journey from a year to a month?"

"I came to my senses and realized I couldn't leave Hannah to Debbie's care of a year. Yet I still needed that journey into the wild. The primary motive of finding a new vision for myself remained the same until a few days ago.

"In my struggle to come to terms with my love for you, I gained the new eyes I was hoping to acquire in the wild. Now I simply want the experience of living in a state of total dependence upon nature and myself. If this seems like an unworthy motive to you, I'll scrap the journey."

"No, you must follow through with your revised plan. I totally support you in this."

"Are you sure?"

"Absolutely."

"Then I shall consider the journey a gift from you, otherwise duty would bind me to your needs."

"That's sweet of you, but you've earned the right to make this journey. It's yours to pursue, not mine to give. Now tell me where you will be living."

"There's a cave in a high bluff overlooking the Tallapoosa River where I camped for a week during my senior year in high school. That cave will be my home. I'll fish the river with fish traps that I've made from split bamboo, and I'll hunt with my bow and arrows in the vast forest that stretches up and down the river from the cave.

"After I roast an evening meal over the coals of a fire in the mouth of the cave, I'll sit looking out across the river as the sun sets in the distant West, and I'll think about you and Hannah until I fall asleep in my deerskin cocoon. But during the day I'll be absorbed into the wild."

"I'm stunned by the primal beauty of your vision, my beloved man."

"Here's something I hope will delight you. I decided last night to delay the journey until the day after Christmas. I'm taking Hannah and Davis to Louisville on December sixteenth. Then I'll drive back here the next day. That'll give you and me eight days to do something together. This means I'm cutting my sojourn to three weeks, which is all I need. I no longer have anything to prove to myself."

"You just put me on cloud nine again. What do you have in mind for us to do?"

"I thought I'd let you suggest something."

"Could we tour the South, maybe spend some time in New Orleans?"

"Sure. What other places would you like to visit?"

"As much of the South as possible. I'll trust you to work out the details."

"Okay, here's a basic framework. We'll drive to Nashville and take in a few things there, including a visit with Susan and her horses. From there, we'll go to Memphis, enjoy some blues on Beale Street, and take a paddleboat ride on Ol' Man River. Then we'll drive through Mississippi, stopping at a few places of interest like Vicksburg and Natchez. Oh, I'll have to take you to Oxford and Jackson to see the domains of Faulkner and Welty. Maybe from Vicksburg we'll swing by Baton Rouge on our way to New Orleans. After spending time there, we'll head home by way of Alabama and Georgia."

"Eight days of touring the South with you. I can't believe my lucky stars. I wish I had the words to tell you how fortunate I feel to have found you. I've been blindly looking for you all my adult life, not even knowing the totality of what I was looking for."

"I know what you mean," he said. "We've had some influence over the direction our relationship has taken, but the big things that brought us together were products of good fortune. I'm as astonished to find you in the center of my life as Samson of Biblical times must have been when he discovered honey in the carcass of a lion."

"Honey in the carcass of a lion? I haven't heard that one. Is it part of the Samson and Delilah story?"

"Before meeting Delilah, he had fallen for a different Philistine woman and persuaded his parents to arrange a marriage. On his way to take her, he turned aside to examine the remains of the lion he had killed on an earlier visit. This is how the narrative reads: *there was a swarm of bees and honey in the carcass of the lion. And he took thereof in his hand, and went on eating.* Ah, the wonder of finding something good, where and when you least expected it."

"So I'm honey from a lion," she said.

"That and so much more."

They talked and talked by the fire in the old den as the night slipped away. Just before daybreak, they returned to their love nest beneath the stars. It was a night like no other for both of them. At first light, they draped themselves with blankets and sat facing east, waiting for the sun to break the horizon of a new day.

About the Author

A native of Roanoke, Alabama, Fred Bassett is a Biblical scholar, novelist, and award-winning poet. His poems have appeared in more than 80 journals and anthologies, and he has published four books of poetry. *Honey from a Lion* is the sequel to his debut novel, *South Wind Rising*. Now retired, Fred holds four academic degrees, including a Ph.D. in Biblical literature from Emory University. He lives with his wife Peg in Greenwood, South Carolina, near their grandchildren.

ALL THINGS THAT MATTER PRESS, Inc.

FOR MORE INFORMATION ON TITLES AVAILABLE FROM
ALL THINGS THAT MATTER PRESS, GO TO
http://allthingsthatmatterpress.com
or contact us at
allthingsthatmatterpress@gmail.com

If you enjoyed this book, please post a review on Amazon.com and your favorite social media sites.
Thank you!

Made in the USA
Charleston, SC
07 April 2014